The Circle of Swords

The Circle of Swords

'Voyage of the Temple Unicorn'

ANDREW DAVID DOYLE FDA

iUniverse, Inc.
Bloomington

The Circle of Swords
'Voyage of the Temple Unicorn'

iUniverse books may be ordered through booksellers or by contacting:

iUniverse
1663 Liberty Drive
Bloomington, IN 47403
www.iuniverse.com
1-800-Authors (1-800-288-4677)

ISBN: 978-1-4697-8135-8 (sc)
ISBN: 978-1-4697-8136-5 (ebk)

Printed in the United States of America

iUniverse rev. date: 02/29/2012

Hugues De Payen - Geoffrey De Saint Omer - Andrew Montbard - Gondomar

Payen of Mondidier - Roral - Godfrey - Geoffroy Bissot - Archambeau Saint Amand

Ordo Supremus Militaris Templi Hierosolymitani

- Magnum Magisterium Porto -

The Order Today

The Grand Priory of Scotland is a component unit of the Order of The Knights' Templar, a Sovereign International organisation whose existence dates back to the first years of the 12th century. Today the Order has almost five thousand members in over forty-five countries and regularly undertakes works of charity and support to those in need.

'Ordre Souverain et Militaire du Temple de Jerusalem'

About the Author

Andrew David Doyle was educated in Dundee, Scotland, prior to joining the ranks of the British Army (Royal Artillery), with a successful career that stemmed almost fifteen years. After which he embarked into the commercial world of hydrocarbon exploitation and currently works globally.

Andrew is currently studying for his Bachelor's Degree in Management and enjoys his new-found hobby as an author, and has recently became a member of the Society of Authors.

Chevalier Andrew David Doyle OSMTH KT Scotland.

Preface

The Knights' Templar Order we observe today in the 21st century is indeed alive and kicking and unlikely to change the way it has fundamentally functioned for the past 720 years, and of which they can be easily located by a simple web search.

As a collective 'Brotherhood in arms', the poor knights had never actually left the structure of society, but 'ran silently' in the ever changing background, and of course still do, controlling or advising the modern commercial world we observe today—depending on one's outlook.

The circle of swords is not about explaining the Order with any scholastic standing or disguising any esoterical messages that have ran rife through the centuries, but a simple, interesting storyline weaved together to capture what is the most intriguing society post-biblical times.

Therefore, this book is dedicated to our global Brothers and Sisters who choose to follow the path of Christ and to the memory of the founder, 'Hugues De Payen', and to preserve the memory of the bravest eight Knights who shed their blood across the many battlefields of Christendom whilst preserving one of the greatest institutions that serve humankind in modern times.

In memory of David Stalker, friend and Templar 19th May 2011

HSE Chev. David Stalker KGCT, EGCSC, FSA Scot
Co-Adjutor General
Grand Priory of Scotland

Introduction

The ancient K.T. Order of the 12th century era is indeed steeped in myths, legends, folklore and many mysterious stories which have added a tremendous amount of analytical fuel for modern media and scholars to shape their many fantasy books, films and documentaries upon. Therefore solidifying the existence of this revered religious order since the year 1119 and onwards into the present day where the Order has not gone un-noticed.

Why The Knights' Templar as an institution has such a fundamental standing on the global stage is very much open to debate. But it is very clear from the many archival records that The Knights' Templar were involved in preserving something which cannot simply be purchased, traded or bantered for in the common marketplace—a is perhaps something that is far greater than mere gold and shiny trinkets.

This inexplicable link to many myths, fantasies and legends have bonded The Knights' Templar ethos together as it rippled through time and history and into the very fabric of our modern day 21st century faith itself.

This belief has permeated through modern society with such potency that it has been firmly embedded by it's shear popularity alone; albeit supported by a fistful of clandestine esoterical meanings and symbology carefully woven within its complex tapestry.

The tale that unfolds tells a story of a special journey in the name of Christendom, and a voyage that is designed to stimulate the reader into thinking outside the proverbial historical box.

Chapter One: 'Novus Conclave'

Hugues De Payen took a few deliberate steps across the open square of the small village. As he began drawing his sword, he took a single deep breath and waited for a convenient juncture before sinking the heavy steel deep into the chest cavity of the now not so brave and cowardly, squealing rapist.

The shock of horror was clearly emblazoned on the face of the perpetrator, coupled with the presence of a cold fear lasting no longer than five quick seconds before the perverted deviant realised he had been 'run through' with a two foot long, cold blade constructed from the best Damascus steel. A precision strike that had been delivered swiftly and cleanly by a new enemy from within the sandy walls of Acre: the *'Templar'*.

De Payen paused for reflection and captured the moment as a snapshot in his mind's eye—momentarily committing yet another soul to what was becoming quite a 'library of death' by his physical interventions on behalf of Christendom—albeit only a few minutes earlier, he had witnessed his victim's active participation in a diabolical act of gang rape and theft on a young woman, that appeared to be barely in her teens.

The girl, in this case the victim, would have certainly been left for dead if it had not been for the gang being disturbed by the sound of the heavy horse hooves nearby, and by the gang's shear arrogance or ignorance, they would have surely left the poor girl traumatised, distressed and potentially pregnant, but sadly left disoriented in her own world destined to become an outcast.

The Knight had already dispensed his understanding of this balance of power and justice towards two other offenders of the gang, who lay not too far away from the girl with similar mortal wounds—both wallowing in pools of their own blood. His interpretation of Augustine rule, often brought on by his self-imposed guilt, would urge him to contemplate his predicament in an effort to determine how far a pseudo Monk and soldier should extend his professionalism in protecting those more unfortunate than most.

This self-imposed authority, willingly employed to deliver justice on behalf of those who were more vulnerable or exposed to rampant lawlessness and tyranny within this turbulent society; a self-imposed rule to keep things in order, albeit, out with the failing laws of the land. After yet another brief lapse in time, he concluded that the ultimate price of death, was in this case, did deliver justice on behalf of the street urchin.

Having removed his sword from an adjacent corpse, Andre' Montbard took a step forward, leaned over the dead body and removed a blue silken purse from the blood stained robes, then, quizzed the curved knife which had been tucked into the belt of the rapist. He thought an elegant weapon however, it's owner either too stupid and certainly too slow to make good use of it's sharpened blade, and had paid the price.

Montbard reached out and handed the silken pouch to the distressed maiden, who instantly grabbed the bag, squealed some distorted phrase in gargled Arabic then took flight, heading towards the outer walls of the village, leaving her dusty and well-worn sandals behind in the soft brown sand.

The Knight stood his ground and watched on in bewilderment as the girl took flight, his physical bodily mass and build was one of a very stout, athletic, strong man, possessing powerful arms that could possibly punch their way through a sandy stone wall—if the need arose. His name was Montbard, Andre, Montbard, the youngest son of a well to do and well heeled French aristocrat, and a man from the landed gentry, a man driven by his troubled past which had urged him to travel to the East to seek answers to his religious beliefs, the answers of which he found very quickly in the presence of a peer known as Hugues De payen.

2

Andre' would show his physical mettle by way of squeezing apples or potatoes into a mushy pulp then would utter, words to the effect that *"This could be your head or your testicles"*, it was his party piece, and a spectacle conducted often in front of many people during most social gatherings.

He was blessed with a heavy crop of fair hair that was encrusted with a series of long interwoven rat's tails that hung loosely down the length of his neck down over his shoulders and was supported by an elaborate embroidered headband made of thick, brown leather.

Andre' possessed a very strong French accent that was clearly identifiable in any dialogue; although a strong Anglais accent with Scottish undertones would appear when in certain company. And more importantly for the Order he possessed a good command of both Arabic and Latin languages, an education of culture that was to compliment his elite class upbringing. Although, he much preferred to moan in the old English language and was on very special occasions inclined to utter shear abuse in Scottish. He turned to De Payen, then spoke.

"Do you ever think they will ever thank us for our efforts?" he said, sliding his steel blade back into it's leather sheath. Then began brushing himself down, muttering a range of incomprehensible obsenities and overtones much towards the "Shitty sand".

"That's not very likely, my friend," came the reply from De Payen, who was pointing to the young urchin. "This girl, 'she', however might remember us though. She will remember us only be because she has survived this brutal attack.

And of course we all know it may well be just a matter of time before this same shit happens again. They are unruly bastards these infidel—they have no conscience, no sense of moral judgement, and certainly no moral compass to guide them"

He replied, pointing to his head, "I would think that in her case, it will be just because she is still alive to talk about it that some will learn. These people have no idea why we are here, Andre'." he retorted, almost in anger. "And let's face it, they don't give a toss whether we are here or not. Do you think they really want us to get involved in their internal politics, us 'Khawaga'?

I think if you ask them, they would all say no and tell us to leave the Holy Land or simply go to hell, you see, gents we are outsiders. But one thing I do know, my friend, is that we, you Godfroi and I, well, we need to get some more bloody reinforcements, and rather quickly.

We need help if we are to survive in this great holy charade. I am getting too bloody tired of killing; too tired to chase my arse through these hot deserts chasing thieves." He cut off, and looked around. "Where's Godfroi gone anyway?" he asked, glancing around the village again. Hugues picked up his helmet and slowly walked across the square heading towards the kibbutz kicking the dust into the air as he walked through the entrance doorway.

Not too far away across the dusty walkway the small figure of a boy stood for a few seconds and watched the Knights in almost total bewilderment. The youth waited until De Payen was out of sight, then he hastily ran headlong into an adjacent alleyway and then disappeared.

A loud, single voice ran out from behind Andre' Montbard. He turned quickly as he walked towards the building. "There were two more over on the far side of the water well. I have since sent them to meet their maker." The voice was deep and commanding, yet the tone sounded humorous and almost rehearsed.

Once they reached the building, Godfroi de St Omer stood near the doorway with his sword draped across his left shoulder. Its long blade glinting in the sunlight as trickles of fresh, warm blood slowly dripped and dribbled into the soft sand, each granule absorbing and congealing on impact.

The DNA elixir of an earlier killing was already staining and tinting his well-worn and dented armour. "Godfroi! Remarked Andre' 'There you are big fella, we were getting worried about you. We thought you might have got lost in the stables. I am sure I heard the horses stirring, I think they were probably panicking, my friend" Then, smiled and followed Hugues into the building.

De Payen stopped and stared into the dark recess beyond the makeshift wooden table. He was day dreaming. His mind had just wandered off into a land a thousand miles into the far corner of the room. A smirk of concern ran across his rugged, unshaven chin. Godfroi wiped his face of blood splatter, then spoke.

"Well, that's the eighth this week," he said, remaining cognisant to the fact that certain elements of the Muslim community were habitually attacking pilgrimage parties. He knew they were easy prey for the many unruly thieves and vagabonds who were targeting the many visitors within the lands of promise, but suddenly he was upset somehow by 'today's' strange events.

The three Knights had often discussed the nature of these attacks between them and knew that the sporadic skirmishes were leaving many followers of Christ either dead by the roadside or potentially dying of thirst, each having suffered horrendous injuries by these indiscriminate attackers, or they had just simply fallen victim to the sun's intense heat rays.

Collectively, the knights were becoming more and more concerned by the increasing numbers of pilgrims who were apparently leaving middle Europe, especially since reports were circulated about the capture of Jerusalem in 1099. And especially now, as the results had been so widely reported across middle Europe, details of which explained that all endeavours had been extremely successful and that the Holy Lands were deemed a safer place to visit.

Godfroi, turned and looked across the window towards his peers. "Andre', is it true that the powers that be in France, are actually promoting the upkeep of these foreign lands in an effort to increase and secure further finance? More money from the greedy French landed gentry?"

Godfroi was aware that Andre' hailed from a very well to do aristocratic family as did Hugues De Payen himself. He knew that he received periodical communications from their homeland and knew deep down that there was also great turmoil across the Holy Land. Nevertheless, his communications brought essential information to share with the Knights about their home country and what was actually happening in central Europe.

The most recent communiqué was from one of Andre's family members, a man named Bernard Clairvaux, who was a simple lay Priest whom had taken great interest in God's Christian henchmen. He had chosen a new place for worship and acknowledged that his uncle Andre' was facing certain death every day whilst protecting the many thousand of pilgrims and travellers to Acre, and he wanted to be part of it; albeit he had recently joined the upper echelons of the Vatican's inner conclave.

Andre' left the room and returned a few minutes later clutching a red leather satchel in his leather clad fist. The bag appeared to be full to the brim with letters, seals and small books. He placed a single parchment on the table top and explained that Anglo French global communications were sparking a greater interest towards these lands of Christ and very careful attention was required to its management especially if it was to reduce further bloodshed. He removed his gauntlet and extracted a few parchments.

"Can you see what the Papacy wants here, gentlemen? Not just promoting the Holy Land or giving due consideration to the safety of the people, but contemplating the wealth and international acclaim and biblical interest it will generate. It appears to me that Europe wants Jerusalem for its own ends."

Hugues looked up from the letter that lay on the desk and smirked again and spoke. "It is true. The Pope wants the Dome. That much can be said. But as I have already stated we are not getting any younger either—you also know that's for sure.

My muscles are torn and my old bones are tired and sore. The psychological scars of Christendom are taking their overwhelming toll on my poor physical frame. I must say, my friends, maybe we should ask our sons and nephews to join our warring efforts.

We could do with some reinforcements around here. I hear somewhere that the Cistercian order has made things difficult for any army. They have drawn a limit as to what age men will be permitted to take up arms and fight for the military. I mean, just how crazy mad is that? How can we possibly build up our defences against these Muslims if we don't have recruits young enough to train and educate, and, of course, I do understand that we are probably seen as cold-hearted mercenaries anyway.

And that might not help our recruiting effort, but we still require resources to manage our business. That's what your dossiers say to me Andre'. No disrespect to your family, or Bernard, in particular. But we are in the middle of a very volatile biblical war. This quagmire of merde is deeply fuelled by those ignorant high and mighty unseen Bourgeoisie bastard classes who sit and proclaim or make false claims that they are helping our global efforts.

But, we know they are not! Let me say something about the local people here in Outremer, do you think they see us as soldiers or freedom fighters? A simple question I pose to you: soldiers who have no shame or conscious thoughts and are just killing machines.

Or do you think they perceive us in a way that reflect any real allegiance to any single country or Monarch, or perhaps is it that I am the only real cynical bastard that thinks that in the eyes of the external world we are just seen as pieces of dog shit trudging through the sands of Jerusalem for what is perhaps an intangible belief?

When, I know really deep down in my heart, I know why I protect the power and the awesome belief of the lord Jesus Christ. My own selfish aims and objectives of desire to bring calm and peace to this holy place, for gentlemen it is in my blood. I can feel it's potency pulsing and coursing through my veins and,' He paused and pointed his finger at Andre'. "I would challenge any mortal man to tell me otherwise."

He then nudged the desk leg. "Tell me Andre', how old is your young nephew, Bernard, now anyway? He asked lowering his tone to a lesser non-confrontational one. "If I recall, last time we met he appeared to be a sturdy young ox if I remember correct. I last heard good things about him and not so long ago he had petitioned to work directly for the Papacy. Is he becoming the eminent scholar we have all imagined or has he become a man of reasonable standing? He could become useful to us in the future; especially as he now has these strong links to the Papal office."

Montbard wiped his goatee beard. "Hugues, you might be right there. I think he is too wrapped up in bloody politics. He is too involved with your bastard upper-classes. As you say, too high and mighty to get involved with the likes of us, I am afraid. Apparently too busy to come and wield a sword, but their money is helpful. Too posh to fraternise or mix pleasures with us: the undercast. Well, with the likes of middle-class yobs like you and I, Godfroi. I don't think Bernard could tolerate all your incessant moaning and groaning. Ha, ha, ha," he said, placing his fingers in his ears.

"If you remember when he first came here with us, he said he hated the sun, and he hated the flies, and he hated the smell of the waters. When I think about it, he pretty much hated everything. I bet he is happy sitting in Rome today.

Andre' clasped his hands. 'I think Bernard is in his early thirties by now; thirty four sounds about right. And yes he is doing well, but those around him, they are weak and feeble minded. Don't worry, I think young Bernard will sort them out soon enough, as he says he is on a mission from God" he remarked, then smiled again.

Godfroi was shaking his head from side to side in agreeance. "Yes, I do recall the constant grumbling and moaning. But he does know what we are up against. He understands our dilemma, and predicament of getting accepted into Al Aqse.

Perhaps that's why he only stayed here a few short months. We should nevertheless endeavour to make good friends with Bernard or indeed exploit his many partnerships. He has connections that will help pave our pathway into the history books one day. His contacts and allies they are powerful men and women, and, if you can recall the efforts of this establishment, they have already recorded our exploits by commissioning those transcripts of the first crusades. I think they have captured all the critical elements in exacting detail. The extracts I read were quite comprehensive."

Andre' nodded again as De Payen coughed. "Yeah, but that was a long time ago my dear Godfroi. Again, no disrespect intended, but your family are all Doctors and Theologians; they hail from the educated classes. I would ask you: what do they know about the art of war or military tactics on the battlefield, how would they deal with twenty thousands hairy arsed Turkish rebels descending on their lands?

They would be lost my friend. But there is a warning here: these scholastic scribes, they are very clever men and would often change the original records to suit their own interpretation of events. And could have easily added their own version of outcomes, could even made out that El Saladin was winning. Surely, we can easily be forgotten in the sands of time. What do you think, Hugues? Does that makes sense?" remarked Andre', looking at De Payen for direct support on his comments.

Hugues flicked a single gold coin in the air, then caught it in mid-flight, clasping it in his clenched fist. "Yes, I wholly agree. The history books are written with a great deal of artistic licence, but remember one thing, and, this is a very crucial point, we do in essence still possess a written record of our earlier exploits, a historical account, and a succession record that we can use to our advantage when the need arises.

If I was to say one thing in response to your question, it would be: remember that history is written by the victorious, and often written in the loser's blood. The losers don't have any rights once they have spilled their sacred blood on the battlefields of Christendom." It was then that the room went very quiet indeed. Hugues took another deep breath.

"Anyway, a change of direction, but don't worry my friends, I am sure help is at hand. I have observed some potential recruits and brethren flirting around and about within the confines of his Royal Highness's not so well-known social outbuildings. I spied a small kibbutz with a red roof a few days ago. It is located just on the outskirts of the eastern curtain wall, and from my observations it's quite a busy little place at this time of day."

Meanwhile, Godfroi cleaned off the excess blood from his sword and faced the two straight on again. "Is that the place where I hear they indulge in red and white 'validus vinum'—drench themselves in strong alcohol? And in huge amounts of it too? We could entice these raw recruits away from their miserable landlords by offering them solace, or even forgiveness, whilst working for your ethereal King Hugues, and of course help them empty their vast wine cellars of their contents whilst consuming as much of it as possible. And we could also smoke their plants in their little heated water fountains." Hugues started pointing his index finger at Andre'

"Oh, yes, wine and shisha—what a wonderful way to relax! But don't get too upset when you wake up with a cold, steel dagger across your throat my friend," He remarked, pointing and pretending to slit his own throat with his hand.

"Especially as you float in vile exultation from a self-imposed unearthly stupor; and, that's exactly my point, we can become very vulnerable if we are not careful. And that's exactly what I mean when I say we need to build up a close knit team: a group of elite fighters, where we can actually have that 'utopia' without the fear of any surprises. We should become a force so strong that we are even feared by those who make the laws and fear our God.

Acre will provide us our good solid training ground and provide a good defence; these closed walls can easily be defended by just a few good men. Well, at least for now anyway. And that's just to start off with. So, I suppose to answer your earlier question, Andre', my vision is precisely that. We are to provide close protection.

Therefore, what we really need is a solid team of very special men to protect it, and we could become an entity far removed from inner city life—far away from prying eyes and ears, and most certainly away from the Temple, until we get really settled.

Our Temple Mount will be our historical start point. It will be documented in the annals of Christian time, as the place where it all began, contained within the sandy walls a historical log of historical battles, and historical skirmishes, combined with discussions and triumphs keeping the memory of the good King Solomon, the wisest of the wise, firmly alive through the ages.

As you know, I have spoken with the King's council, and it appears that Baldwin is desperate to take control of his lands and restore order to the surrounding countries. He feels he is somehow losing his grip and feels that he may lose his crown soon."

Just then, the prayer call resonated from the nearby village; the Shaman stood high in his muddy mosque calling for prayer. The Knights each bowed to this ritual and played to its existence within the Order—a control measure in the years that followed as their mark of respect.

If war was to be had, then its bloody outcomes were to be considered. The mosque construction and design was built to be filled with people at prayer, and the many congregations were easily contained within the many villages as temporary prisons, or safe havens, as the battles and skirmishes were being played out by the Generals of the day. And the simple lay folk could be protected.

De Payens had often notionally built the mosque strategy into his contingency planning, where he would enact a notional war at key times in the Egyptian calendar for impact and review the outcome gauged against religious devotion. These prayer gatherings would ensure that the simple folk were in a collective audience and not exposed to imminent war, and of course what no better location to keep the rich pickings hidden away from the very folk who were stealing from them.

The rudimentary tables and shrines that adorned these places of worship held many secrets far beyond the knowledge of their keepers. The mosques were used not only to house the many that prayed but played host to the gold and rich pickings held by the Order from their many encounters. Vaults were hidden underneath the house of prayer, and more importantly specific shrines identified for foodstuffs and wine were stored as contingency for potential longer term sieges.

Jerusalem was, and is, riddled with underground caves and passageways, and only one map had been produced for strategic purposes during the turbulent times. De Payen had acquired that very source of topographical information and had it made into a woven rug that hung over the doorway. Godfroi, meanwhile, was busy wiping his face upon the very tapestry that held the most relevant of detail.

A secondary part of the siege plan was to ensure that the spoils of war were easily accessible and were also moved under the blanket of secrecy, and today the Temple may still lay claim to most of these hidden treasures.

De Payen smiled again. "But more important than that gentleman, is that we, as a collective group, will know that it all started from this very location. A point in time when Acre was but a clutch of donkey hutches and nomadic dwellings, a village littered with sheep droppings and human excrement, oh, and that reminds me.

You know, Andre', Godfroi, I have to ask you both a question: I have no idea why you two hang around this shit-ridden, hell hole with me. And yet you don't ask for much in return; neither do you complain. And yet, you place your life on the line in support of our needs. Why would you gentlemen want to do that?" There was a distinct, quieter moment for reflection between the assembled Knights as De Payen sat back in his chair and smirked.

Montbard smiled first and tapped the heft of his sword. "It is because maybe I like the smell of sheep shit, 'merde' perhaps. Maybe that's what keeps me here?" Then he laughed loudly again.

Godfroi pursed his lips and ran his big, hairy hand through his thick, dark hair, front to back and started pulling at the tiny knots as he spoke. "I have lands that I inherited in France. I have enough of the good life waiting for me, if, and when, I return to Europe. But these trappings were bestowed upon me.

I did not earn them. I did not banter for their delivery. Nor did I win them in battle. These are trappings of the aristocracy. They are gifted, not earned." He stopped and took a deep breath. "But here in your empirical 'shit hole', I have a certain level of self-worth.

I fight to both survive and to be part of something very, very special. And I honestly care for the many travellers who do not deserve to die because of the confusion that this hostile, uncaring land brings, and work to the fact that pilgrims deserve to visit the lands of the Holy, and bear witness to something even more special: belief. And I see myself in that role.

For the past five years, I have seen many sad and unnecessary deaths, rapes, murder, deceit, dismemberment, horrific acts of torture and injustice coupled with corruption beyond corruption. I suppose I just hang around to see what the hell happens next." Godfroi was nodding in agreement.

"I have watched you closely, Hugues. You struggle to find order amongst this ever increasing chaotic world of depravity and depravation; a place where order is unlikely to rest its shield. And yet, you yourself, Hugues, you don't ask for anything in return either, yet you still strive to correct it.

King Baldwin is good to you—us—he likes you and he trusts you, and you yourself, well you are a bit of an enigma to me . . ." There was a moment's pause. "You sort of inspire me too. Although you're not the best swordsman in the world by a long way, and certainly not the best cook in the land either. But, may I say that you do me much justice by simply having me around. And in reality tolerating my arrogance and my unrelenting humour; well my friend that to me is nice. So here I still stand, with nowhere else to go."

Andre' suddenly motioned the assembled Knights to be quiet by placing his finger across his mouth. "Shush, can you hear that?" he said.

Hugues took two steps towards the door and took a quick glance outside. To his surprise he spied a young native girl sitting cross legged with a piece of cloth grasped in her hands, rocking back and forth.

She was sitting near the old town's Byzantine well, an ancient water well that descended down to the level of the aquafir, the table of fresh water that lay just a few metres under the blanket of sand, and was probably dug by the locals as a water source easily three hundred years ago. This part of

Jordan was literally littered with underground tributaries each having been penetrated at most built up areas.

The young girl was singing loud enough for him to make out the older Aramaic tongue. He turned back and asked Andre' what she was singing. Andre' smiled again. "Why, my dear friend, she is singing your Lord's Prayer—isn't it haunting? De Payen took another look and listened intently. He could distinctly hear the words 'Abwoon D' Bashmaya' over and over.

"Yes, haunting," he said, then sat down after taking another glance at the young maiden.

Montbard reached out and closed a single window shutter then sat down opposite De Payen, who was still playing with the gold coin. He was spinning it across the table top as if it was a child's toy.

"So, tell me, my good friend, you said yesterday that our history will unfold to tell the big wide world that this team of elite mercenaries brought peace to the Holy Land by protecting visitors who needed protection from the varying groups of raiding infidel and murderous Muslims, who were desperate for wealth but more importantly 'hell-bent' on destroying the faith of the western world. Is that really your vision, Mister De Payen?"

Andre' asked the question in anticipation of having the option to join in and share this pragmatic view of the future world. He then placed a hand over the coin and stopped it spinning. Hugues momentarily sprung to life, having drifted away from the on-going conversation, almost lost in deep thought.

Andre' continued, "Your dream is to escort thousands of pilgrims who have chosen to undertake this arduous journey from middle Europe and across the desert and eventually through to Outremer. A simple adventure for them but for us a monumental task. Our role is simply to provide protection and safety for every one of these ill-informed people. Hugues, that's thousands upon thousands of visitors over the years. We couldn't possibly cover that many people. But what a challenge!"

Andre' gave a little thought towards their own personal crusade which had brought them together. Their journey was undertaken several years back and an adventure which would replicate the ones that most pilgrims of the day would take, a time out in an effort to pay homage to their biblical icon, Jesus Christ.

Their pilgrimage was a mark of their own devotion towards Christianity in general, but sadly they had collectively witnessed many acts of greed and violence. It was clearly the systematic rape and pillage against many people who had suffered tremendous hardship and torture at the hands of those who failed to understand the complex western culture. Of which, according to De Payen, was orchestrated by their own local commanders and leaders.

This was indeed the pivotal point where the three Knights came together and chose the unrelenting task of providing this welcome protection. Often between them discussing the potential of their services being requested by leading officials and could lead to undertaking many errands on behalf of the Monarch, King Baldwin himself, or similarly secret tasks and exercises for other noble figures of authority. And thus, primarily lay the seeds for their Templar services.

Montbard would often recite to the many clients that the Templar's were either employed as protectors of people or were the long term custodians of other people's wealth, and that was not always a bad thing.

Hugues De Payen stood up and spoke with sudden authority. "Godfroi, Andre', I have had a notion about bringing many knights together for our new order. I have taken the name from the former Jewish temple over at 'Al Aqsa'—that's the name for the old mosque."

Godfroi started shaking his head like an adolescent child being talked down to by his elders. "I know what you're thinking, Goddy. You think I am stating the obvious, but we do have the opportunity to inhabit the royal palace and this very structure lies in close proximity to our stables and ultimate goal. I have asked King Baldwin if was possible for us be accommodated within the noble dwellings as I wanted to ensure that we are at his disposal night and day when required by his highness. There is an annex in the palace that would suit our exact needs. It forms part of the east enclosed wing and has two exits. The royal scribe says that King Baldwin has agreed in principle to our requests, but we will have to wait until he decides on the scope of our services."

De Payen laid out a small page of parchment on the table. It was perhaps the only sketch or map of the Al Aqsa mosque in existence. Godfroi sneezed then stood next to Andre' who had momentarily raised himself out of his seat to view the very informative map.

Both of them were now facing De Payen who had started spinning the coin on top of the map. Andre'" was quick to remark, "What, are you saying? Are you telling us that you just asked the Israeli King if you could move into his royal palace as a resident with some of your friends, now! That even amazes me. Hugues, you have some balls—I will tell you that! Furthermore, I also think you have given this a far greater deal of thought than you are letting on, my friend, haven't you, you old dog?" Andre' opened the window shutter and leaned up against the wooden framework, just as the sun's rays lit up the window frame then illuminated the map on the table.

Godfroi momentarily began scratching his head with the tip of his dagger. "Well, what did the King actually say then?" he asked with keen interest then prompted, "C'mon, Hugues, stop pissing us about. You know we are itching to find out. Did you really honestly ask King Baldwin rule of all the sands in the Holy Land for his support? And I do mean honestly."

Hugues stood up and puffed his chest outwards. "Gentlemen, may I present to you both the only set of keys to Al Aqsa. Then he lay two heavy steel keys down on the table top. Montbard and St Omer stared at the keys; then gazed at each other for a few brief seconds. De Payen remained calm; expectant of a comment or three. None came.

Chapter Two: 'The Knights' Templar'

Al Aqsa.

It was an extremely hot and dusty morning as the three mounted Knights made their way into the enclosed palace courtyard to conduct their planned reconnaissance trip of their new acquired dwellings.

The annex building lay one hundred feet west of the older stable house where a single doorway led up into the aged towered structure of the Al Aqsa Mosque. The Knights, having dismounted their horses, had entered the inner dwellings with haste and anticipation. Then collectively began making their way up and beyond the high curtain wall.

After a minute or so they were confronted with another set of broad stairs leading upwards into an almost secret hallway or alleyway, through which a modestly decorated tunnel led directly into the King's court. At the midway point, in the newly constructed alleyway, there stood two guards. Each placed on either side of the marble walkway with simple clear orders that no-one was to enter the next doorway unless they were adorned in the new Order's attire of the Knights' Mantle bearing the Templar insignia.

Godfroi stepped almost gingerly into the mosque and began removing his footwear, when Andre' spoke out. "No! No! Godder what are you doing, this is our domain. Within these walls we have our own customs to adhere to first. We must remain ready for battle at all times. We cannot simply allow ourselves to be distracted by cumbersome rituals that leave us vulnerable. The time will come when we will pray as a collective group—but not now. Put your boots back on."

Meanwhile, Hugues had entered one of the anti-chambers and was taking his surroundings into his memory. He remained very mindful of the historical events that resonated in the sandy masonry. He then entered the great hall with great pace and was somehow clearly excited when he spoke. "Is this not the just the best place in the world to form a religious military order from? I mean look at it!"

Godfroi spoke out in quick response, "Hugues, it's a flea pit. Yes, it's big and open, but it does need a bloody good scrape and clean!"

"I know, it has been untouched for nearly twelve years," retorted De Payen, who was now walking across the floor again, counting his paces. "Fifteen, sixteen . . ." Then he stopped at thirty something steps. "Thirty one, by thirty one point four paces—that's perfect." He exclaimed, then headed for another side chamber door on the other side of the hall. Then he raised his voice towards Andre' as he passed by. "Guys can't you see it from here? This will become our newly acquired headquarters.

The 'new Knighthood' will evolve from within here. We will grow not only as a powerful monastic warrior troop but as a strategic international entity of great importance." He then pointed directly at the two Knights. "Godfroi, you and your banking experts, they can financially clean up from here. I will ensure that you will be assisted by clerics, illuminators and administrators.

We will hold commune and conclave and pray to the lord for deliverance whilst counting our newly acquired wealth. Our reality will be to evolve into a team of highly trained, professional killers and guardsman, but unknown to those ill informed, we know that we already own lands in other countries across Europe, and this gentlemen is where our risk lays. We had better make sure that our adventures do not wholly displace our families, France will show no mercy if he upset the Vatican.

But, we together as a team we will become very famous and will be known as seasoned diplomats and envoys. We will be serving both the Kings and Lords of many supporting lands, and eventually empowered by papal bulls and decrees from the Pope himself, and that I know for sure will happen. We could have succession with Papal support and even from uncle Bernard himself."

Andre' stepped forward. "Hugues, have you been at the wine again? This plan of yours all sounds very complicated and seems to balance on a notional whim and prayer! Are you not getting a little bit ahead of yourself my friend? I mean we have just got into the building, and already you have hatched a new world order of things."

"Precissimo! Andre'," remarked De Payen. Pointing his index finger straight into the air. "But sadly, you, my dear friend, lack a certain vision. Let us stop and think for one moment, shall we? Number one: let us contemplate the fact that we are now housed within the royal palace. Number two: we also have full support within the ranks of the Vatican's leadership framework. Number three: the buildings themselves are already protected structures by the King's Army. And if you look at your many sketches you will see that we already have stables and safe havens at our disposal."

He then pointed out of the window. "Just out there we have a certain freedom. And look, we have rooms for at least another six to eight Knights; a body of men who will have a single chamber each, imagine that one of their very own. And finally number four and the most important item of all: we have each other to make it happen."

Andre' Montbard was now thirty-nine year's old and was shaking his head, he appeared almost motivated by Hugues's ramblings and had never really got excited about anything, and he was now shaking his head in total agreement. Well, that's what he would say if asked to explain anything about getting excited.

And for as long as he could remember was brought up with a modest lifestyle and never really had suffered growing up as a child—having been supplied with all the trappings of a comfortable, rich life back in France. The rich pickings of the rich classes which were literally thrown at him.

For Andre', now was the exact time for him to get excited, and he did not know how to enjoy this new experience. He knew his social skills were immature, or deemed almost cold even. But he wanted so much to integrate and be part of this new, lively and exciting group.

"So what do we do then?" he asked. "Do we find our space and dance about the room like idiots or do we all go and get drunk and fall over, or what?"

Godfroi, pushed the door fully closed, then spoke, "Andre', look at us? Do we look excited?" Andre' shook his head and pointed to De Payen. "Okay, granted, yes I must admit, he does look a bit happy. I mean look at him," he said, as De Payen marched out of the chamber. "He is like a blacksmith with a new batch of steel just delivered by the Grand Master Hammer-Smith of the cosmos himself."

Godfroi clapped his hands. "Yep, I must agree with you there. He does, doesn't he? That because excitement can bring great fear or great relief. This example over there is one of relief. It's not the same as running your steel blade through someone and saving your own skin—that feeling is another experience entirely all together. But it is still exciting. You must decide how excited you want to get."

Andre' began nodding as De Payen came back into the chamber, having looked in most of the various other anti-chambers that were connected to the tower. "Precissimo!" he exclaimed. "Gents, we are heading the right way. Trust me—I feel it in my water." Then he marched off into the final anti-chamber.

Andre' smiled, "Yeah! It does feel good. I think I know what you are saying. Thank you, Godfroi. I must write to my uncle Bernard and let him know that you are all watching over me."

"Oh, no, Andre', don't do that. Your uncle will know that I am leading you astray, my friend. As he knows that there are many other pleasures and delights in this big, wide world than just killing." Then laughed as he walked off to find De Payen.

Chapter Three: 'The Recruiting Campaign'

De Payen returned to the central chamber and turned to both Godfroi and Andre' Montbard. "Well, then gentlemen, that leads me into another point, I need another seven like-minded Brothers like you two to join me. I need more friends and trustworthy men. People whom I can trust with my life. And more importantly, Brothers in arms who are not afraid to engage in battle; Brothers who are willing to die for our cause."

De Payen stopped his ranting and stared directly into the eyes of Andre' Montbard, "Will you be one of them, Andre'? Will you join me on this madcap campaign to restore law and order into this damned, barren wasteland, this grotesque rat infested desert, and I do of course mean as an equal?"

De Payen pointed across the room. "Godfroi has already agreed to join me. Between us we can bring some sort of stability to this hostile shit-ridden environment where we can work to a universal but very simple strategy. A plan where we, as a collective group, can protect new-comers to the Holy Land. We can only offer temporary shelter for them, a safe haven against any potential harm and keep these ill-bred moronic infidels at sword's length.

Let's be practical here—we are already doing it anyway, but let us add a new dimension to the equation. Providing protection for pilgrims from start to finish of their intrepid journeys to and from the Temple Mount, wont be a walk in the park, but, of course, my friend, there is a potential bonus in it for all of us: a great opportunity to thrive and prosper. We can ask for small donations or request a small fee for our special services, 'Le-Protection'.

Who knows, perhaps in the future great kings from afar will demand our services and ask us for protection. Lords will trust us with their woman-folk, but of course our vows of chastity must remain pristine, we will remain untarnished, and that part of our life, my friends, will be judged by the power of the sword."

The Knights began making their way through the chambers and back into the outside world. Montbard laughed loudly and walked into the rickety outhouse. "Don't you think the great Allah might have something to say about that?" he said, flicking the heavy linen screen to one side. "I don't think he will be happy with you re-directing all the incoming monies into his sacred land—especially into the coffers of Rome," he shouted, pushing the heavy linen curtain to one side again and looking back at them.

De Payen laughed. "Good point, but I did ask him about it. It was in one of my many visions but, in his defence he did say something to me, this great Allah! But, as I do not speak enough Arabic or Aramaic to interpret his message effectively, I thought I would find out my own way by exercising my own wit and understanding by observing what happens next.

Although, my friend, I do know one thing, and that is that his holiness, the Pope in Rome, would help us secure our future existence here. The Papacy would support our campaign if we apply enough pressure and diplomacy towards regime change, especially if he sees the potential in procuring a vast amount of riches for the Church of Christ."

Andre's head suddenly popped back out from behind the carpeted doorway. "The Pope. Did you say El Pope? Thee Pope! The holiest of Papal ones!" he exclaimed, tilting his head to one side as he spoke. "So, Hugues are you saying for my many, many efforts, I will actually receive clemency or Papal forgiveness for my many, many, sins, after all! I mean, this is Outremer and not middle Europe after all!" he exclaimed, and stepped back into the room. His tiny mind scrambling to grab the notion that he could receive a legal pardon for his unquestionable and deathly past.

De Payen smiled again. "Depends on how many sins you have to divulge, my friend. I would presume that one sin is just added on to the next," came the response, in a more defined and almost humorous tone. Godfroi was laughing loudly and began collecting his belongings together. "Now that would be worth fighting for."

"It is," came the shallow response from De Payen, who then sat down staring back at Godfroi.

After a few days, several potential temple dwellers had assembled in the grand hallway. King Baldwin had once again been very accommodating in permitting many guests into the inner sanctum of his domain; albeit they remained under the watchful eye of the palace guard.

The invitees had begun parading themselves like roosters in a hen coup trying to grab the attentions of the prime hens, each candidate presenting their case in front of Hugues De Payen and Andre' Montbard, asking to join them in their crusade to avenge Christ for his untimely demise.

Each demanding to join the quest against the many brigands of marauding Muslims, and each clearly explaining the way in which they would despatch tyrants and villains with the sword whilst offering to obey the laws and virtues of the church, coupled by pledging allegiance to Hughes De Payen himself as their Grand Master.

Andre' had come to the conclusion that there were more potential murderers than potential monks in the new found community, and he became quite uneasy at the prospect of this hidden population navigating the darkened alleyways of Jerusalem in the stillness of the night, potentially preying on the vulnerable local community.

After careful selection, a few seasoned veterans had been singled out and had signed up for what was to form the core team of this new Christian, military order. These chosen men were the more silent types of the invitees, the more mature who had let their skills as swordsman and thinkers determine their future careers.

Andre' sat quietly and watched the few potential Knights integrate with one another within the thick, stone walls of Al Aqsa. Each man was smiling as they conversed. One Knight in particular, Gondomar, a man of fair build and dark complexion had a particular humorous streak in him. He would wait in the side-lines until it was quiet then he would flick or ping a few hard peas at one of the other Knights; then make gestures towards another Knight, intimating that they had thrown the peas.

Andre' stood close by Gondomar, he coughed, then spoke. "It's amazing what a little distraction can do," he said. Both men now standing up and watching as two adjacent Knights had begun mimicking mock battle steps. Then he turned and faced Andre'.

Gondomar, not wishing to be seen as flippant, spoke out. "It's always the same; one can observe the subtle indications—a bit of misdirection it can provide great opportunity. It has certainly fooled a few guards in my day."

Montbard smiled. "Indeed, but these men may save your life one day. I would suggest best stay on their good side for now. Let the infidel worry about the peas when the time is right." He slapped Gondomar on the back and walked away.

Chapter Four: 'The Nine Swords of
                   Christendom'

Hugues De Payen held up a scroll of vellum and read out nine names. An incredible silence rang out across the internal hallway of what was once King Solomon's social guest halls. Godfroi had laid six swords of forged steel on the large round table, each of which a veritable and welcome donation from a benevolent well-wisher.

The table top had been etched with the initials of each chosen Knight, in their order of succession and the heft of their new swords were laid out adjacent to their initials. Godfroi then read out the vows of chastity and poverty and asked for obedience before the patriarch of Jerusalem. They all agreed and vowed to join the local regular canons of the Holy Sepulchre as newly appointed postulate Monks.

Each Templar remained mindful to the fact that they had absolutely no intention of joining the church as full time Monks for any specified period of time, and they anticipated another ceremony was to take place, a ritual ceremony that was to be re-enacted within a few days' time; a gathering that would be attended by King Baldwin II, who would be acting as their witness as they each took their rightful places on the global political stage.

Each man swore and agreed to obey the 'rule' of the day. The very same 'rule' driven forward in earlier years by Pope Nicholas II and the Roman Council of 1059 and adopted and integrated by Bernard for the order, but the Knights Templar had ultimately insisted on not being fully ordained into the ranks. Therefore, were legally able to wield a sword, whilst remaining cognizant that it was strictly forbidden for a man of the cloth to take up arms against any foe.

The Knights' Templar had found a balanced solution to the church's dilemma, and a balance that fitted well with the ailing King Baldwin's hidden agenda, a plan that was provide stability in his Kingdom. His father, Hugh, the Count of Rethel, would have wholly agreed with his strategy, had he lived long enough to witness this new order being formed, and perhaps would have joined Hugues and Bernard in the longer term.

It was also widely known that King Baldwin II had close links with Godfrey of Bouillon but, perhaps not a link that would suggest genetic connections or near family relationships, but ensured that their close and trusted friends and colleagues knew of their strong relationship.

A bond of friendship which would forge understanding and co-operation between the Temple and the ruling classes in the years to follow, and became very evident as daily life unfolded. Suffice to say Godfrey was close enough to form an allegiance as Brothers in arms for the purposes of success, and perhaps Baldwin may have even planned to serve the Order from within the ranks on both sides—once the Order was fully established.

The newly established Order's first real quest of the day, was to rid the alleyways of the inner city of Jerusalem from those who were wreaking havoc in the wee small hours within the walls of Jerusalem, and within a very short time frame Hugues and his team had cleansed the inner city from the hidden enemy and brought a level of stability to the many market places.

The Order roamed the inner walls under the cloak of darkness and dealt with the unruly in the most vicious of manners. In a very short time frame, the Templars had earned a great level of respect from the local population; a respect and acceptance that were almost unthinkable just a few months prior.

The master plan had simultaneously been hatched to source the riches of Christendom and make plans to remove the many riches out of the reach of the infidel in Outremer. The Knights were tasked to frequent the many outbuildings and lodges and take the local community into their confidence and learn what they could from many of the old wives' tales or stories that appeared to have lost impetus.

The Templars would gather weekly and recount their many tales of rags to riches and discuss any folk tales where an element of secrecy evolved or existed. After a few months Godfroi had compiled a relatively long list of potential locations for the storage of wealth, but the same location kept recurring: 'Solomon's Temple'.

On reflection in the few years that ensued, one could attribute the Templar's vast portfolio to their careful and strategic asset management skills, including the control of their vast maritime fleet of ships with almost two thousand vessels at their disposal.

A fleet which traversed the globe containing riches beyond even 21st century ideas of greed, and was indeed the established merchant shipping fleet of the early days. An enterprise that boasted continuity into the modern era, having negotiated the middle ages.

In their extensive acquisition portfolio, the Templars were also reported to have owned a series of fortresses, castles and churches, globally. Mostly accrued as donations from the more wealthier families, often with powerful, influential connections, coupled with some higher echelon elements of the church; a collective group who anticipated that these new breed of Templars were becoming a force that was not only taking the Middle East by storm, but was also making a significant impact across central Europe.

Introduction of Abbot Bernard of Clairvaux—Cistercian

A major figure embedded within Templar history is one Bernard of Clairvaux, an informed intellectual and highly influential member of the clergy who was born under the title 'Bernard de Fontaine' in the year 1090, in Dijon, France.

He was refuted to be one of the greatest theologians of his time and is credited with writing the construction of 'The Rule'—a series of guidelines as instruments in guidance for the evolving order.

Bernard spent considerable time gaining recognition for the Order which was eventually awarded by way of Papal endorsement as the 'Templar Order' by the council of Troyes, in the year 1129.

It is permissible to think that both the Templars and the Cistercians were close allies, as both had connections with Troyes in some shape or form, as did Bernard's family links and therefore, in recognition of his efforts as a Cistercian Monk and his Templar involvement, was also recognised as a notable pillar of local society. Eventually being canonized in his lifetime as a living Saint at Citeaux and was relocated to a monastery in Clairvaux by the ministry.

Chapter Five: # 'The Advent of the 'A Orbis of Murco'

William of Tyre and his entourage had arrived in the small village of Acre with little or no fuss. The guard troop assembled in the middle of the square and quickly dispersed in a flash of swords and brightly coloured armour glinting in the sunlight, coupled with the chinking and clanking of their rudimentary protective bodily armament clearly a display of presence.

William stood up in his stirrups and looked around, just as his small group of his most trusted body guards had surrounded this local dignitary. The standard human four by four shield, then the guard of soldiers quickly dispersed across the small, grey square in an almost orchestrated formation, hiding and skirmishing between the many alleyways and squared edifices of the local buildings, almost sealing off all exits and entry points into the square—or so they had thought. The rider sat back down in the saddle.

Above them, poised stealthily on the rooftops of the clay buildings, six figures stood in quiet contemplation, each watching as William's troops shuffled and settled back into their strategic positions in securing their Lord's safety. Twenty feet away, in an outbuilding, two Knights stood in total silence and watched.

After a few seconds, a shout resonated across the square. "De Payen!" the echoes ringing out as a loud cry from the lead horseman bounced across the many walls. "You have a mystery benefactor. We come in peace. See, we have here a white flag raised to make you aware of our honest intentions". The horseman held the flag aloft on a single wooden pole then stood up in his stirrups again.

"We have brought you some offerings." The rider did not appear to be an infidel; his attire was too regal to be anything but a Lord and his guard were certainly rehearsed in providing 360 degree protection. A simple circle had been formed, and at its centre point, their prominent Commander spouting out his commands.

Hugues De Payen recognised this early first visit as a significant step towards obtaining the recognition that the Order desperately craved. The public relations of the 12th century political mechanism had kicked in and a Lord of the manor had sought them out. Firstly, by his efforts in travelling to what De Payen thought was his own personal sanctuary, or training ground, away from the Temple Mount, and conversely bringing them offerings from an external alien source.

The village of Acre had been deliberately selected by the Order as their operations centre: the small clutch of houses lay within two arterial routes in and out of the local area and were ideal for the Orders purposes. De Payen, Godfroi and Montbard had spent a great deal of time living amongst the people there, trying to blend in with the locals and build a quiet harmonious relationship whilst building a reputation through absorbing the culture.

This location was also the mid-way point to Jaffa and the small village that would eventually house the many thousands of pilgrims who passed through the lands. The pilgrims could take time to adjust and acclimatise to Outremer for the first couple of days of their exposure in the Holy Land, until the time of their exit.

A few moments later, Hugues had made his way to meet William of Tyre face-to-face, and had exited the small outbuilding just off to the rear of the visitors. Simultaneously, there was a shuffle of armour and another chinking of metal as many swords were instantly released from their scabbards. De Payen bowed his head slightly forward. The sun had just peaked over the building tops, sending showers of rays of sunlight across his steel helmet almost temporarily blinding the horseman.

Then he stared directly at the rider, just their eyes made contact, the rider was momentarily unnerved and shifted uneasily in his saddle—he was clearly apprehensive. "Salam el al malikum," came the response from the Knight. "Malikum El salaam." Retorted the mounted visitor. A customary gesture in acknowledgement of his societal standing.

De Payen remained respectful but was clearly harbouring the notion of entrapment. The last thing he wanted to do was get caught unawares by stupidity, let alone fall into the simplest of traps. Andre' Montbard and Godfrey had done their homework and recognised William as soon as he entered the square but not as the squire in charge of the team, but more of a bystander hidden amongst the troops.

"Who, may I ask, did you say provides such an offering?" asked De Payen, staring up at the horseman.

Tyre remained mounted and slowly removed his silver gauntlet. He coughed a little then spoke. "It appears your efforts are not being overlooked, or dismissed. Nor are they being underestimated. I have been given orders or a request to pass on to you. They come from the powers on high; they hail from one Bernard of Clairvaux. This request has been sent from across Europe."

The voice of the horseman was not an ignorant tone nor was it fully Arabic.

De Payen gave it credence as either German or Italian, but it was certainly not Arab. "I bid you welcome," he said in response.

"Bernard says don't give up on your quest, and insists that you will accept these gifts as a token of his intended future friendship and a gesture of his long term support for your holy cause. He also says take care of his kith and kin, as he is precious to him, whatever the words kith and kin actually mean in your particular language as I am not fully rehearsed in middle latin. However, that was his message." The rider was by then a bit more composed and took to twisting in his gilded saddle.

Andre' suddenly took a step forward and thrust his sword deep into the sand, pointed end first and left it to sway in the warm breeze. "No matter where you go or where you venture to, no matter where you hide in this forsaken land, your family always seem to find you. How comforting is that?" he said, quite loudly and slapped his chest and again gazed at William. "I am kin," he explained. "It is what we call our family members where I am from. I am sure you can work out the rest." The rider nodded in agreement.

The horse was suddenly startled as one of the guards had adopted a juxtaposition almost next to De Payen himself. In doing so, Hugues flinched as another single sword was passed across his eye line.

It was a slow and very deliberate gesture and was presented from his left side, the steel being held by Godfrey Buillion. The sword was then very slowly presented, hilt first, towards the lone guardsman. De Payen froze momentarily; trying to fathom what was unfolding before him and was almost annoyed at himself for being so stupid.

Meanwhile, Godfroi de St Omer had made a quiet, stealthful skirmish behind the group and waited patiently, should things go wrong. Godfrey Bissot had recognised that one of the guardsmen was William of Tyre himself, and not the rider at the front of the entourage. A simple ploy adopted by the gentry to protect the master. Godfroi had luckily been at court when William had entered the palace as one of the King's trusted messengers.

Hugues De Payen glanced at Godfrey and Andre', then nodded his head and thanked them.

William spoke up, "Clairvaux also asks that your special Brotherhood be asked as to what costs your services can be acquired? He also reports that although he has adequate support from the Cistercians, he feels they do a good job, but sadly, they cannot provide your specific line of support by way of the holy sword.

Therefore, he wishes you to be provided with clothing and more steel and sufficient funds to be able to stand on your own ground." The small square went very quiet as the two groups waited and watched. There had been a moment of disturbance as a flock of small birds took flight.

Andre' was standing on the right hand side of Godfrey and whispered something into his ear. Hugues offered William a hand of friendship and openly accepted the welcome gifts. Standing all too quiet in the back ground was Geoffrey Bissot. He watched and waited as the many interchanges took place. He had taken it upon himself to remain as secretive as possible with every intention of preserving Hugues De Payen's life.

"We will do God's bidding with these gifts. Come, join us William, for we are about to eat; not a feast by your standards of course but an honest meal and little compensation for Bernard's generosity."

William of Tyre and the assembled Knights sat around a large, circular wooden table; a large plinth of timber, almost three inches in quickness and endowed with many gouges and chunks evident from its surface platform. The table dominated the small room and barely left enough space for the assembled group to sit comfortably.

Montbard spoke out, "It is an interesting article, this table, don't you think? The obvious cuts and sword indents here, there and over there, signs of bygone times I am afraid. And this big one here, this huge slice mark, well, that was me I am afraid. But all relevant when this table was once employed as a fine par of doors to our residence. Served us well in the protection of our humble abode, and now look at it, a piece of our history in the making." Andre' was almost proud of his table and explained that the design and shape had been fabricated, or cut down to size from, what was once a pair of old oak Temple doors.

"The two halves placed together making a fair sized tablet and of course very crudely joined, cut into a circular surface, and representative of a symbol with no corners, a neutral point, a shape with no start and no finish. A symbol of continuity.

Well, that's according to Andre'," he said, tapping his breast. "And you can blame Godfroi for the rough edges," he said, slapping his chest again. "He is not the best 'le carpenter' in the world and an even worse butcher, especially with a saw." Andre' again smiled a huge, broad smile and gave a gentle slap on Godfroi's back. "But he wields a sword like any crazed axe wilding homicidal maniac, but, only when he needs to."

Gondomar then joined in the conversation and ran his hand along the leading edge of the table and removed a few splinters with his fingers as he went along it's concentric outer edge, stopping only for a few seconds to withdraw his dagger and cut a larger sized splinter from the table top. He then ran his hands across the relatively smooth surface, then spoke.

"You could eat your food off this table," he said, then faced the assembled Knights who had all started laughing again. "This particular visit to Acre was reflected in his chronicles of the 'Kingdom of Jerusalem' by William of Tyre and places the foundation of the Knights' Templar between the years AD 1119 and 1120 by charter.

Therefore, now the Order was widely recognised by many scholars that the prime Knights' Templar and was undisputedly formed by Hugues De Payen, officially in the year 1120. Albeit the Order may have worked together sometime before this official launch date."

'The Breaking of Bread'

In the small room, each Knight had sat next to one another; their swords placed tip to tip, forming what is now a recognisable symbol of unity. William of Tyre reluctantly removed his sword from its sheath and placed it gently on the table top, between De Payen and Montbard.

"I see every man has his place in this new world of yours?" said William.

Andre' was very quick to respond. "Indeed it is the order of things, my liege, and an indication that we accept all changes to our structure, as an order, and we must retain this level of conformity to ensure reliability, stability and, dare I say it, 'order'."

Another voice spoke out. "Befitting, don't you think. Now, that we have collectively agreed in moving this fine piece work of dodgy craftsmanship to better lodgings," he said, pointing to the table, "this table is now part of our order, and that this once old pair of wooden doors will be transported from here into the old wing of King Baldwin's and the great King Solomon's temple."

William gave a quick glance in Hugue's direction, who acknowledged and smiled. Geoffrey was getting excited, as was Andre', and he continued in explaining the workings of this simple table. "It is to become our focal point and neutral place for open discussion," explained Geoffrey Bissot as he sunk his teeth into a good sized lump of bread.

William responded almost in admiration. "I am sure it will witness many great discussions and decisions, and will bear witness to the evolvement of this new Holy Order that will shape our alliance in the years to come."

Godfrey placed both hands on the table top. "If I should be so bold to say, that our Lord will share our offerings in the many years to come, and will provide us with great guidance and direction, in bringing an end to this tyranny and civil unrest that the great Lords of your lands have failed to stop."

"Indeed," William promptly replied. "Tyre was a very astute and clinically observant type of individual. He would always take time to weigh up the oncoming enemy, and often think well before committing himself to either verbal or physical entanglement. His strategy had obviously served him well and kept him alive, and he deduced that Godfrey was by no means a small man; his chiselled jaw and dark hair presented a strong and awesome figure of a man that suited any Knight's description, as did most of the people in his immediate vicinity."

Godfrey had an uncanny and unstable presence about him, where conversely, William was almost awestruck and bemused at the same time with Hugues De Payen, in his unique ability to manage such people with great ease in the way that he did. William had no reservations that each man in the tiny room would die for this one man alone and, more importantly, what he could not understand was that they would do it without question.

William then spoke up. "Godfrey, you may well be correct, but as you are all aware, there is great confusion amongst Allah's children. The people have no direction. El Saladin commands farmers and slaves. He has no real army to command as a military arm, just a mass of lay people who are coerced into fighting for their family's security. But, you, gentlemen, are very different," he said, pointing his finger around the room.

"As Temple dwelling Knights, well, you are already feared by the law makers of the land, and you are just coming together as a new force to be fearful of, and this is very much widely acknowledged by our leaders." Hugues then slammed his jug down on the table and stood up. "Chevaliers, a toast! To William of Tyre."

Each Knight stood up and toasted the good Lord in succession, then saluted their new benefactor, Bernard Clairvaux. It was after this salutation that Hugues De Payen then raised his wooden goblet again and toasted the first real **Order**. "Gentlemen!" he said, in a stern and very commanding tone. "To the honour and the glory of the Knights' Templar—Outremer!"

Non Nobis Domine, Non Nobis, Sed Nomini Tuo Da Gloriam!

Each Knight drank a full chalice of wine and remained standing in quietness for a full thirty seconds until De Payen lowered his head and said, "Amen." The Order followed in obeyance.

Just as Roral was about to tuck into a large chunk of bread, he was momentarily stopped by Godfrey as his large hand was placed firmly over the crusty brown loaf. "Gentlemen, as we are now a band of Brothers and of course a collective team, it is only right that we observe a few rules and regulations from the onset: feasting should be conducted after we say grace and acknowledge that the food on our table is perhaps more than most would have in their homes. I would like to ask we take a few minutes in silence in thanking God for this meal, and humbly thank Jesus for the provision of it."

After a short period of silence, William spoke out, "Carry on, Godfrey, this is very interesting."

Godfrey leaned forward over the table top then spoke again. "We should be caring, in as much that our 'scraps and leftovers' be granted to those less fortunate than ourselves, and that unbroken bread be retained for another meal. And finally, that one tenth of our bread be given to the Almoner as our charity."

"Hear hear!" came the reply, with a thumping of goblets on the table top.

"Tell me, Brother Godfrey, how many of these 'rules' are we to follow? These so-called laws we are to adhere to. Just as a matter of pure interest, I might add?" asked Gondomar, placing his thumbs under his chin, contemplating how he was going to remember them all—as literacy was not one of his stronger points.

Godfrey continued, "My Brother, I think there are approximately six hundred and eighty six rules. We will take time of course and ensure that we all receive a verbal reminder now and again, but only when time allows. But in your case, Brother Roral, we may have to make up a few new rules to cover your weird and wonderful and very unhealthy interest towards goats and sheep." A bout of uncontrollable laughter ensued throughout the room—Roral's laughter, louder than most. Then he stuck his fist in the air in playful gesture of thumping Godfrey.

Godfrey responded and smiled as Hugues turned to William of Tyre. "If we can laugh at ourselves, then we can surely laugh in the faces of our many enemies."

The Knights celebrated and drank wine whilst breaking bread into the wee early hours of the following morning, and good conversation was had.

In order to understand some of these rules, it is widely accepted that the many rules would have been amended or revamped as daily life unfolded for the Order. They were not only placed to control the Knights' behaviour but also designed to provide a framework to apply a consistent approach and an understanding of what the outcomes of such actions were and could be controlled, or at least anticipated accordingly.

Roral had decided to take it upon himself to read and absorb each rule. He would be the first to admit his writing skills were not the best, but his memory served him well. Roral craved order in his turbulent life and thought this would serve him and his new found vocation as a scholar.

At each main meal or gathering, Roral presented one rule per sitting, accompanied with a short prayer of thanks, to keep the 'rule' alive. And by the end of the third year together, the Order was a much wiser, orderly collective.

Roral had taken custody of the 'The Medieval Military Manual' and took great pains to understand its content. The manual was by no means a small document and produced copious amounts of more rules and regulations that were simply too complicated to apply. Therefore, the order, under Roral's guidance, integrated the manual within the seven main sections of the primitive rule as a compromise. It was from that day forward that Roral's function, and day job, was to interpret what he could from the mass of information aided by a team of scholars to assist him.

The Temple had openly acknowledged some events that unfolded over the coming years and taken the necessary steps to record their many exploits. Sadly, King Baldwin died in the year 1118 and never quite saw the Order evolve into the most significant army that Christendom had ever encountered.

The Knights' Templar were evolving quickly, just as the Hospitallers had previously done and who were now in their 6th year of succession and making good progress towards re-establishing that omnipotent Military Order status, they once enjoyed.

The early rivalry between the two orders was never a great secret and history reflects that a high tolerance was endured by both sides as they evolved in harmony. Hugues De Payen and his eight man team domiciled collectively in the Al Aqsa Mosque on the temple mount, deep within the palace confines and had formally named themselves Templars.

The Order took much needed time to get their momentum together as a military force whilst lurking under the facade of the poor Knights' umbrella, but was, in reality, secretly searching the many hidden caves and caverns that lay directly under the Temple Mount at Al Aqsa.

It was thought that somewhere deep below the stables were riches that stemmed beyond gold or money and rumoured to be riches that reached into the very soul of mortal man. Scholars may argue that such riches as treasure maps or esoteric books of the afterlife or the Ten Commandments themselves lay within the many hidden chambers of the Temple Mount, and common intellectual knowledge would point towards the actual Ark of the Covenant itself being located there.

At this time, it was rumoured that many of God's signature pieces had indeed been found along with many relics such as the holy rood or true cross, the chalice of life or the Holy Grail, great riches of the early Kings of Israel, and perhaps other relics that shaped the world in which we live in today. All special religious items that may have been physically discovered by the Templars and were moved beyond Outremer for safe keeping—or had they?

Andre' Montbard had removed his sword and was picking through some of the debris that lay on the sandy floor of the cavern. He flipped over a single coin with the tip of his sword and was amazed to find it was a single gold piece. He picked it up and placed it in his leather pouch. A few moments later he had found another coin. After a series of visits through the maze of caves he had accrued a total of sixteen coins.

It was when Montbard and Godfroi were making their way toward the smaller tunnels in the maze of rabbit runs that they discovered that most of the trails were leading away from the Temple Mount's central dome as opposed towards it.

Some tunnels had long, broad avenues of brown and red sandy rock, others were dug through the light brown sands and interspersed with stone and a dark type of hard calcite rock, and each corridor below the Temple, led to nowhere in particular. Andre' flicked a small stone from the face of the rock wall then spoke.

"These tunnels must have taken years to dig," he remarked', and incidentally one who kept ducking his head every few steps in order to prevent bumping his brow off the low cut ceiling.

"Short bastards as well," remarked Godfroi, who stood over six foot tall and had similar distractions and many more bumps and bruises on his head, having removed his helmet earlier.

"Yeah and my back is killing me. Let's take a rest—I am knackered."

Both Knights found a suitable spot and sat down. The pair had found a total of five extra tunnels which had been excavated with precision and led to many older graves of the many ancestors of the Israelites, and of which several significant sarcophagi had been discovered and remained undisturbed.

In particular several graves of biblical significance were found still intact when they were unveiled and were each endorsed with a special mark on the parchment of map that Godfroi had maintained. After a few days, he had compiled a comprehensive map littered with symbols and signs that only he and Andre' could decipher.

It would be prudent to note that the first Crusaders had indeed found some riches of Christendom and had made their lives somewhat more comfortable on the rich pickings that once lay secreted in many hidden caverns since 710 CE.

The historical booty had been strategically positioned under the old Al Aqsa mosque many hundreds of years prior, leaving a legacy of riches that had been waiting to be plundered and exploited and ultimately placed back into circulation under the watchful, but distant, eye of Pope Urban But now it was time to make safe these very important articles of faith.

The recce team quickly returned to the Mosque and found De Payens at his desk. He was pondering over some routine finances, and had just finished signing his name when Montbard, Gondomar and Godfroi burst into the office in a hail of excitement and chaos.

Hugues was amused as the huge, cheesy grins blatantly ran across the faces of the Knights. "What's all the excitement about?" he asked, anticipating good news. The three Knights looked at each other, then all three spoke simultaneously.

"Stop, stop gentlemen," he said, putting his hand straight out in front of his face. "You will confuse the hell out of me if you all talk at once. You have obviously all been at the ale again, or you have something more important to share? Gondomar if you will please explain."

Gondomar straightened his tunic and placed a single coin on the desk, then spoke. "Hugues, whilst we were traversing tunnels, three, four and sixteen, we discovered a series of vaults that contained more sarcophagi, a bit like the ones we had found last week but in this particular case these four tunnels all led to the same central tunnel where I found several single coins.

Each coin had been placed in the soft sand, every thirty one paces or so along the central tunnel number sixteen. And now I know that these tokens were actually distance markers because at the end of the tunnel well . . ." he cut off and looked awkwardly at Andre' Montbard.

"But that's not why we are excited," remarked Andre'. Taking over the conversation. "I think we have found her!" he said, almost reverently.

De Payen did not react much, apart from staring deep into the eyes of the three men in the room. Then he spoke, "Have any of you touched the tomb? I mean is it intact."

The three men nodded out of synch and retorted, "No and yes."

De Payen grabbed his armour. "Show me!"

After visiting the tomb, Hugues sat with Gondomar, Godfroi, Roral, Geoffrey and Andre' Montbard, who were now sitting around the wooden table. He then laid out Godfroi's now very important map. "Gentlemen, I am about to call conclave to discuss the holiest of plans we could ever imagine. I know I do not have to ask, but I want total secrecy beyond secrecy regarding this meeting."

The next morning's conclave assembly Hugues De Payen would hatch his master plan to the select few men in the world he trusted. He would discuss the relocation of the 'finds' and ensure that they were managed under yet another secret operation, laying the foundations as to how the Temple would procure and gather the many 'physical articles of faith' and made them ready for transporting the treasure and riches out of the Holy Land.

"Tomorrow, after our meeting", he said, "we will assemble at Acre as a collective group and I will explain our forward plan in succession, and gentlemen, please do not bring your laymen nor your servants, and do not tell anyone of our meeting. God be with you all, merci."

A strategic program was installed in order to protect the riches for the future. It was also during this time that many visitors started to appear in the Holy Land. Mostly ranging from across middle Europe including Italy, France, Genoa and Switzerland, but more specifically Asia, Russia and the Ottoman Empire.

The Knights' Templar global community had assembled under the most secret shroud of anonymity, yet in a few short weeks the Holy Land was buzzing with many examples of the Order's influence.

In particular the Teutonic Templars or Germanic persuasion of the Order had increased their standing in the Holy Land and had stood back whilst supporting the endeavours of the Knights' Templar in their greatest crusade.

Each supporting Order was thus, providing extra resources to bring law and order into line as well as procure and make safe the Vatican's new acquisitions for the new world order, a show of which had assembled en mass and the outside world could not make head or tail of what the Order were up to.

Hugues De Payens despatched a single communication to the Vatican it read:

Illumination: 'Unleash The Temple Unicorn'

Chapter Six: **'The Journey of The Temple Unicorn — Scotland to Outremer'**

Far away in the Northern hemisphere in Scotland, a single galley ship, sixty-five foot in length lay in the dock of the old Dei Donum (Dundee) harbour. Four heavy, hemp woven mooring lines appeared to be struggling, almost moaning whilst taking the strain on her fastenings.

The vessel was being systematically laden with copious amounts of stores comprising of sheep, ale, pigs, oils, bread, linen, corn and other provisions for her impending long voyage, east to the Holy Land. Although the mooring lines were still squealing in protest at being over pulled and were contorting and twisting their fibres in retaliation to the tension, they still managed to take the strain as the heavy cargo was loaded.

From the black and sticky appearance of the hull's timbers, the ship's woodwork had been coated with a type of sludge resembling black tar bitumen; only this brew was made from animal fats and honey. The aromatic, musty aroma was still lingering in the warm air as the figure of the new Captain stepped on board.

The vessel's many sails had been refurbished and refitted with heavy, double-edged or seamed sheeting, thirty feet plus and upwards towards the top mast and sitting central three able bodied seaman sat cross-legged and had straddled themselves across the three beams of the square-rigged frame work, and were in the process of making fast a new type of white canvas mainsail, one of the very first triple-mast ships in existence.

Below, on the immaculate, wooden decks, a crew of five rope and cargo riggers were busy with rigging the many ropes and boltrope lines that retained and secured the huge main sheet into place. After a few minutes of intense activity, the few remaining ropes had been tidied up, as each bostay and brail were neatly gathered and tied with figures of eight at the tail ends and stowed in ship-shape fashion against the fresh oak bulwarks.

After an hour or so, and on command of the Bosun the crew began slowly deploying the ship's main sheet. Stage by stage the huge airfoil was lowered—the first time since being hoisted aloft after many weeks under a shroud of secrecy and darkness.

In the centre of the mainsheet was a huge symbol with an insignia of the Scottish Knights' Templar Order, 'The Cross Patte', and an indicator that could be clearly seen from a fair distance off. A single eight pointed red cross was now in full view for all to observe.

At the fore edge of the ship's bow, two hemp sheet coverings were draped over the ship's name plate, and had been tied off with loose ropes which dangled downwards and stopped just above the waterline, each shielding the name of this awesome, new watercraft from prying eyes.

Captain Duncan was clearly tired as he sat down at his desk and removed the new leather bound document. It was pristine and contained within its wrappings a brand new, red cover with a series of Chinese papers, each folded into neat little squares.

The binding of the outer edge was not one that he had encountered before, he paused for thought then began writing in the Ship's Log. It had been twelve days since boarding the vessel in dock and he was making ready for potential sea trials of his new vessel.

The Temple Unicorn, Captain A. Duncan.

The Ship's Log had several entries and read along the lines of:

> *I am Adam Duncan, the appointed Captain of the Marine Vessel,*
> *The Temple Unicorn, and have been charged by my peers and by*

the authority of his holiness the Pope to sail my vessel to the Middle East or Holy Land and conduct a port call at a place known as Acre or Jaffa, or conversely, a designated marine port inlet in a middle eastern location. The task is to secure some precious cargo.

Due to the nature of this holy quest, I am also compelled to record the relevant details of my intrepid voyage; therefore, my ship's log has been recently started and is set in no particular order. I have also taken the liberty and started my own personal journal to compliment my most inner thoughts during the course of this ad hoc journey, of which this entry being my first.

I have found myself having to explain some of the detail upon which future journeys may depend upon, and have all the intentions to include some finer details, therefore, I will try and keep my ramblings in some sort of logical order or format.

I will endeavour to avoid the many maritime technicalities of this journey but in most cases have touched on some sensitive subject matter as crewing problems and the importance of transporting such a precious cargo across the globe.

I am already fearful of my crew's lives, and my own life, especially having had to remove one of the crew already by way of the sword. And have since replaced his role with a close friend and long term travelling companion. His name is Brother Knox Andrews. I fear we have already been compromised or as an alternative offering for contemplation; 'we' have been tested?

Sea trials complete, and we are now en route southerly.

After a period of time the ship's log reflected some six hundred and twelve entries, a few entries have been extracted and placed below, others have been discussed within the pages of this voyage account:

Location—The outcrop 'bells rock', six hour's headway, south from Dundee, underway and en route—La Rochelle.

In the smallest and craziest of ships, we plunged boldly into another stormy and icy, cold sea. The winds were quick to rise and our vessel was tossed and bounced like a cork in a bottle. I have had reports of water leaks—not too badly at first but still a concern. I have sent the Bosun to check below decks.

We have taken a hit by a freak, huge wave, which inclined us fully broadside to port and almost capsizing, leaving us inclined with little or no freeboard. Our positive buoyancy saved the vessel. Furthermore, our forty-foot mast was almost horizontal into the cold, icy seas with mainsheet deployed. We had inclined so far over that three top flyers or flags were saturated in sea water.

I feared that I would lose my complete crew on the first day of sailing, and within the short time of attempting; taking a few frightened, final deep breaths we were upright again. We had almost been submerged under the waters.

I have no explanation to provide for this event as yet, except that I can say that the design of the ship's double hull may have a degree of trapped air that kept us buoyant and returned us to positive buoyancy after acute inclination to our port side. I have had the cargo reshuffled to add greater stability to the vessel; all appears quiet.

My crew, as a collective team, reported that each man was grasping one another and finding pieces of the ship's framework to clutch on to, and luckily they all survived. Apart from losing a few chickens and another sheep, we are alive and in good shape.

The Templar order in Scotland had taken delivery of yet another sea going vessel; another ship added to an existing fleet of almost two thousand that the Order had procured or employed over the past few years.

But this particular vessel however was very different: this ship had been specifically designed and constructed with heavier and more stable hull ribbing support—not unlike the older Greek sea-going craft, designed with sporadic supports but a series of calibrated joists that tested the naval architects' wildest dreams.

The vessel was loosely designed on the keel design of the Baltic carriers. But this special vessel was being made ready to carry a cargo that the Templar Order and the Vatican would deem the most precious cargo in Christendom, or indeed history, and required a very robust craft indeed, and a vessel built of one of their own special design.

Because this craft was designed to carry the most holiest of relics in Christendom, the galley had been constructed with a thick double skin of wooden timbers, and several wooden doubler boards had been affixed to her keel, making the vessel somewhat sturdier and heavier than conventional ships of the day, but much slower in the water. A secondary mast and fly jib had been added to compensate for her displacement.

The t'ween decks were modestly furnished with red wood and finished off with tiny gold cross motifs of the 'fleur-di-lis' of which had been inset into the wooden braces every few feet along the length of the forward facade, almost mirroring church, ornate woodwork.

Normally, the vessel would have been a chartered vessel from one of the subsidiary order or locally known as the 'Peiron' and a future group managed by the pirate Knights, hailing one Captain Red Beard as one of their prominent Skippers, but on this specific charter no outsiders were permitted in any shape or form to be contacted.

This select crew were chosen from over one hundred potential sea farers to escort her precious cargo back from the Holy Land. Each man hand-picked by Captain Duncan himself; each chosen for their individual traits and superior mariner skills.

The young galley rat was close family but that was to remain a secret throughout the complete journey. On the other hand, Garth Bertie was the only master helmsman available at the time of recruiting and he had previously sailed with Duncan on several voyages—undoubtedly both trustworthy and loyal, albeit, he enjoyed the ale and women as much as any other sailor.

Bertie wielded a sword with little or no effort, and Duncan was more than comfortable with him around. His side kick and companion was known as 'Young Wishart', who hailed from a village on the outskirts, known as Lundie, several miles from old Dundee and was deemed the First Officer of sorts.

His family were all seasoned mariners and had conveyed many, many tales of voyages and mystery during their global exploits. A family who had undertaken extensive trips in support of the old, black market trade, conducting frequent 'booty' runs into deepest Africa and Asia, but sadly not many of their lineages remain alive today and the desire to die had worn off.

Rumours resonated within the ranks that the last family excursion resulted in multiple fatalities when the expedition had encountered a family of pygmy cannibals who had trapped and killed most of the crew as they traversed within the dense jungle forest undergrowth, or had ventured into unchartered areas in the darkest regions of Borneo and Indonesia.

After the '**illumination**' trigger word had been reported from Jerusalem via France, one of the most detailed Maritime plans in history had started to swing into action. It was a plan that would require every morsel of intellectual property the Order possessed, and was to be conducted in the utmost secrecy, all information regarding Al Aqse was secretly reported within the ranks of the Knights' Templar, that the on-going searches for relics of religious significant standing were coming to a final conclusion, and that a single discovery had been made early in the year 1127.

It was requested that an escort party be assembled and sent to the Holy Land in order to take custody of the 'Holy relics' as cargo, and the Vatican staff rejoiced in procuring Christendom.

The appointed vessel and crew was to sail onwards to a series of undisclosed locations having first acquired the precious cargo from the Holy Land, and would then have to endure a single voyage without a single port stop that could stem into almost twenty months at sea.

The Templar fleet of the day consisted of just over two thousand galley ships at this time and had set the commercial world of shipping into motion. It was also a new and developing world for the Temple and its very complicated infrastructure which moved vast amounts of wine, bread, weapons and general cargo across the globe for huge financial reward, and it was not long before the coffers were overflowing.

The trust of the Temple was such that any slave cargo or human trafficking in particular would not be tolerated and the strict movement of people on their vessels was controlled with perceived outcomes. Therefore, the standards were also applied for sensitive cargo such as political prisoners who were carried to many global locations under the auspice of 'visitor' and not detainee and a relative amount of freedom was permitted.

The primary relocation plan of the Order was to despatch the fleet of vessels to Palestine, then sail them onwards to the Holy Land in bulk, and as an added strategy to compliment the markets, a further fleet of fifteen vessels was to be sent to strategic locations globally to assist. This was the message being communicated to the outside world and was carefully controlled by the inner network of the Order.

The main thrust was a fleet of Templar ships had left the port of La Rochelle in early March as a planned advance party and were to be placed strategically in each country; their overall role was to escort the returning vessels out of the Mediterranean.

Additionally, another sea going vessel 'The Temple Gael', a ship of a similar doubled-skinned galley design, was duly named '**The Temple Unicorn III**' and had set sail for France in the later months of 1127. The vessel was to make directly for the port of La Rochelle in France and was to remain at quayside no more than fifteen days. The Captain's orders were to restock her cargo with endurance for the next four months, then set sail on her Christian voyage to the Far East, stopping off at Porto in Portugal and to await further instructions.

If the many rumours in the city were to be believed, in such a short space of time for these manufactured rumours to circulate, it was very soon clear that the Temple had indeed been compromised. The Temple Unicorn III remained north and the remainder of the fleet went south.

The current rumour was that there was more than one vessel named The Temple Unicorn in the fleet, and that it already contained great wealth and treasure, and conversely, if The Temple Unicorn was already being mentioned in conversation and if contemporary rumours from abroad were to be believed, then her journey was already in peril, six months before she had even left European waters.

Being the custodian vessel of any acquired wealth of treasures, was indeed a target for less worthy and unscrupulous custodians or pirates who would certainly mount a full scale attack on any vessel for booty.

The notion of striking a vessel at sea was pointless as no-one would dare attack a Temple vessel underway. But they could attack them when they were at their most vulnerable point, and that vulnerable point would be in any of the sea ports across the Middle East where she was destined to be docked.

It had only been a few weeks and now the rumours had already been circulated to central Palestine. The Temple took great pains to ensure that any relics or indeed any precious cargo would not fall into infidel hands, or even worse, end up in the unscrupulous European hands.

They had procured several vessels similar in shape, size and design structure to The Temple Unicorn, and ventured further into complicating things and went as far as naming a further two vessels: **'The Temple Unicorn II'** and **'The Temple Unicorn IV'**, respectively. This was a deliberate ploy in order to hide the primary vessel's movements.

Although each was destined to support the future of the global Knights' Templar movement for the next millennia, and was therefore necessary to provide protection to a single vessel that was significantly different from the rest of the fleet. A ship that was only recognisable to the Order staff if one knew which symbols to look out for: symbols which were so obvious, that the ill-informed would simply accept them as external decoration.

The motifs and designs consisted of many small effigies, crosses and lambs, depicting foreign fruits that had not quite reached middle Europe yet, carvings that were embedded into her overall woodwork. But suffice to say that The Temple Unicorn was an elegant and 'marked' vessel and was to become a very lonely place for the crew over the next eight to ten months.

The Atlantic base held the main thrust of the Templar Fleet and was home to the trades that operated within Europe extending as far north as Ireland and Scotland, of which had been a safe haven for many years.

In the port of La Rochelle, France, the Temple had a strong presence during the tenure of Eleanor of Aquitaine, who had granted specific rights under charter exempting the Knights' Templar from certain duties and, in the year 1139, saw the Templar Fleet witnessing prosperity and security into the early 13th Century.

One notable event in the Temple's history was that Jacques De Molay had travelled with the Templar fleet at some point as the transition of relics was being implemented. Where he had boarded one of the larger vessels named from the Temple's fleet in Malta and was busy laying foundation plans to ensure that The Temple Unicorn formed one of eighteen ships which were to be docked in France at the same time; a strategic ploy where the vessel could be easily hidden amongst the vast blanket of timber frames, ropes and rigging.

In the years that ensued after 1307, which was very a notable date in Templar history, in that it was that during this period of time of chaos and uncertainty the Templar's fleet personnel, consisting of highly trained, loyal personnel, took flight to many countries across the globe and, who eventually forged many alliances and secret pacts with many foreign governments to seek revenge.

This strategy was to seek compensation from the very greedy and very short sighted French King and his unscrupulous supporters. Rumours in contemporary history would lead the many **'would be'** treasure seekers and scholars to many strange and far off locations, places such as Oak Island in Canada or the islands of Cyprus, Malta in the Mediterranean or venture farther afield to Ethiopia, or far northwards to the outer Hebrides or the island of Iona, leading them on a crusade in search of the many riches that were hidden away from society to stem commercial greed.

For the many Chinese whispers that are in circulation today, each element driven by the notion of acquiring acute potential wealth, a drive based primarily on such dilemmas as the money pit in Nova Scotia, Canada, or the riches that were supposedly contained under Chateau Le Rennes in France, one has to remain sceptical of where the Temple would actually hide such riches if they did indeed exist, and an institution that would certainly not make things too easy for treasure seekers to find if it were true.

The many would-be treasure seekers would have to return to the Holy Land and start from scratch in order to understand how the order functioned, let alone, tangibly touch the riches of Christendom. If such a quest is to be embarked upon, then prepare to be disappointed as the Holy Land still contains Temple riches which are indeed today very questionable, and little supporting evidence or documentation perhaps exists to prove any credible sources for corroboration; indicators that say, such relics were actually discovered from Al Aqsa Mosque, or indeed raise the question of where they would be located today.

The spin doctors of medieval Europe had begun to spin a very mixed web of deceit and mystery, coupled with the production of many parchments and briefs that had been despatched to middle Europe, and of which were made available after the year 1128, to substantiate the existence of such treasure.

The many fabricated documents that were circulated—the contents of which included simple translation errors that polluted and contaminated the documents with many mixed messages and metaphors from across Europe—were rife. Basic communications stating that the Knights' Templar had found a host of secret treasures that once belonged to the Queen of Sheba or King Solomon himself; a half-cocked attempt by the ruling fractions to discredit the King in residence and trigger yet another holy war.

For King Baldwin II it would be most upsetting in the fact that he had lost the country's secret wealth, an issue which would also echo through the upper echelons of the aristocracy of Israel, informing the people of the fact that their progenitors and rulers had secreted great wealth away from prying ears and eyes, whilst the poor people perished on the streets under their intolerable tenure.

The rumours in the inner city were rife with tales of corruption and coercion and many reflected that Solomon or his son Menelik had secreted vast amounts of gold, diamonds and other jewels which had also been taken as spoils of war over the centuries, and had hidden these vast quantities under the Temple Mount in the old stables, which in essence still belonged to the people of Israel.

After the executive orders were sent to Scotland, Gondomar and Roral spent several weeks recording what they thought was a plausible inventory and presented it to Hugues, who was now the Grand Master and was still annotating some symbols and markers onto Godfroi's map.

He sat at the big, round table and was busy trying to remove some wax from his left ear with his finger, then he reached out in order to pick up his scabbard knife, of which he was about to place the silvery pointed of the blade into his appendage, when Roral coughed a very untimely cough. "Don't think you want to be sticking that in there, Hugues. Here try this. You might do yourself some damage there my friend," he said, passing him a small piece of wooden splint, then he turned and faced the window recess.

"How do you plan to move the many sarcophagi? They are bloody heavy you know," he said very loudly, making his way across the room to one of the anti-chamber doorways. Then he slowly pointed to the door indicating that someone was listening behind.

"They are very heavy," he cried, then snatched the door open in one swift movement, and stepped aside as a young street urchin fell through the void, landing fully on his back. Both De Payen and Roral had removed their swords with lightning speed and were about to deliver a series of blows and strokes of the very worst kind, when they both suddenly stopped.

The young boy on the floor appeared to be no more than fifteen years of age and began shouting, "No, meester!" came a loud squeal. "I am not listening. I am coming with news. Good news for you—much honest." Then he raised his hands in defence.

De Payen was quick to realise that this individual was the same street urchin that had already been chastised for entering the Royal Palace a few months earlier—yet he was brave enough to return. He picked the lad up and sat him down at his table, then gave him some water to drink. Then he posed a question. "So, tell me how did you get into this part of the palace this time?" he quizzed.

The boy wiped his face, then spoke. "There is a tunnel that leads to that door from behind the wall. It is inside the brickwork, Meester Huggies, but you have to move the big stone first, but only small people like me can get through it. But I have come to warn you of trouble Mister Huggies, not to 'Ali Baba'.

I am hearing that the soldiers of Meester William are planning to overthrow your temple peoples here, and want to replace the Knights' men with Muslim sympathisers, but the people of my house tell me to warn you firstly now.

Because these sympathisers are not for the people, they are '*Khawaga*', they are non-Egyptians, and are deemed aliens in our midst. These are El Saladin's secret people from Turkey and they want you all very dead!"

Roral had quietly rolled up the map and the inventory list as the young man spoke. Then stood by the doorway watching as to how Hugues would distribute his line of justice with the urchin.

"What is your name young man?" Hugues demanded.

The boy responded, "Aladdin Al Ahmed Mohammed," the boy whispered.

Roral spoke out quickly. "Easy for you to say!" he replied, and watched on with great interest as De Payen walked past Roral giving him an almost comical gaze, and then walked behind the boy.

"Well, Aladdin, I want you to show me this tunnel of yours. Can you do that for me minfadlak? And, I also want you to help me, as I have a kabir problem that only you can solve for me. A big problem that requires lots of courage and stealth. Will you help me, minfadlak?" The boy was nodding and appeared more than eager to show De Payen the tunnel.

After a short time, the boy was gone and De Payen was either very relaxed or he was far cleverer than Godfroi gave him credit for, and surmised De Payen had just hatched yet another cunning plan.

The Knights discussed the plan further and agreed that all the tunnels under the Temple would be filled in, and sealed. The plan was to leave no trace that the tunnels had been excavated deeper than the normal rabbit warren.

There was no specific inventory of what may have been discovered in the vaults during the compilation of their work, explained Gondomar to Andre' Montbard as they were putting the final touches to the inventory, but he had constructed a listing of tangible objects discovered by the Order that he had physically touched:

Inventory List:

> *The Head of John the Baptist, The Holy Chalice, Veronica's Veil, The Sadarium, The Holy Rood or parts of the Cross, The Shroud, Prior to Turin, The Ark of the Covenant, The Crown of Thorns, The Head of Judas, The Nails of Christ, The varying Ossuary of the Saints, The riches of Solomon's gold deposits, The Spear of Destiny, The crockery of the last supper, The Robes of Christ, The ten commandment tablets., The golden fragments of many ancient artefacts, Clothing from ancient Kings, Queens & Rabbi's, Samson's hair, Sixteen Glass Orbs Ancient Swords and ritual sepulchre.*

The simple gathering of many such items of huge iconic status were almost inconceivable and the fact they that they were brought together in one place, at one time was an event that would never have been conceived by any governing monarch of the day. The risk of a collection of such riches brought together could never have been made safe under the current regime, but the Hospitallers and the Holy Knights' Order together, could achieve the impossible. They possessed the knowledge and the trust of their patronage to ensure total security.

Chapter Seven: 'The Concerns of Christendom'

The Nag Hammadi Parchments

De Payen and Montbard walked amongst the few Knights chosen to manage the many relics, it was at the newly built quayside when Hugues De Payen was stopped and confronted by three heavily clad clerics who wished to discuss something so important that they dare not mention the subject in an open public place. Hugues had invited the assembled clergy to meet on board the vessel to discuss the subject further.

"Grand Master," said the lead cleric. "We need your assistance: we have in our possession the most holiest of written accounts that our country needs to keep safe, but they must remain here in Israel. These parchments cannot leave the people."

De Payen was bemused. "Why are you telling me this?"

The cleric stared back at his fellow clergy then back at the Grand Master. "We wish to take them to safety, and ask if you can provide us with an escort." Hugues smiled. "And what do you call these parchments?" he asked, anticipating an answer.

The cleric leaned closer to Hugues and whispered into his ear, "These are what we call the hidden gospels of the sacred script. We are to take them to Nag Hammadi near to The Dead Sea and secure them in the valley within nine hidden caves in the mountains."

De Payen wasted no time and provided four of his Knights to escort the clerics and their paperwork to their new destination, whilst remaining mindful that the Order would know the whereabouts of the sacred parchments should the need arise to source them in the future.

It was not until as late as the 1940's, when a series of hidden gospels or accounts came to light, as they had been secreted in the caves as reported and were near to a small village locally known as Nag Hammadi, where today exciting and new revelations are being discussed.

If these writings are to be believed, then the world may have to shift its empirical view of Christianity, given the nature of the detail contained within these parchments, and we must remain mindful that these are indeed speculative conclusions, but nevertheless have to be treated with extreme caution. And even after authentication of age and content, they may still just be considered as mere fabricated fables.

The 'Nag Hammadi' supposedly provides an account of fact written about the time of Christ and in the language of the day by what appears to be an informed group of scholars. Any tangible or corroborative evidence that proved 'if true', or alluded to the most sensitive of subjects of a biblical nature, then they would have to be treated with the most ultimate of caution. Especially when casting wholesale dispersions on the Church. Accusations that have cost many lives and would cause concern for many institutions attached to the Papacy. Therefore they are treated with the utmost sensitivity.

Physical artefacts or corroborative evidence such as the Nag Hammadi scrolls simply explaining the close liaison between Mary Magdalene and her relationship with 'Jesus the Nazarene' would certainly be very contentious. Items such as the physical nails from the cross or the actual blood of Christ would spark potential ecclesiastical war and safety precautions must be in place to manage any further media exposure and place very strict control measures upon them for information management protection.

These ancient documents or parchments would indeed be precious, and in particular the Nag Hammadi documents that were found tied together and placed in clay jars with some other relics for safe keeping or for further transportation, are indeed an archaeological conundrum, but were secreted in a series of caves near to The Dead Sea. The real question asked by scholars was "Why?"

The disclosure of such information would place the Papacy in a very awkward, global religious position indeed, and the Order knew it had to protect this level of detail from the inquisitors and the people of influence at all costs. Reporting any intimacy and love between the two that led to the fact that the couple could have in reality made their way out of Palestine and into continental Europe was intriguing and would be an event that would certainly cripple the 'establishment' very quickly.

Further rumours and speculation would lead the reader into thinking that Mary Magdalene and her entourage had travelled to either Ireland or Scotland, and perhaps the powers of the Vatican would have to retrace their Papal steps and back track their belief doctrine into re-assessing their global footprint and more importantly so, perform such steps in the eyes of their 1.2 billion people who supported their cause.

However, in true human fashion, it was not long before many more tales and stories had emerged around this time. One account that strongly resonates amongst scholars is in the form of a young girl simply known as Sara or Sarah (where a certain belief would place Sarah as the black Madonna), and who would ultimately carry the bloodline of Christ himself in her DNA, and into the next generation. And if her existence was proven, **could and would** undo the Church's global divination footprint.

Another speculative account takes us to middle Europe where it is rumoured that Mary Magdalene and her entourage had sailed to Provence, having first accompanied Sarah and Joseph of Arimathea to Iona, in Scotland, and eventually into Southern England—more journeys conducted under yet another blanket of biblical secrecy.

Further accounts take us to France, St Maximin to be precise, where the head of the 'one' either John the Baptist or the Magdalene herself is celebrated annually across this elegant part of France and is paraded throughout the streets in celebration.

It was quite easy to see that history would have to be re-written or even deliberately distorted to affect the sensitive balance of power and influence, and a shift toward the unknown was never a good outcome. How could the Papacy regime bounce back from such disclosures? And it soon becomes apparent why the **'Holy See'** reacted to certain information being communicated in the way that they did, and perhaps still do.

The acidic potency of open speculation was never a good thing and the distortion of information intentional or otherwise is a difficult argument to establish, whereby early, informed scholars could be perceived to be lining their own pockets by scare mongering or producing conspiracy theories, and then extort monies to remain quiet.

The Order in the ancient world dealt very swiftly with such problems and would often despatch a Whispering Swordsman to execute their wishes, and of course the person in question, which often or not ended up by the accused knocking on death's door with a warrant with his or her name clearly written upon it for entry.

The immediate thinking for the Order of the day is that this was not beyond rational thought and the Vatican had to ensure that they remained in total control of both artefacts and the written word. If not, they would certainly open a huge set of religious doors for discussion.

The Pope himself had deemed this issue too risky to accept and ordered the removal of God's signature pieces from the Holy land, and ensured they were to be secretly dispersed across the countries of Christendom, ranging from Portugal to Spain, Egypt to Russia, Edinburgh to London and Italy to Switzerland, for their safety.

'The Chinon Parchment'

In the year 2001, a document now known as the 'Chinon Parchment' was discovered in the Vatican's vast archives; a document which had been apparently misplaced or misfiled during the year 1628.

The paper itself is a comprehensive record of the trials of the Knights' Templar and clearly shows that Pope Clement had absolved the Knights' Templar of all the imposed charges and heresies in the year 1308, before formally disbanding the order in 1312.

If these parchments were presented back in the 14th century as fact, then perhaps we would have witnessed yet another cycle of events where this single disclosure would have brought the Aristocracy of France and its lineage instantly to its unstable knees and the Order would have evolved into a new global regime.

This would have occurred for two reasons, if the Order were to disclose specific details or simply by proving divination had never occurred and that Jesus was just a man, and not a super entity that he was revered to be, and more importantly, if the wider world were to learn of such information, then the cycle of belief would be set back thousands of years, returning to paganism with more unwarranted sacrifices and chaos would again ensue—sending the world back into the middle ages.

The Papacy could never permit such an event to happen. Secondly, the King of France would be discredited, disrobed, dethroned and most likely come to a sticky end as the Temple took its unrelenting revenge.

The Templar's therefore remained mindful of the potential collapse of the international social and belief structure, not only at home but globally and they could do nothing to avert it, nor would they be permitted to, until the time was right.

Further rumours quickly spread like wildfire throughout Christendom regarding the removal of many holy riches—stories such as the Holy Sepulchre or the Ark of the Covenant itself, the Holy Rood, Veronica's Veil or the sadarium, the head of John the Baptist and perhaps the Holy Grail itself, to name but a few which had indeed sparked great interest from many unwelcome sources.

Each artefact was slowly becoming an object of desire for Kings and Queens across the globe, and they had despatched many treasure seekers to procure the many hidden riches for their amusement, the attitude of the day certainly has fuelled many myths and legends today and we still see that fokelore is rife with fantasy.

Chapter Eight: 'The Temple Unicorn'

The Voyage

The Temple Unicorn slipped her moorings in the early morning mist and slowly made her way through the cold, deep waters of the river Tay, stemming or heading into the vast expanse of the cold North Sea. Then taking a southerly course in order to shadow the coastline southwards towards the lands of the Angol she echoed the coastline. Eventually crossing the twenty-six mile expanse of open water of the English Channel, making a direct 'beeline' for the warmer continental waters of France.

The voyage to the Holy Land was to become the most secretive voyage in maritime history, and a journey that cemented The Temple Unicorn's epic journey in the unknown maritime chronicles and history books, with an entry denoting that 'The Temple Unicorn and her crew secured the most holiest of riches in Christendom', having first sailed to and from the Holy Land. The vessel and her crew were instrumental in securing God's signature pieces from antiquity, thus preserving them well into the modern day of the 21st Century.

The newly appointed Captain of the Unicorn was one Brother Adam Duncan, a local inhabitant of Dei Donum and a veteran sailor with fifteen years of salty existence under his belt. And an individual who provided the Order with enough sea skills to deal with the harshest of enemies and the most volatile and unpredictable of weather conditions that nature could throw at him.

Duncan would often comment about the most inhospitable weather being supplied by mother nature across the globe and discussed horrendous sea storms and hurricanes that had ripped the masts clean off the decks near the Bay of Biscay, and remained mindful that he was due to traverse these treacherous locations in the not too distant future. But he enjoyed reciting his tales to the less informed members of his crew.

He was no mild man of nature. He was calibrated and yet unwittingly humorous and certainly strong enough in physical stature of despatching any wannabe Captains who challenged his position. Although simultaneously possessing a very cautious character, and as a hardened, seasoned mariner would survive the copious quantities of ultra-high strength potato wine or apple ale presented to him for consumption. After which he could remain relatively compos mentis enough to maintain discipline amongst his crew.

That was until he would pass out completely, then it was up to the next Officer in line or the Boson to take command of the crew in the Captain's unconscious state of presence or absence. The Bosun himself was a strong stature of a man and was slightly larger than most. He was stout, yet supported an athletic frame.

He possessed arms that required very little muscular exercise, acquired through many years of wielding his sword in the name of his landlord. During a turbulent time in Scottish history and a time in history that ran amok with many arguments of land rights which had taken their deathly toll, coupled by his years as a sailor pulling and throwing ropes which provided great strength and endurance. But nevertheless, he was a happy and humorous, mild man by nature.

First Officer, Brother Kyle Wishart, on the other hand, hailed from middle Scotland or the green belt, a beautiful scenic backdrop of middle Scotia, a land barely held together by the spilled blood of the land workers on behalf of their land owners who had endured many land-right disputes and claims who himself had survived the many battles that had developed.

The many highland and lowland clans had toiled their lands within the highland regions and had separated, where possible, the boundary lands with stone walls or makeshift fencing. The Lord of the islands, on the other hand, were not so forgiving and were systematically accruing land as they made their way southwards, creating a huge divide within the Scottish ruling classes.

To the north of Dei Donum, Dundee, towards two glens, laid two distinct valleys, known locally Glen Clova and Glen Prosen. These rural areas housed the residence of two famous families who dominated Scottish rural life through the ages: the Stuarts and the Ogilvys.

From one of these families was Duncan Ogilvy, a man of twenty years, who had left the comfort of the family environment and chose a life as a mariner as opposed to a politician or Queen's Council, as did many of his peers of the day, each individual setting out to discover a new world under his own choice.

Duncan Ogilvy was very different from the common-or-garden variety of men. He was an early scholar and had a good education, and spoke fluent Greek, which was not a language spoken much in the earlier years, but in the 12th century it was almost non-existent—unless you were Greek of course.

Duncan and Wishart had sailed several times together and had each learned and maintained a good working knowledge from both the academic and physical aspects of Maritime life, and between them had forged a good, solid partnership, based on a harmony of understanding and trust.

"Wishart?" the Captain asked in a Captain's loud demanding tone. "What do you know about fabric? I mean like these silks and cottons here—do you know how they are actually made? I mean woven?"

Wishart stared at the cloth and smiled. "Do you want me to make you a night dress, Skipper?" he asked, almost sending Duncan into a fit of uncontrollable laughter, then spat out his ale, then wiped his face.

"No, you oink! I want to know how these silks are so well put together. They are soft, colourful, and smooth to the touch. I was wondering if they could be used as a linen to wear under our new armour—you know, adding a little padding and comfort."

"What armour?" came the reply. "There was no mention of armour in our many conversations Captain, until now of course."

Duncan stared back at him with a playful glint in his eye. "Mr Wishart, we are on a King's errand. A task sanctioned by the holy Pope himself. Do you think it's because we are only sailors that we have been granted this momentous task? Oh no, my dear friend, we must protect our precious cargo with our lives and that is why we will require armour. I have some special bits of armour for you my friend, 'cus you are the largest of the apes around me."

Duncan smiled again. "You worry me sometimes, Skipper—never know if you are taking the piss or being serious. Which is it this time?" Duncan sneezed. "I am deadly serious, my friend. We have armour for every man on board this vessel, and it will be issued when the time is right, along with shields and swords, all provided by none other than the Pope himself. Even more intriguing is that it was delivered directly to Scotland under secrecy to enhance our holy quest. Would you like a beer?"

Wishart ran his fingers over the blue, velvet piece of cloth, then placed a small piece over his face. "Yes, I see your point. You should ask Brother Dunsilk—his family are all weavers. He would be best suited to answer such a question. He is in the galley at the moment. Shall I call him?

"Yes, great idea. Call Silky and we can see if we can get the bloody roughness out of this bloody sacking cloth. It is giving me many itches and rashes."

After a few minutes Dunsilk appeared at the Skipper's cabin door. "You want me, Skipper?" he asked, taking a prominent stand in the doorway. "Yes, Silky, can you make me a shirt of this material to sit under my normal clothing? I mean like a padding to make it more comfortable."

Silky rubbed his thumbs together. "As good as done, Captain. I have already begun to make such garments for the cook and the Bosun."

The reply was a good one, the Captain smiled another smile then retorted, "Okay then, please make sure every man is treated equally with an undergarment. Make me a couple. But tell me how do you get the cotton so soft?"

Dunsilk picked up a piece of the silk, then spoke, "Oh, no, no, Captain, we can't make that on board here. This is the ultimate article. This is fine silk. It comes from a beastie known as a silkworm, or a type of spider, little beasties that leave traces of millions and millions of tiny threads that are gathered together then they are woven together. It can take two or three months to make a single garment. What we have is softer hemp, or cotton strands made from flax or jute but, just as good to sit under armour."

The Skipper stopped the man in his tracks. "How come you know about the armour?"

"Oh! That's easy, Skipper, the cook was using one of the breastplates as a frying pan, a pan for the meat when someone asked about it. I managed to overhear."

It was during this conversation the ship took a sudden jolt and the Captain instantly grabbed his sword then made his way up to the top deck. "What was that crash, Bosun?" he demanded, whilst quizzing the sea around him.

Mr Ogilvy waited a few seconds before answering. "A huge beast. Maybe a whale or a sea serpent. It came from nowhere Skipper, underneath the hull and straight into the keel. Then it came alongside and nudged the rudder. I bet it's got a headache though. It was a mighty crack on the ship's ribbing." Kyle Wishart stared into the oggin and sure enough the body of a huge, grey mass just lay under the waterline, not doing a lot.

"Shall we kill it?" asked one of the crew. Wishart turned and looked at the sailor. "Not today young man, not today. We have enough blubber around our fattened guts—no need to add anymore. Mr Bertie send a man down below to the lower decks to check the cargo holds, see if there has been any damage. And let me know, soonest."

Brother Bertie tipped his hat. "Aye aye." Then he sped off and found a deckhand.

The Bosun had acknowledged and grabbed another deck hand and made his way to the aft of the vessel. The last words heard by the Skipper were from the Bosun in his capacity as crew mentor was:

> *"No, you idiot, that's not a plumb, that's a tow fish. We are taking a depth sounding not a speed test, you moron. The tow comes after depth, which comes later. And it looks to me like you left your brain in your father's other pants."*

Duncan stared across decks at the cook and shook his head. "Bosun," he shouted. "Please ask Cookie to stay down in the galley and not to venture onto the decks willy nilly like that. These men need food. It's not good for him to be on decks all the time. Get him below. Goodness he might even burn the bloody ship down if he doesn't watch than fire. It is not good practice for the finest of galley rats to be splicing ropes and cooking food at the same time."

"Aye aye," came the reply.

The Skipper then gave another command then proceeded below decks having given the Ballaster a few directions to shift cargo in order to make best speed.

The square rigging sheets were soon in full deployment as the mass of canvas sail filled with a huge volume of easterly wind, and The Temple Unicorn made a full 12 knots, heading southwards towards the Straits of Gibraltar, and the wind was still picking up.

After La Rochelle, the Bay of Biscay loomed ahead, and for any seasoned mariner who knew the area remained mindful that this was a potential ship's graveyard. Each sailor knew that sailing in and out of this treacherous body of water was not a walk in the proverbial maritime park.

The ship was a unique vessel and the very first of her Templar Class and an obvious design for her purpose. The ship's displacement was 710 tons mainly due to light ship additions equalling 150 tons of a timber built, double skin and decking frame.

Her overall length was 105 feet, and her breadth 34 feet. The marine oriented reader of this document will soon realise that the internal arrangements are not a common design to galley class vessels of the day.

Unique to The Temple Unicorn was a single, lightweight 'liftable' rudder, which allowed the vessel to run in very shallow water, and once lifted the vessel would then be steered by a series of oars until the water depth was again at keel depth; this was controlled by the Coxswain or the Bosun who could re-deploy the **oak 'island' rudder** at any time.

Wishart stood on the deck and was throwing fragments of burnt paper into the sea, "I take it you do not want them, Skipper?" asked one of the deck crew.

"No, too late now anyway. They were only sketches of the ship—nothing to worry about." Then he walked aft toward the open deck hatch.

He had destroyed the sectional midship's drawings and hand sketched schematics and had carried out this requirement on the specific orders from Tibald Gaudin, one of the highest ranks in the order. He smirked as he viewed other maps and documents. He was not so confident with academics, they, the foremost cartographers of the land, had furnished his ship's library with sketchy, almost dicey versions of the fore runner to the 'Typus orbis terrarum' or maritime maps and he double questioned their ability to produce exacting detail. It was not that he was anti-establishment, but he knew desk jockeys could not deliver the level of detail he required for such a trip.

Suffice to say, earlier charts were somewhat vague on detail and very unreliable, yet these ancient mariners still managed to negotiate the many treacherous waters of the globe without them. Captain Duncan would always shout, "Depths and soundings, Bosun, depths and soundings as we go." Especially when in the shallower waters, Duncan appeared to have a morbid fear of running aground and being stuck without any chance of recovery.

Maps in the early 12th century were as often as valuable as the cargoes of the largest vessels themselves; ships that traversed the waters of the globe on which their trade routes were well documented with little options for any deviation.

It is not beyond the realms of normal logic that the Templars had copied all the key maps of trade routes that were in their possession, and of which were certainly used in later years to patrol the global oceans and intercept the many unsuspecting trade vessels that sailed the high seas, attacked for 'booty'.

"This particular body of water has probably claimed more lives than the Saracens and the Sadducees of ancient times put together," exclaimed Duncan, as he pulled two pieces of rigging together and waited for them to be tied off.

Then the Bosun started a wee yarn or two of his own. "These waters are the seas that took many a mariner to meet Davy Jones in his underwater locker of maritime hell, and of course the soul never rests as it walks the aquatic ethereal plains of existence amongst the undead. Legends and myths say that Calypso and Poseidon roam the bottom sands and wait to claim the souls of unfortunate seamen who were caught unawares as casualties of the torrential winds and hurricanes or ships that ran aground on the many sub-surface rocky escarpments. Each unfortunate casting their tortured memories into oblivion."

Wishart was listening intently then interjected. "Bosun, stop frightening the men, they will not want to sail back with us once we get our cargo."

The Master of the vessel returned to his cabin, and found the ship's log book. He read a few extracts and then added some notes:

> *Sixty-Eight—Our many, older sea charts and parchments have suffered many updates and changes. We are at the stage that my collective crew of master mariners have agreed on every detail, so far, of the various stages of our journey. I have kept my conclave to the original fifteen men, and chose to keep all future locations secret apart from our next, intended port visit.*
>
> *Seventy-Six—Have instructed the crew to make ready for sailing at first light, and to ensure that we conduct a strict stowaway check*

whilst de-ratting the storage bunkers. I have been informed that all cargo is stable and sea-fastenings have been inspected, albeit three sheep are missing.

Eighty-Nine—I have not slept this night; the vessel appears to have a presence. Not sure if the crew feel the same way but it makes me uneasy. Brother Knox Andre' reports having been confronted by a white figure of an angel. I have no rational excuse for his reporting of such ghostly sightings. I am compelled to think that the crew may appear to be over excited by the details of our voyage or consumed by alcohol. The latter of which is my gut instinct.

Ninety-Two—My crew again have reported strange shadows appearing over the vessel. I am of the opinion that new rigging and upright staves may add shadows that my crew are unfamiliar with, or the ale is too strong for their weakened minds. I remain sceptical.

Have limited alcohol to three shots per man, per day.

I have decided to stop numbering my entries into ship's log and added dates. I am of the opinion that readers may find it more informative.

AD. Captain. March 1127

Bosun reports cargo movements in the lower hold. Have sent Wishart and Bertie to establish cargo fastenings. Ballaster reports that livestock appear to be overly quiet. I have an inclination that the animals may be infected. Have had the crew thoroughly clean all areas.

I, myself, have chosen to assist the cook in the galley, and have also set standing order for one Officer in the galley to assist 'Cookie' one hour per day.

AD. Captain. August 1127.

It was now nearing midday and the cruel North Sea had calmed down enough for the crew to take things easy for the meantime. Wishart stood forward of the midship's shelter and stared into the green mass of the 'oggin', when a voiced piped up.

"So what do we expect to see when we get to this La Rochelle place, Mr Wishart?" asked one of the crewmen, who had formed part of the afterguard, a task where the crew had just finished stowing the aft windsheets in ship-shape fashion in their stow baskets.

Wishart rubbed his thumb and forefingers together, then wiped his chin. "The new order is something very different to what I was aware of, or so I hear. I have been led to believe by the Captain that there are several layers of grades and ranks that we should be able to recognise before we reach the warm waters of the east. We must be able to distinguish between certain levels of this new ranking structure that the order has imposed. The complete order is made up of three distinct ranks, and is supported by many other Brothers within our ranks. So everyone we meet may not be a Templar.

Wishart began walking amongst the crew as if he was lecturing about some great maritime ancient journey as a returning expedition leader, stopping now and again either to straighten a rope or to pull a knot.

"So! What we have in our sights is the 'first class level' formed of full Brotherhood members who are our Nobles and they are classed as free men. Easily recognised by their white mantle, which is adorned with our red eight-pointed cross and should support a healthy beard. And not like yours my lad," he said, placing a hand on the shoulder of the youngest crew member. Your sad, cat's whiskers may be some time yet and it may even take an act of God to bring your goatee out for an early drink," he said, laughing aloud whilst kicking a wooden strut. Then he continued, "Our second layer of Knights consists of Sergeants, or middle ranks, who hail from the free upper classes. These are executive ranks and act as men at arms, sentries, grooms, stewards, etc., but still our Brothers nonetheless. But with a wee bit of power. These are recognised by our Templar cross on a black or brown woven mantle. And that's why we have brown mantle's Brother," he said, staring across the deck space at Brodie. "To place us in the working class, the third and final layer are deemed the brains of our outfit, they consist of clerics, or priests who are indeed our chaplains. But be very careful of the third order, Brother Brodie, these priests can read and write and they have a degree of literacy that can put a man in chains, and may be rehearsed in several languages. My advice is to stay clear of these people until you get to know them—very dangerous. This level of our league of gentlemen are the educated; men who hold 'quill'. These are the clerics and scribes who maintain records and basically keep our manuscripts in good order. Men of knowledge—some of which are accountants who count our wealth, and only differ by their mantle colour. They will don a green cloak emblazoned with a red Templar cross upon it, and they will be clean shaven."

Brodie stared on, then wiped his brow. "So they give us our money for our journey then?"

Wishart wiped his beard and chin again with his left hand. "Sort of," he said, then gazed across the vessel's main deck again.

"Get the Bosun to clear away the main mast ropes and, Mr Brodie, the place is like a store room, and get Cookie to prepare some meat for lunch. I am getting sick of fish. We should be in port in a few hours. Don't want to hit France on an empty stomach. The Captain also tells me that their wine gives him the gout and a dose of the runs. Did I tell you, men, that these foreigners, especially the Frenchies, eat snails and birds' eggs over there; big, bloody green things, yugh. And wee birdies' eggs: quails they are called, a bit like a pheasant, just a wee bit smaller. God in heaven preserve my health and don't let me suffer at the hands of French cuisine," he said, then marched off down the decks to meet the Skipper and the Ballaster.

A few hours later, The Temple Unicorn silently slipped through the quiet, calm waters towards the harbour's port entrance; the area was locally known as the straits of Pertuis d' Antioch and sat on the Western Atlantic margin, and of which had been very easily navigated by the more than able crew. Especially today having passing through the non-hostile trail between the two major islands, lle De Re and Ile d' Oleron. And of course the continental coast, the layout of which are strategically placed and instrumental in bringing unwanted merchant ships to an instant aquatic grave.

However their passage was eventless, only the cry of the seagulls and other birds disturbed the otherwise peaceful atmosphere. This was an indication of the power of the Temple, no vessels to sail and no idle chatter of new European vessels sailing within the normally busy waters.

The long, wooden jetty could be seen jutting out some one hundred feet and appeared to have been constructed as an add on to an older rickety framework: a mixed bag of uprights and stays, that sat just above the waterline, and a warning to unworthy mariners who failed to follow the leading lights into the harbour. The legs and uprights were saturated with crustaceans and streaming lengths of seaweed clung to the framework. And of course all enhanced by the salted, musky, pungent smell of a sea port which lingered in the air for months.

The long, thick, wooden bulwark had just started grazing up against the jetty's woodwork sending showers of tiny splinters over the walkway as the Helmsman brought the vessel alongside and to an almost halt

A single shot of hemp rope, half a cable in length was making its way through the air towards a single, lead bollard some thirty feet away. The monkey's fist thumped down just short of its target and bounced three times before eventually finding the left foot of a young French peasant who grabbed the fist and pulled the rope, eventually draping the large loop over the wooden bollard in order to secure it.

Captain Duncan tossed an apple and a single gold piece at the youngster who took a long stare back at the Captain then took a bite of the apple and made great haste heading towards the marketplace and the local public houses.

"Why would you want to do that, Captain?" asked Wishart, struggling to understand why a peasant boy should be given a gold coin for such a simple act.

"Because, my dear Wishart, by the time we tie up and get ready for shore side. The message of our wealth and status will reach all the right ears in a very short space of time. Once the French take sight of our colours, they will be desperate to send their wealth away from Europe to support the Order in the Holy Lands. This is what we do, remember, this is our worth." Then he laughed out loudly.

The Execution of King Louis XVI.

720 years after the Order was in place, the Templars would be exonerated from any charges of heresy by the Vatican. This was supported by the most recent discovery of the afore mentioned 'Chinon' papers which only added fuel to the conspiracy as the timely misplacement of these significant records within the Vatican's library came to light, and perhaps could be seen as an act that could be interpreted as a deliberate ploy to keep the lid on the Order's profile.

Let us not forget that the concept of time is an element that has a habit of healing long awaited deep open wounds, and most scholars will regurgitate, with perhaps great detail, the execution of King Louis XVI. Especially as he stood on the scaffold housing 'Madame le guillotine' on the 21st January 1793, and stared across the assembled masses that had congregated to watch their King die.

As the King was marched through the Place de la Concord, he was recorded to have accepted his fate as he handed himself over to the grand executioner and shunned the assembled crowd.

It was not long after his brief introduction to his people, that the heavy blade fell, and the King of France was dead. It was not a day for rejoicing but a day to mark the tides of change, and according to some historians at approximately 10:15 hours, just as the executioner held up the blood drenched severed head of the late Louis XVI, a man was said to have dipped his fingers in the royal blood and said, "Jacques De Molay, thus you are avenged."

Templar history will record this as an indication and a warning of no matter how long the Order must wait, they will seek revenge on those who chose to desecrate the ancient and esoterical ways of the Grand Priory and The Knights' Templar, and all conspirators will be judged.

The crowd would have jeered; knowing full well the significance of the King's death, and the many Chinese whispers would have been circulating on the run up to the great event, yet, was always hovering or sprinting silently in the background as the wheels of deceit had been put in motion since the year 1307 to bring France to its knees.

History will account for the pre-planned kangaroo court that witnessed the last Grand Master and his servants burned alive, having been declared heretics, and the punishment dispensed by court that would have been served on a common witch in the later 16th century, and not befitting a Templar Grand Master, therefore deemed another opportunity exploited to further disgrace the Order.

Although today, as the body of supporting evidence unfolds, we are again drawn to the Chinon papers that exonerated the Templars of all wrong doing, conveniently hidden away in some haphazard administrative error. But sadly it was too late for any recovery for the Order as the extensive and immense damage had been done.

The advent of the great French revolution of 1789-1799 is a notable period in European history that one could argue was a direct product of attrition and long term planning by The Knights' Templar Order and of where history also witnessed the deaths of Marie Antoinette and Louis as casualties of Christ but very indirectly placed within the wider fabric if medieval influence.

Scholars would of course scoff at this notion and point the finger of concern toward the many misguided story writers and historians, looking to make a quick impact on society whilst boosting their own popularity during their own existence. And of course the establishment would request substantial evidence and burden of proof against any presented theory. But history is history and we all must move on from any misguidance or conspiracy theories that may have been contrived through time.

The heroic soldier monks who served the many pilgrims visiting the Holy Land were indeed a welcome light at the end of many proverbial tunnels endured by the followers of Christ. These early settlers had moved in their droves to the Holy Land since the early Crusades which had taken place and many sympathisers have indeed decided to stay and support the on-going war effort, and of course to serve their British King, one Richard the Lion Heart at this time.

The crusades started in the year 1095 through to 1291, as the overall time frame that the European world attempted to secure the many routes to Damascus. After the fall of Acre in 1291, the world changed for The Knights' Templar. By 1165 the Knights had branches in every major city including Palestine, which holds significant standing today in the modern world.

A sad notable event was in the year 1119, where a group of almost 700 pilgrims were attacked and left for dead, because the Saracens had stalked the roads and track ways that led towards the river Jordan. Visitors were easy pickings, and rumours stated that nearly sixty people had been thrown into slavery.

This is an extreme example of why something must be done and quickly to secure the followers of Christ. These concerns were lodged to both the Vatican and the King of the day.

After many such incidents, the council of Nablus was assembled mid-January, in the year 1120, to address the issue. As a direct, result King Baldwin II had indeed met with two significant Templars and Noblemen, Hugues De Payen and Godfrey De St Omer.

Baldwin took to the notion of a small, special group who were not quite mercenaries but more of a monastic order with allegiance to Christ, and they certainly appeared to be more dependable than previous groups of so called local supporters that he had employed.

He had, on many occasions, stripped the Commanders of their rank or had them flogged or even killed. The nightmare he endured was the constant threat of being overridden by his own trusted cabinet. He was becoming weary and the menial tasks of office were becoming a heavy burden as his own soldiery became worse than the bands of robbers he was trying to control.

Baldwin searched further afield and was alerted to a self-controlling band of men who were not exactly creating problems but were policing an area they had deemed their own. The King was enthused by their self-reliance and made enquiries as to who these men were.

To this end, he found out that near to the small port of Jaffa, a new regime was coming to light and the port had been made safe by the Templar presence, and the village had become the entry point into the Holy Land for many thousands of pilgrims.

King Baldwin had found a solution to his problems. The newly formed Knights' Templar was in the country and at hand to support his efforts. Baldwin could not understand why they would want to escort and protect these visitors, but they had constructed an infrastructure that resembled a small stable local community.

Chapter Nine: 'A Grand Errand'

As news of the arrival of The Temple Unicorn hit Acre and Jaffa early 1128, there was an uncanny atmosphere of both apprehension and uncertainty within the palace dwellings. Baldwin was unsure and found himself in new territory and had despatched William of Tyre to investigate the arrival of this vessel. As he, as King, was not fully aware of any new type of craft being brought into port, nor was he informed of such a visit of any dignitories.

Baldwin was somehow perplexed, for the first time, suspicious of why a special guard had been assembled for this arrival, let alone being arranged under almost secrecy for such a simple occurrence, and he half expected the Pope himself to step off from the ship—considering the amount of preparation that had been made.

Tyre watched as the vessel was tied off against the jetty, then turned to Hugues De Payen who sat quietly absorbing the routine. "Is this a special vessel?" he asked. "And why so much activity to ensure this vessel is given special privileges, like the royal berthing spaces? And that's quite a welcoming party!"

De Payen instantly felt a slight tension in the air and fused it quickly by stepping forward and stroking his beard. "My Lord, you mentioned this planned errand, or shall we say a quest to Cyprus. A noble quest to find your country's new Queen. Now, surely you must agree that your new Queen should travel in style?

We cannot permit nobility to travel on a simple thing like a common cargo vessel. Oh no! That will never do. Come with me and I will take you on board and show you our new acquisition; a visit around the pride of our fleet: Le Templi Unikorn." After a few hours, all was quiet and the hustle and bustle had died down.

William of Tyre was introduced to the vessel's Master Captain, Adam Duncan, who took time to show the internal make up and new design of the vessel. Albeit he was thinking on his feet in order to disguise the fact that the vessel was more designed for a specific security purpose of removing God's treasures from their current location than just for general cargo storage movements and a visiting dignitary.

After an hour or so on board, William was happy and returned to the Al Aqsa mosque to report back to Baldwin, secure in the fact that there was no reason to doubt the vessel's visit as anything but to show off a new design of craft that was designed to protect her cargoes, but elegant enough to carry a Queen.

Captain Duncan approached Kyle Wishart and placed a heavy hand on his elbow. "Mister Wishart, I have a very uneasy feeling about this William of Tyre, and definitely his 'aide de camp'—that William De Souza. He appears to be rather slimy, don't you think?

He looks very dodgy to me. Did you see the way he nonchalantly touched our unicorn? As if to say, 'Yes, this would make a fine ship for me!' I think he may try and relieve us of our transport home, Mr Wishart. And that will never do. So here is the deal: when we are fully loaded, we sail first tide, no messing around, no waiting. If any of the crew is missing then they can join the ranks here in Acre. Speak to the crew will you."

"Aye aye," came the reply.

That was the last order Captain Adam Duncan had given to any of his crew. It was during the next morning that his body was found floating in the shallow waters of the dock, with his throat slit from ear to ear. Although his clothes were ripped and torn, he had not been relieved of two gold coins that he carried in his pockets.

Wishart was now more than agitated and knew he would be next in line if the crew did not remain ultra-vigilant for the next few days. And a degree of stress and tension filled the air as it was announced that Hugues De Payen himself would sail with The Temple Unicorn on her departure, at least for Wishart the Knights were now protecting his interests.

It was the third day in port and the vessel had been alongside loading and unloading her various bits of cargo in preparation for sailing. De Payen was making some very secret last minute arrangements with the newly appointed Captain, Mr Kyle Wishart, and was discussing duties.

"We have some careful preparations to make. Do you think you can handle the crew as efficiently as Mr Duncan has?" he asked, and tapped the top of the sea chart.

Wishart stared into the hardened face of the Templar. "With your guidance, I see no problems sir." These were the exact words De Payen wanted to hear. Although his presence in any room was dominating, he remained cognisant that in the short space of time, he knew Wishart, would make a Grand Knight—let alone a good Captain.

It was then that Kyle Wishart pushed the cabin door closed and spoke. "I should let you know that Captain Duncan's body will be buried at sea. His family have always stated that this was Captains Duncan's wishes, therefore I will require a bit of time in the Straits of Gibraltar. And I should also disclose that I was the Captain's closest confidant, and has shared the most intimate of details with me Grand Master."

"Well then, Mr Wishart, you will have no doubt in thinking that the Captain's death was not a simple act of robbery, but an assassination in the making. We must raise our awareness until we sail out of this shit hole. Oh, and Mr Wishart, I believe that if there is any one person that can get us home in one piece, then I am sure it will be you. And may I ask: are you okay to change cabins? After all, the Captain, is the Captain."

Wishart became suddenly aware of his status as Captain and was moved by the request. He had just found out that the Order did in fact have its own internal framework to stick to and promptly moved into the Captain's cabin. A few hours later, there was a knock on the Skipper's door. "Entre!" he shouted, and waited for the visitor to enter.

Several seconds later, the door swung open and eight of the largest men he had ever encountered entered the cabin; whereupon he almost dived for his sword. But was quick to realise any attempt to thwart these monsters off was futile. He watched as each Knight assembled in front of him.

The Knights of the Temple Order had made their way into the small cabin space and stood quietly as Hugues arranged his mantle and introduced his closest allies. "Captain Wishart, allow me to introduce to you to Mr Geoffrey De Saint Omer, Andre' Montbard, Gondomar, Payen of Mondidier, Roral, Godfrey, Geoffroy Bissot and Archambeau Saint Amand. These men are undoubtedly the most loyal humans on the planet; they have my utmost respect and my allegiance.

I place these Knights at your disposal. But their primary function will be to protect the many artefacts now stored on The Temple Unicorn. These men are under Orders to serve and protect. That basically means, Mr Wishart, no-one will be permitted to come to the next level below our decks unless escorted. And I trust you could make that clear to your team?"

After a short period of discussion, each Knight had taken their respective areas of concern and De Payen left the Captain to make ready for Cyprus. He then made his way to his bunk and sat in the wooden seat and browsed the cabin again.

His discussion with Captain Wishart had been very comprehensive. Wishart had left no stone unturned, right down to the warm taste of the ale. De Payen smiled and gazed out of the open door and into the small wooden corridor.

"Well, it's not Al Aqsa. But it is home for the next couple of months," he muttered, then made his way back on to the upper decks having made an entry into his master's logbook:

1127 AD: The Grail (or manna-machine) is found. On Bernard's orders the Templars bring it back to France.

1128 AD: Official foundation of the Order of the Temple. The machine is kept in the custody of the Brotherhood. Later, it is venerated as the idol Baphomet.

'Apparition: Hugues De Payen'

Later that evening, De Payen had nodded off and was asleep in his bunk when something disturbed him. He stirred a little bit and then jumped up, fully awake, searching for his trusty blade of Damascus steel. Something in the shadows had alerted his sixth sense and he was aware of a presence in the small cabin; although nothing was readily visible.

He just knew the atmosphere was not quite right. After a few moments, his eyes focused through the darkened shadows. Then he spied the shadowy outline of a man's figure, about ten feet away. The apparition stood silently in the corner. Then there was an aromatic hint of something in the air—an unusual smell, he thought, not rosewood but more of a wet pine. He took a deep breath and waited.

For the first time in a very long period, Hugues was somewhat disturbed. The hairs had already sprung to attention at the back of his neck. He smelled something else through the rosewood aroma: it was musky and he would swear that he could also feel vibrations racing up and down his spine and legs—and not normal.

If he was not mistaken, he could hear the distant peel of bells as they rang out in the distance. Obviously that could not be possible and he must be mistaken. They don't house bells in mosques in Egypt. He then glanced at the outside world through the small wooden porthole. It was still dark outside.

He was very much aware that he was also sweating profusely and he sniffed his own body sweat. The temperature in the small cabin had seemed to soar, from blistering hot to an almost unbearable skin irritation. All his senses were working overtime. His olfactory glands in his nasal tract were working double time and actively sought out the dankness of the galley's wooden surroundings.

As for the nape of his neck, he just knew the tiny hairs had already sprung to attention without any prompting. It was then that the atmosphere turned to a very icy cold and inhospitable atmosphere. A faint mist had built up around the deck boards near his bed and with a single, sudden shudder, he clenched his elbows inwards then shook his head. Nevertheless, the figure was still present, and he felt very uneasy as it stared back at him.

A slight movement from the apparition and the Knight grabbed his blanket even tighter for some comfort, and simultaneously prayed that he had left something that resembled a two feet long steel bar wrapped within its folds.

His sword was somewhere, but where, it was normally at the other end of the bunk and his dagger was draped in his belt slung over the chair nearer the door. He prayed for something—just a tangible object to grab on to. He inwardly acknowledged that he was vulnerable and had nowhere to turn. He contemplated fleeing the cabin, but something held him back. Fear was his only companion and his legs were not going to help him escape.

He observed two distinct white flashes of light at eye level coming from the direction of the spectre. Yet he was still physically frozen. He could not find the drive to attack the intruder and funnily enough nor did he have the inclination to, let alone the confidence to make any silly gestures. He just stared on for a few more seconds then plucked up the courage to speak out.

"Who are you and what do you want?" he asked.

The tall, dark figure remained still as Hugues waited semi-expectantly for an answer. The dark shadow moved left slightly then emerged closer from out of the darkness. The Templar took a deep breath as he spied the face of the spectre. And he was still transfixed, gazing into his own middle-aged unshaven face—easily recognisable with his strong jaw and goatee cut beard. The long robes were not so readily identifiable.

Then he took another deep breath as he stared at himself staring back at him. Questions sprang to mind: 'What the fuck is going on? Why was he having to confront himself?' Raising himself up slowly from the confines of the blanket, he asked out loud, "I ask again, What do you want?"

The visitor raised a long, thin and almost misty structure of an arm and pointed at him. "You!" came the reply, with enough force that he could feel his hair being pushed back by the volume of air pressure, just as his eyes started struggling against the stinging volume of thrust against his eyeballs. And he began uncontrollably blinking.

"You have much to learn about yourself. You will have to learn quickly and must become very decisive. Think on your feet. Quick witted if you wish to live long in order to prosper from this journey. There are unforeseen dangers and traps ahead of you. Obstacles that have been ingeniously engineered to catch you out. Do not let anyone have the upper hand over you."

De Payen sniffed and felt himself nodding—agreeing to obey. Then he wiped his nose with his hand. The voice spoke on. "You must remain vigilant. You must apply attrition towards your enemies, and above all you must trust no one. Keep your friends close and your enemies closer. For you, Hugues De Payen, you will be the keeper of God's signature pieces." The figure again pointed directly at him. "These holy artefacts will shape mankind in the many years to follow. You are to trust but only one person . . . and that person is yourself."

There was rush of fresh air and the Templar fell forward, tumbling out of his bed. Three hours had passed, and he found himself still face down on the wooden floor, clutching his tunic tightly. The bitumen smell was capturing his olfactory senses again. He was cold and very much alone as the coldness wrapped itself around his torso.

The morning had come very quickly indeed. Hugues had not slept well nor had he the inclination to. He was panic stricken as he stood up and quizzed the confines of his cabin. It was quiet enough and he was very much alone. "Merde," he murmured, looking for some water to splash across his face in order to wake himself up.

In the light of the morning, Captain Wishart was busy reading a letter which had been somehow delivered to the vessel. After reading its contents, he updated his ship's log.

KW. Have followed Captain Duncan's Log with dated entries:

> August 1128
>
> *Today I received orders to ensure that an item, 'The Crown of Thorns', was to be delivered to the King of France by December 1129, as a pre-ordained measure. That leaves us several months to make the necessary arrangements.*
>
> *Note: I am frightened by my own volition. There is something much stronger than just will power amidst my crew, and we have permitted three visitors to traverse the Ship's interior. I have no issues as these dignitaries come from on high and our Grand Master wishes to ensure that the King has no misunderstandings of our journey. Today I met the most awesome Knights on the planet. I do not trust William De Souza."*
>
> *KW. Captain.*

Chapter Ten: 'Al Aqsa — Mosque circa 1127'

That very morning, King Baldwin had summoned Hugues to court and had sent his high court official to the vessel and asked for the Knights' presence at the palace to discuss his impending departure. Hugues De Payen had invited a new face at court and that face belonged to the sea mariner Captain Kyle Wishart.

The rumour that was already circulating the court was that Duncan had been murdered in an attempt to inject the vessel with fear, hoping that the crew would be afraid to stay on board and the ship could be taken over by the Lord Advocate himself as a spoil of a very quick war. De Payen on the other hand had other ideas—as did King Baldwin.

Hugues and Wishart had arrived at the palace where Baldwin was in the process of judging an act of intrusion and was about to dispense justice as they entered the chamber. The King gave De Payen a welcome gesture in acknowledgement of his presence at court, whilst at the same time drawing a silver sword from the leather scabbard held by one of his courtiers.

At the front of court, kneeling down in silence was a young boy—barely fifteen years of age. His head was half covered with a red silken pouch. And he had no doubt as to his whereabouts or his future; considering he was found within the confines of the inner palace without permission and had been arrested a as result.

Baldwin spoke out. "What am I to do when my guard allow these young delinquents like this example here to enter my palace? And how do I address the council again, telling them I have yet slain another wrong doer?"

De Payen stepped a little closer and spied the face of the youngster who was clearly distressed. Then he spoke up. "Your eminence, if I may be so bold as to offer an option for your consideration: why don't you summon your chief guard to the chamber, and let this young man explain to the court how he managed to infiltrate the palace walls in the first place? And, if his reason is a good one, then perhaps a show of clemency and example of your great management skills and permit this young uneducated individual to live? And in conclusion, your highness may learn of a vulnerability within the palace walls. Thus, putting an end to anymore unwanted or unwelcome guests into the Royal Palace. And conversely your highness, you could discipline your guard by way of ensuring that they report on a stricter periodical basis for say, one week, reporting to the same person at the same time every evening. A balanced approach your highness. This action achieves two things: one, is that it creates an inconvenience to other guards and the message of disruption and inconvenience is quickly communicated. And secondly, the guardsman will feel guilty about the undue attention he has created for his fellow colleagues and never allow such an event to occur again."

Baldwin drew the Knight a very odd, long kind of stare, evidently amused by his decision making and approach to the problem in question, and decided to take De Payen's advice.

He then summoned the Guard Commander to court. Very soon thereafter, the King had discovered that there was a secret entrance into the palace from the stabled vaults and of which was duly sealed within a very short time with mud bricks and mortar. As a direct result no-one died unnecessarily. Suffice to say, the Order had just recruited their first spy and it was not the first time this urchin had met Hugues De Payen within the palace walls.

In the follow up discussion, Hugues also explained to King Baldwin that he would like to sail with the vessel back into Europe in an effort to recruit more Knights and could take the opportunity to guide the new Captain in the ways of the Temple.

"It was also very convenient that Mr Wishart had become the Skipper, in light of the untimely death of Mr Duncan," explained Hugues to King Baldwin, whilst staring directly at William of Tyre, who appeared to be uneasy at the tone of his conversation and had added that the Captain had been robbed and murdered, and that is body would be buried at sea; albeit he had suffered an ailing illness and may never had made the long journey back to Europe in any case.

William of Tyre, was very annoyed, the look of anger on his face had said it all. De Payen made it very clear to Tyre that his days may be numbered if he was to upset the workings of the Order ever again. And all without saying a word, by just simply placing a small crucifix in William's hand and smiling.

Prior to the vessel arriving in Acre, it was during one of the follow up investigations that De Payen had discovered ancient Aramaic symbols scraped on to the inner walls under the stables. And as he began poking around to locate other tunnels that may have been dug, he soon discovered many hidden tunnels that ran under or into Al Aqsa.

Although he kept his findings very quiet, he never mentioned the markings to anyone but his inner conclave, and it was not long before the Templars had begun using the stables as a cover for their many excavations.

Earlier in the week, De Payen had instructed the young urchin who chose to warn them that trouble was afoot, was ordered to get deliberately captured by the guard and vowed he would not be punished as a consequence.

As a matter of regal course, it was very early during the excavation periods that Hugues De Payen and his team were despatched on a major diplomatic mission to middle Europe.

The quest was bestowed on his team and they were to sail in 1127 to France.

The Templars were accompanied by William De Bures, Prince of Galilee, and some high ranking officials in order to persuade Fulk of Anjou to marry King Baldwin's daughter, Melisende, who was the sole heir to the throne of Jerusalem and much was at stake.

After The Temple Unicorn sailed from the Holy Land, the remaining troops of the Order had remained in Acre and, as history informs us, the Templars were losing their fist-iron grip on control.

The vast Templar fleet had left La Rochelle under a very strategic mobilisation plan and were almost non-existent by the middle of 1307. After a very systematic clean out by the Order, all that remained in the harbour of La Rochelle were a few merchant vessels and a few recently procured third party vessels that were hired to keep up the pretence that the harbour was still active.

But it soon became apparent that something was not right and by the middle of the year the great harbour was almost near desolate and had become a barren quayside—less a few small insignificant craft that were tied off at indiscriminate moorings across the once bustling marina. The picture to portray was one of a few cargo stalls interspersed with varying sizes of fishing nets and reels that lay strewn in small bundles.

The only real activity was the scurry of rats and cats that lived amongst the community; each animal left to scavenge the now very desolate port for what little pickings were to be had. Conversely, a stark contrast from the once bustling community that had brought great prosperity and wealth to the French nation, and the animals. A community that had vanished silently into the mists of time, almost reaching into obscurity as quickly as it had emerged.

Two thousand, four hundred ships simply vanished off the face of the earth in an orchestrated effort. The notion of escaping the French authorities from possessing the many vessels was indeed a real commercial threat and many anchorages were slipped under the clandestine blanket of night fall, and mobilised under the strict direction of the Templar executives.

The Pope gazed out of the Vatican's stained glass window and smiled. "The Order is gone but will never be forgotten," he whispered, then sat down at his desk and put quill to vellum. It read: Papal Bull.

Chapter Eleven: 'Cyprus and Malta'

'**The Temple Unicorn**' was already underway and it was the first vessel to leave the global port near Acre. She had sailed in silence and was en route to La Rochelle, sailing just before dusk as ordered by the Skipper.

A secondary decoy vessel named The Temple Unicorn **II**, had recently slipped her moorings about the same time, and almost in darkness but under a 'not so' quiet and orderly departure, she was reported to have set sail for the island of Malta—deliberate strategy to alert any would-be spies or looters to inform the secret societies that the 'booty ship' had left port from Jaffa.

And was en-route out of the Holy Land. The primary vessel, along with her priceless and precious cargo secreted within her deck spaces, was making good headway sailing north bound for the island of Cyprus. Unlike her sister ship which was destined for Saint Thomas' bay, Malta.

Wishart watched and listened to the crew around him, each reciting some of the events they had witnessed prior to leaving the quiet harbour. His original crew of fifteen had increased to a total of thirty souls; each new person adding to the already strained logistics on board the vessel.

The long voyage back to her homeland was not communicated specifically to the crew first hand as originally planned, but the general crew were spoon-fed tiny snippets of information on the strictest need-to-know basis to keep them semi-informed and above all interested.

He had told the crew of their intended location this one time, then splashed out some ale to alleviate the increasing tense atmosphere that had sprung up amongst his crew and passengers. Hugues De Payen, for most of the first couple of days, remained in his cabin and found Wishart a most able Captain.

Albeit De Payen was no mariner and took solace that his choice of Captain was indeed correct. He left the confines of his bunk and searched the vessel for the Captain and soon found him up to his knees in ropes and marlin spikes with one of the crew, on a teaching spree of ropes and knots.

"Mister Wishart," cried De Payen, in an attempt to catch his attention. "May I have a word?"

Kyle slapped the young Brodie on the back and made his way to where Hugues stood. "Of course, what can I do for you?" After a brief walk across the upper decks, the Grand Master had decided against all his better judgements to enlighten Kyle to the real plan that had been hatched fifteen months prior and explained the master plan to move the artefacts across the globe.

He also explained that the object of previous visits by the Temple Order to Cyprus had been politically driven and although that was a long time ago, it was designed to drop off a single person on the island to setup a marriage. The main aim was to negotiate the marital arrangements with Fulk of Anjou, as per Baldwin's wishes.

Hugues explained that this voyage had an equal significance in preparing the Order for the future, albeit they were also returning a very specific piece of jewellery back to its original owner, amongst other great pieces.

Secondly, the Order also had secret battle plans to activate, the planning for setting up their new fortress, or plan 'A', which was to build a fortress on Malta; a battle keep that resembled Jacob's Ford but on a more stable structure. It was only after a very short period of time that it was deemed too far off the beaten track, and plan 'B', the location being Cyprus was chosen. However, we know today that plan 'A', Malta, was the better decision.

The real details of the journey were never fully communicated to Hugues De Payen during this period in time but were held secretly within the intellectual grey matter of William De Bures, who was under direct orders from King Baldwin, and the important visitor who accompanied the vessel as far as Malta, after the Cyprus stopover.

Hugues De Payen, yet again, had another reason to visit the Port of Paphos as he had secreted within his robes a pouch that contained a set of very ornate jewellery pieces. These jewels were rumoured to have belonged to the Queen of Sheba herself and mother of King Solomon's son, Menelik.

The first consignment of precious jewellery of the Ethiopian Queen was being delivered back to their homeland. The meeting was a convenient disguise and added credibility to the journey, and a new alliance was made with another country.

The vessel was to initially visit the port of Paphos in Cyprus for a two day stop over, then sail onwards to Malta in order to offload both personnel and cargo; the vessel eventually sailing onwards to the port of La Rochelle. But, unknown to her crew, the vessel was never to see the busy port in France ever again and Malta was still an open option.

Secret orders had been recently issued along with travel instructions that would see the vessel sail directly to Scotland, after leaving the waters outside Porto, in Portugal. Therefore, after offloading twelve per cent of her precious cargo and thirty per cent of her passengers, the point where the Scot's contingent were to join The Temple Unicorn III, thus leaving the Knights and a few sailors to both sail the vessel and to protect the cargo.

Kyle Wishart had a clutch of envelopes hidden in his cabin. Each letter was hidden behind a series of bulkhead panels—several sliding plates conveniently installed as elegant wooden panelling secreted within the Captain's cabin bulkheads; a design feature added by Duncan and Wishart with the assistance of a master carpenter during the early shipyard work. Ingeniously the carpenter had constructed a series of secret closets, or 'cubby' holes, that were used to retain the orbis—orders that were only to be opened at specific time intervals.

Wishart gazed at the many panels and would often get confused as to which were the sliding ones, and which were not, and momentarily reflected on whoever had planned the complex route to and from the Holy Land was a very well informed person indeed; a person who was very much more aware of the miniscule and finer details of both naval warfare and land tactics. His thoughts veered towards Hugues De Payen—he was a very influential individual, and so were the eight Knights who accompanied him. According to Kyle, they were more of a challenge than the Grand Master was. Yet each man obeyed the Captain's many orders, religiously and without question.

The intrinsic details of the instructions were in fact dated and signed with concise timings, stock control, weather details from earlier voyages, and other information that Wishart and Duncan struggled to work out—albeit he instinctively chose not to open any of the envelopes prematurely or out of turn, and the Grand Master knew it. But he was nevertheless always amazed as he read new orders that contained pre-ordained exacting details.

It wasn't until the vessel had released its visitors and secured the precious jewellery on the island of Cyprus that Wishart received a small piece of vellum. The message had arrived indirectly from a Bernard Clairvaux. The parchment had the words '**Prior Du Sion**' written upon its outer page and contained several inserts.

Each 'dossier' had been scribed in very neat handwriting, and was clearly addressed to the **Navigator and Vessel Master**. Wishart absorbed its content and after consultation with the Grand Master sailed directly to Gibraltar via Malta only stopping for a few hours and anchored off the Northern coastline to relieve his vessel of some personnel.

He had mentioned his other letter to De Payen who acknowledged its subject matter but never asked to see the actual letter. Wishart thought for a moment that De Payen could have written the letter himself and had it delivered to him, but then again, 'Who knows,' he thought. The Order of the Knights' Templar had many ways of skinning the proverbial cat.

Once the Ship had arrived at St Thomas's Bay, several vessels of wine and thirty large containers were offloaded, and it was here that one of the Arks of the Covenant was offloaded; forming part of the normal cargo, but it was unceremoniously removed by employing the small water craft only. It was again an operation that was conducted under the darkness and in the silence of night.

The original plan was to drop anchor and remain with her ship's manning level at optimum, in case a hasty retreat was called for. Of course things went well and soon the artefact was bound for the highlands of Ethiopia. Aqsa being the treasure's intended final destination.

The second Ark was to be picked up by the second vessel The Temple Unicorn **II** and she was to make her way to the North edge of the Suez River where the artefact was intended to be offloaded and transported overland. The plan being to transport the Ark back to her final resting place in the hinterlands of Ethiopia where it remains today.

The Grand Master's orders were very clear and very concise: the vessel was not to put into any port until north of Malta but nearer to the rock of Gibraltar at a point known today as Europa Point, and it was picked specifically as the strategic drop off station—mainly due to the shallow water depth where the vessel's oak island rudder could be lifted to accommodate the ship's shallow transit draft and oared into location.

Even though the vessel was under orders to send her small craft ashore and that the mother vessel was to remain out of dock, Wishart decided to employ the use of the unique rudder system to alleviate any potential of being followed into the shallow rocky waters by the Spanish.

Wishart knew that the transportation of any cargo to and from the vessel was made very awkward and could be treacherous, but he insisted that two trips by the smaller gig craft would have to be made.

It was here that the crew were met by the Templar's Spanish contingent, who took stock of several artefacts such as the Shroud of Christ, The Sadarium and Veronica's Veil, along with parchments and other relics of the Saints, consisting of several bones housed in their ornate cases. The

Grand Master himself, Hugues De Payen, being present as each artefact was handed over to the new custodians.

Wishart contemplated going against these orders at one point, but in a moment of epiphany he chose not to fully dock in the port of Gibraltar itself; a decision that was to maintain control of his crew and his vessel through yet another dangerous stage of the journey—although it slightly hindered the transition and offload of some of the cargo.

"Very good decision, Mr Wishart," remarked De Payen, commenting on the recent display of command and control asserted by Kyle. "The Temple will survive for eternity if all men were as trustworthy as yourself."

Kyle quizzed the look on De Payen's face; he appeared to be genuinely impressed and responded, "Any mariner knows that carrying cargo in these straits is dangerous. The Spanish hunt these waters religiously, but they do have deep keeled vessels and will never come within twenty cables from the shore for fear of grounding. But you can bet your last gold cross that they are lurking somewhere out there, waiting for an opportunity to strike at us when we are most vulnerable."

"Exactly my point, Captain. You have already thought about it. Well done, well done indeed." Then he marched off below decks.

"I had no idea that you would opt for the most awkward way, but this clearly displays to me that you will deliver our souls by the letter of the Pope himself, not many men would make such decisions."

'Captain Duncan's Funeral'

Early in the morning, fifteen Knights, clad in their full regalia had assembled on the main deck of the vessel. Captain Wishart had been provided with a full, white mantle, emblazoned with the Order's eight pointed, red crest, which he wore with humility hanging over his thoughts.

De Payen stood next to him, watching as the crew placed the body of the late Captain on the long, wooden plank. The body had been tightly wrapped and enshrouded in fine, white muslin cloth and a single sheet of silk. His belt was wrapped around his waist and his sword was placed along his torso.

Captain Wishart waited for an appropriate moment as the vessel drifted quietly, then he said a few words. "Captain Adam Duncan, friend and sailor, a man who served us well and led us through many dangerous encounters, we this day commit your body to the deep sea and ask that Davy Jones makes your pathway to heaven an easy route. We now release your tortured soul to the Lord above. Amen."

The Bosun, Mr Bertie, assisted by one of the deck hands raised the wooden plinth slowly, and the body of the late Captain Adam Duncan slipped quietly and as gracefully as possible into the cold, deep waters.

Wishart turned and nodded to De Payen, who remained quite still, somehow disturbed by the pomp and ceremony of a simple burial at sea. He was unaccustomed to ritual on the battlefield or in death, but acknowledged that each man, who had paid his dues with his life, commanded great dignity in death by those he has left behind.

Wishart made his way to his cabin and wrote a few words in his log:

We have this day committed Adam Duncan's body to Davy Jones. Thank you, Adam.

KW. Captain October 12th 1128.

The Rock of Gibraltar:

The Demise of The Temple Unicorn II

The small boat and a crew of four went ashore and returned within a few hours. It was on their second return to the vessel that the crew brought with them grave and sinister news. Brother Bertie, Knox and Andre' were on their return and found the Grand Master and the Skipper, then they began to tell a story that made them all momentarily freeze in their leather moccasins.

"Captain, you need to hear this," said Andre' as he took a seat down on the wooden beam opposite, staring at Mr De Payen, and leaning over the rudder arm. Then the Captain listened with keen interest.

"Three days ago," began Bertie, he continued account in graphic detail in an attempt to explain the demise of the sister ship, The Temple Unicorn II. His story went something along the lines of:

> The hustle and bustle from outside the bedroom chamber was loud enough to wake the town's clerk from his slumber. Outside in the narrow alleyways chaos ensued as the nocturnal population of the Maltese port of Valletta were fighting the mass of flames from the long quayside.
>
> At first thought, what appeared on the surface to be a simple fire on one of the vessels was in fact an act of terrorism that continued to burn down six adjacent vessels that also lay alongside, and the fire was en-route towards the twenty wooden buildings that ran the length of the jetty.
>
> The bells of the two nearby churches had started to peel in no recognisable pattern, summoning the town's people to leave their respective homes and help save their precious town from burning to the ground.
>
> Hundreds took to the streets with buckets and receptacles filled with water, making a chain to and from the water's edge. The night sky was ablaze as the flames reached up over sixty feet into the sky as the surrounding thick, black smoke started to choke the townsfolk, just as the heady aroma of tar and wax filled the town's streets. Many people were screaming as the potential impact of the fire had begun to set in. There was a huge silence, just as a nearby building exploded into a hail of fiery debris and shot wooden beams and glass across the harbour.

At the centre of the melee of this horrendous fire, The Temple Unicorn II was consumed by fire and the remainder of the crew watched on as the mast appeared to be disintegrating in front of them, and the rigging almost all but gone. Pieces of the ship's balustrade lay as long charcoal pieces along the length of the bulwarks and the main deck consisted of a series of burnt out holes each bellowing smoke—clear evidence that three small ignitions had been deliberately started.

After nine hours the fire was brought under control, as the townsfolk and the well-to-do inhabitants surveyed the extensive damage to their once ornate and beautiful dockyard, which now resembled a naval battle field amid their harbour walls.

The many wooden upright posts of the jetty were all that remained of the one hundred foot long quayside and the walkways were all but gone. Smoke was still spiralling upwards from many buildings as the final dowsing of water was applied. Six masts, the remnants of fishing vessels, just barely breaking the water's surface, sunk and destroyed.

Many locals were demanding answers, the cries were echoing across the harbour walls: "What happened here? How could this fire occur in our town? Where are the night lampers? Were they not on duty?" A single high pitched voice stood out from the jeering crowd and the Mayor raised his hands, ushering all to be quiet. Then he grabbed a street urchin and asked the question: "What did you see young man?"

"It was three men your worship," came the voice. "They were dressed in red robes and carrying lit torches. They had boarded that big vessel there," proposed the street urchin. The small town had recently been plagued by an influx of Romany gypsies and this little chap was one who stalked the inner township at night, and he was now pointing to the smouldering Templar vessel that lay in the dock.

The Ship's Captain had confirmed that twelve of his crew were dead and that a substantial amount of cargo had been removed from his vessel before the fire had been ignited. "This is unacceptable and an act of terrorism and theft orchestrated by your town's senior people," he added, raising his arms in defiance. "Only a few people knew the cargo we were carrying and now because of 'loose tongues', it has all gone.

The only way into the dockyard for the past two days has been with your authority and that authorisation lay under the control of the harbour master or port Captain's watch, both of which had suddenly disappeared off the face of the earth. Find these two scoundrels and you will find out who nearly brought your town to its knees and who ordered the murder of my crew.

We, the Knights' Templar, will not rest until retribution has been exercised and our cargo returned." The Captain stormed off across to the other side of the jetty leaving the town's folk to contemplate what would befall their town if the Templar Order decides to take revenge.

Having listened to the account, Hugues grabbed Roral, Gondomar and Montbard and took time to comprehend the message and acknowledged the demise of The Temple Unicorn II. Their journey had just taken the most sinister twist of all, and he feared the worst case scenario, and that was the question of corruption and secrets being applied. He hated not having all the facts at hand, but knew things were given a certain series or orders to follow.

Hugues De Payen had made an entry into the Ship's log, under the watchful eye of Kyle Wishart. It said:

Stage five Completed. HDeP GM St John's. K.T.

Kyle made a follow up comment under the same heading:

We have heard news that one of the Temple's vessels has been the subject of a horrendous fire whilst in the port of St Thomas Malta. Our greatest fears were confirmed and the crew have been severely disturbed by this revelation.

KW. Captain. December 1127.

After explaining his thoughts to the Templar crew, the vessel made all haste, heading into the safe but deadly waters just off the coast of Portugal, near Porto. Collectively, the crew would have to remain vigilant in order to escape the Spanish and French King's naval fleets—if they were to survive this important leg of the journey.

"Captain Wishart," shouted Hugues, spying the ship's Master in the lower decks of the vessel. "We must talk, if you have time. I would like your opinion on something," he asked. Wishart nodded and motioned De Payen toward his cabin.

Hugues wasted no time and explained the circumstances around the demise of the vessel in Malta—in that it was a deliberate move to buy precious time for the vessel to navigate the narrow Straits of Gibraltar with safe passage, having taken a northerly left turn and was now heading up into the volatile waters that lay within the Bay of Biscay, her next way point for her unscheduled stop was to be at Porto, Portugal.

The Captain and De Payen discussed some of the recent events that had unfolded over the past couple of years. As Wishart sat back in his wooden chair and rocked back and forth, be began contemplating his current status.

Meanwhile, Hugues De Payen drifted off into dreamland and relived some of his memories that saw the fall of Jaffa and the old world of Acre as distant figments in his imagination. The Battle of Hattin, the fall of the Jacob's Ford, and, sadly, the ultimate fall of some of his best Knights in arms, together were a horrendous series of events that were an unforgettable memory; all atrocities that were peaked with the fall of the heavily defended city of Jerusalem.

Wishart momentarily aimed his thoughts towards De Payen and his Knights. His job was to ensure the safety of the one man who had brought it all together, and a man he probably feared most of all in his meagre time on the planet. De Payen was a firm and great leader and testament to his Order; he was a man of principle and diligence; a man who would make decisions based on fact and not conjecture; a man who would apply logic to his approach to business.

He had the best defenders of the faith in Christendom on his vessel, and a team of highly skilled killers under his command and yet they relied on him. He was a simple working middle-class Scotsman chosen by the Order, for the Order, on behalf of the Pope himself. Kyle Wishart for the first time in his life gave himself a pat on the back and smiled.

'The news of events in Malta had rippled through the Arab world many times over, and the overwhelming forces of El Saladin were again indeed not a memory that was going to quickly dissipate,' thought De Payen, considering the horrendous bloodshed and recurring wars across the sands of Outremer.

After all their crusades and the many years of inhabiting the Holy Land, he knew, somehow, that a mass conspiracy was afoot and the Templar Order were about to fall with monumental repercussions—and there was nothing he could do about it. His thoughts were about leaving the Holy Land at this time and he should, perhaps, view things as a blessing in disguise for his safety. He had served his purpose several times over. He knew it and so did his trusted Knights.

The Captain had once again contemplated making an unscheduled port call for food, half way up the coastline as the ship's stores and fresh water supply were running low. Some of which had been contaminated by the not so fresh water below decks. The crew had taken to fishing, but after more discussion, Hugues had permitted the Skipper to make the judgement.

Kyle laid the ship's log on the table top and flicked over a few pages and stopped where he had made a series of notes. He pondered again. It was only a few weeks back when he had sat with the late Skipper making a few entries. He knew as much about the journey as did the Skipper. And he skipped over most of the long winded notes and read a few to himself:

> *We have been at sea for 91 days and a pungent smell has been detected in the lower t'ween hulls. I feel we have the ingress of sea water that has gone stagnant and producing hydrogen sulphide toxic fumes.*

Our mid-shipman has found four jars of incense and has taken the initiative to keep small, lit fires in bowls with droppings of frankincense deployed over the decks to stem the odour. I have placed a man at each fire bowl to ensure no incidents occur.

Three: I have also despatched two men to bail out the bilge and am locating shallow water in order to inspect the hulls for any damage. I have had many volunteers who appear to have given their souls to the Lord to ensure that this cargo reaches whatever destination chosen. I am humbled, as I am not driven by their passion, especially with so little information afforded to them; loyalty is indeed rife amongst the crew and I am honoured to have them with me.

There appears to have been a disturbance in the sarcophagi in the aft hold; the tomb of Pilate has slipped its footing and is now hard up against the tomb of Her Holiness. I am confused to the fact that the lid of Pilate's stone case has been dislodged or removed. The sealing faces are all free of sealant but none is evident on the decking. There are several scorch or burn marks on the lower end of the kiste.

I have quizzed Mr Bertie and he is unaware. The shadows continue to be evident but my crew appear to be okay at present. The most recent sighting, according to the cook, was that he was met by a tall, dark figure in the lower alley that runs port to starboard. The Knights we have on board have been, for most of the journey, quiet and extremely helpful. They are an odd bunch of men but have a very close relationship with one another.

I have to admit that I have had the uncanny feeling of more than just a presence. My chambers provide me with both solace and peace, but I have seen shadows lurking in the recess aft of the cabin, as has the Grand Master.

The Bosun sat crossed legged on the warm deck boards and was eating the peel of an orange when Wishart spoke out. "Two hundred years of bloodshed, glad I am not a foot soldier these days. Can you imagine the shit you would have to endure in those hot sandy deserts?" he said aloud and found a bottle of ale.

"Every day three hundred and fifty Knights or so would march to meet Saladdin's Army and twenty three men would return. Each man saturated in the blood of their opposers and their own, day in and day out for fifteen nights. And I hear they still fight again tomorrow. What drives such devotion in a man?" he stated, then took several slugs of the ale.

Although, the many crusaders were reported to be still fighting and many stories of indiscriminate skirmishes flashed across the Holy Land the heroes of Christendom were still being talked about, on an almost daily basis.

Wishart cast his eyes over the crew, but at least his crew were out of harm's way for now. Especially as the main thrust of the Templar population were starting to withdraw their numbers from global strategic locations and had slowly merged into the ranks of the Hospitallers and further rumours reported were that many Knights had fled into middle Europe to Switzerland with a fair degree of booty.

Wishart shielded his eyes from the bright sun as it reflected off the still waters. "Skipper what about these Arabs? Surely they were wholly committed to preserving their Al Aqsa mosque as they had indeed done for hundreds of years? Do you think they are as proud of their religion as we are of ours, or even as our adversaries?"

He took a swig of his ale and thought about the question for quite a long time, then offered an answer. "You know, Mr Knox, I never gave that concept much of a thought. I know that our religious beliefs were consistently being destroyed at source, and our fellow countrymen were being slaughtered daily, and in the words written on the holy scrolls, *'there are many lambs to the slaughter'* on the killing sands in Jordan.

The very place where all men should be wholly protected, but I would, however, appreciate it much more if we continued to discuss this particular subject elsewhere, intriguing thought nevertheless, as we all have differing opinions. And now is perhaps not the best time, but I do value your thoughts, Mr Knox. But be my guest to ask the Grand Master, I am sure he will furnish you with more detailed responses than I can." Knox lowered his head and suddenly fell silent.

Hugues De Payen had heard the line of questioning and sat down, balancing on one of the upright wooden pillars, then faced Mr Knox and spoke. "A lucky few had been chosen to secure the riches of the Holy Land and we are protected under the direct orders of the Pope.

Likewise, the Muslim community have been guided by their own faith, Mister Knox. They have fought and died for their own values and beliefs, and so have our men. We apparently fight the same war based on differing values.

Before we left Acre, Andre' Montbard had received a communiqué that stated his Holiness had been recently threatened with death and was placed in the most awkward of political positions—a position that he could not escape from. It was engineered by the King of France himself. He had made a few critical decisions that served the order to good end. His holiness had made such decisions in the night and under the utmost secrecy, unbeknown to the French King. Decisions that would seal the King's fate in the days and weeks to come.

But more so, this was not the first time the Pope has been placed in this awkward situation, Mr Knox. I fight for what is right and just. I take up arms in order to preserve what is important for a far greater cause. We believe in our values to protect and preserve, whilst taking up arms for those who cannot defend themselves.

It is that simple. We have fought many wars and battles than just mere skirmishes in the sand, and so have my Knights, but without you gentlemen and your sea skills we would not survive Mother Nature and conversely with our skills as soldiers we could not protect our holy riches, or indeed protect you gentlemen from invaders and maybe yourselves. You see there is a fine balance and we all have our little parts to play."

De Payen swigged some of his ale and spat it out over the bulwarks of the vessel and into the sea, "We thrive and survive together, and you are a good man, Mr Knox, I can see it in your eyes." Then he walked off.

Meanwhile in Rome, the Pope's recent decisions were made in favour of the Order and his own preservation, and if discovered that he was scheming against royalty then he would have ended both his ecclesiastical standing in Europe and ultimately paid with his own life very rapidly.

An example lay down by King Phillip, 1307, where the Pope of the day, Pope Clement, was coerced to agree a compromise to rid the world of the Order or suffer the consequences were clearly presented, and if the King had any inclination of his involvement in global Templar strategies, he would not have survived his next meal.

The Pope was caught in a difficult situation and valued his life more than his post, and was deeply disturbed and frustrated as he took stock of how many deaths had occurred in the name of Christianity. His Papal letters and briefings were written and hidden from prying eyes.

On board the vessel 'Temple Unicorn' the holy men at arms sat quietly in front of the two large doorways to the upper deck buildings. The guards below decks, whose job was to secure the more valuable cargo, had just swapped over shifts and were discussing how they would each enjoy the exposure and their wealth after their intrepid journey.

These new, odd additions to the deck structure clearly dominated the main decks by design and were designed to distract, rather than hide. The voids below decks contained four large sea chests, three large vases, six smaller chests, a range of library documents—most of which were wrapped up with leather strapping and there was a single golden cross, almost three foot in diameter. Eye candy for would-be robbers if they got this far into the bowels of the vessel.

However, secreted below two decks down in the bowels of 'The Temple Unicorn' were a few significant items which had been secured in the most secret of chambers and were each draped with specific red and blue velvet sheeting. The larger artefacts were hidden in one of the few aft void spaces stuck between the thick double skinned chambers.

One casket was draped with a single Templar flag and another casket was sitting adjacent to the stone coffin draped with a red, velvet sheet, barely covering the golden wings of the cherubs that adorned the top of the golden box.

Parts of the wooden floor decking were layered with an extra or second wooden skin and hid any signs of entry. The hatchway would have been easily mistaken or dismissed as a simple but crude deck repair—an initiative solely to secrete her cargo from hostile intervention and steps to secure the cargo; especially relics that would spark great interest in the many hundreds of years that were to follow.

'The Templar Fleet'

The real fate of the many Templar ships is not clearly recorded in historical detail and only a few vessels of the fleet can still be traced with exacting detail today. Therefore, it is widely accepted that the Order were forced to adapt to their conditions as a result of their expulsion from society since France had declared them heretics, in its quest for the Templar's vast riches and had deliberately ostracised the complete army en mass. It was indeed a red flag to a French Papal bull.

It was only natural that these men would take an alternate course of employment and with their newly acquired fighting skills, were in a good position to dictate terms in their favour. Their clever fighting skills would serve them well and would set the many future scenes for swashbuckling adventure films through into the 21st century.

In reality, the many ex-Templar vessels became safe havens for its many crew members, who in essence became an army of highly trained men who either remained as maritime core crews and evolved with great cohesion, or had separated or jumped ship at one of the many ports of calls in their travels. Suffice to say that some crews remained together and may have traversed the world's oceans seeking booty as new age pirates, whilst searching for payment for their ill treatment by the King of France.

Rumours of great bloodshed, torture, kidnap and murder hit the high seas and anger ensued, as the many Governments began to feel the commercial strain of losing precious cargoes from varying affreightment contracts. The embarrassment of losing precious cargo to those who originally once protected them was indeed very unwelcome.

The Order had many ships to transport personnel across the continents, such as pilgrims, soldiers, immigrants, passengers and indeed new recruits to and from the Holy Land. In essence the Templar fleet was moving great amounts of cargo of varying descriptions across the vast expanse of the Mediterranean Sea between the east and west populations for good reason, and that was wealth.

But not only a commercial fleet, but a shipping fleet that we could term, as a Naval Military Fleet arm, albeit the primary function would be transit general cargo and the inevitable sale of newly constructed ships designed for arms and people was a very desirable commodity.

The details and schedules of the Order's vessels are easily corroborated from the copious amounts of port records that were retained by global harbour offices, and of course by royal endorsement for the licence of imports and exports. Certain shipping notices were never placed in the public domain and The Temple Unicorn's movements were never really communicated openly, just a few secret parchments passed by several custodians as they passed by in the night.

Within the hinterlands of France, copious amounts of vineyards had also sprung up and had fallen under a great deal of Templar control, and as a direct result, many ships laden with huge wine vats became the only cargo that was being transported from the port of La Rochelle—almost on a weekly basis and was sustained for several years, not only to the Holy Land but into middle Europe and beyond.

Such was the high demand for wine, the Order was driven to hire additional merchant vessels to complement their existing fleet; a decision that was made to keep up with the high demand for the good life—a lucrative enterprise that paid the order very handsomely.

It was not until the January of the 1292 that Nicholas IV ordered the Masters of the Temple and the Hospital to procure their own vessels, which were subsequently sent to support the Armenians during their hour of need, and the Order was not only a land operation but was now a fully-blown, integrated, military marine entity.

The new Marine Corps ran for several years until war had subsided as control reigned strong across the holiest of lands stemming into middle Jordan and the borders of Iraq to the west and Syria to the north.

Conversely, the enthusiasm for active 'Templar' involvement had dwindled somewhat and the holy wars were diminishing. Where large amounts of the Order remained in quieter surroundings and enjoyed the comforts of their commercial labours, key figures of the Order were spending more time pursuing politics and economics, rather than war tactics.

It was over just a few short years that the commercial aspects of the Order were more acceptable, and as a direct result, the Order lost its overarching identity. However, during this transition period, many swords were drawn and many quarrels ensued and arms were taken up against fellow Christians.

The Order, once highly dedicated poor, monk soldiers and sailors of God's population, had turned to crime and soon became known as global rogue traders or high sea's pirates and were seeking revenge on France as their remit, although risking being burned at the stake for their collective actions and group 'think'. But they would nevertheless march and sail into the history books.

The many Knights had been rejected and expulsed by the people of France and indeed middle Europe and, as a final slap in the face, the Pope of the day had also turned renegade and was compelled to side with the King. The Pope was deemed the one person in humanity that they had sworn an oath to support and to obey in the course of their duties.

But, with hindsight and historical records it was to become known that sadly the Pope of the day was too weak to oppose French rule, and a man who would not risk his own skin for any defiance towards the French King's demands.

In the ancient and modern world, the population at large would, of course, agree as not to be seen opposing the King of the day as the penalties were extreme and the consequences certainly could prove to be fatal.

The King of France reigned with an iron fist but had misread the signs that the Temple would instantly crumble under his wrath. His fate was sealed the day he conceived the notion of rescinding the order, especially with such an ill thought out plan.

Chapter Twelve: **'Queen of Sheba and the Ark of the Covenant'**

In the many years gone by, the Queen of Sheba had offered her queenly womb to the King and eventually spawned the son of King Solomon, but had decided to return to Ethiopia as Axum was her capital of her native country and that was where she belonged.

Yemen was a distant country and yielded as perhaps the secondary location for Sheba's continuing existence, and would frequent between both lands to maintain her sovereign profile for all of her people.

Sheba's son, King Menelik I, was born in Ethiopia much to King Solomon's annoyance, it was just a few short years later before Menelik returned to Jordan and found Solomon and pursued solace from his father, where the King recognised and accepted him as his son and heir.

The Queen of Sheba herself had converted her religion to Judaism and simultaneously converted her Queendom as a result of her understanding of her faith. Today the Falasha are the remnants of the religious culture and belief system we see today in Jewish Ethiopians.

History tells us that the Ark of the Covenant left Israel in approximately 650 BC; Zodak's son and Menelik travelling with the Ark in their possession, bound for Ethiopia.

The pilgrimages to Axum continued and although uncertainty was still very prevalent, many people chose to walk the path of righteousness. Only those pilgrims of true heart or 'in the know', will receive God's unbridled attention and be blessed with divine vision.

The Knights' Templars today still have significant roots in many countries; Portugal and Ethiopia perhaps are two countries that may even have more standing than others, but we extend our thoughts towards Scotland at this time. Just as the Grand Priory can communicate that in the year 1128 Hugues De Payen had travelled to Scotia in search of further financial support and new recruits.

'The Ark of the Covenant'

The Ark of the Covenant is one of the many such objects that stimulate dreams of wealth and power by many modern dreamers, and a singular object that would certainly generate varying levels of controversy and perhaps denials by those amongst society who are non-believers.

The Ark was hailed as an object 'not of this earth', and why should it be? Especially if God sent it to protect the tablets that would eventually lie within its secreted chamber. Tempting as it may well have been, but the Order was not going to test their many scientific theories by allowing a mere mortal man to commit suicide by physical intervention, even it was assisted by the Lord above.

Mortal man's inquisitive nature would drive many to die in order to seek the hidden power that is contained within its chamber. The Ark is one of those objects that must be carefully managed in such a way that man does not inadvertently suffer its awesome power of destruction.

The Ark itself was known to have powers that could elevate the chamber off the ground either by some super conductive magnetic source, or it defied gravity by an anti-gravitational push. The scholars of the ancient world had certainly kept their theories very secret. The Ark was deemed most unsafe and possessed qualities that mirrored electricity.

Death was on the cards if basic controls were not applied. Therefore, the Ark had to be hidden away from prying eyes and uneducated people and more importantly protected from unscrupulous rulers.

The Ark was subsequently taken on many journeys before the Order had located its true location and shipped it overseas accordingly. It had travelled from Israel in earlier history since the advent of false idols and was taken away after the apostate Manasseh introduced rudimentary demi Gods for his own corrupt and egotistical worshipping reasons.

The offices of the High Priest, Zadok, had been identified and his very own son had been driven by a calling from the Lord above. His special calling was to take the Ark to safety. Such a task that could never be performed without ultimate authority from the highest ruler of the land.

Chapter Thirteen: 'A History Lesson in Short'

It is widely acknowledged and understood that at some point in time Hugues was summoned back to the Holy Land on business grounds. The visit certainly occurred between 25th April 1124 and 24th May 1153 and confirmed by the charters set by King Alexander II, King David's grandson, confirming the following;

> *Charter of Alexander II confirming to the brethren of the Temple of Solomon of Jerusalem all the rights and liberties which Kings David, Malcolm, and his own father William had granted them, as their authentic writs testify, to wit that all the men of the brethren should have the King's peace, and intercourse with all his subjects in buying and selling their merchandise free of bane and toll and duties of passage; that none inflict or consent to the infliction of injury on them, that heir cause be first heard in judgment, and that they first receive their right; that no one bring a man of these brethren to judgment, if his masters are unwilling to stand pledge for him, unless he be a convicted thief, etc., that they have all the liberties in all parts of Scotland which they have in other countries; that none take a pledge from them or their men unless for his lord's fine; and that if any one of them ignorantly take money out of their own land it shall be restored to them immediately without any fine. 20 March, 1236. OSMTH archives.*

The Knights' Templar, based in Scotland at this time, declared that the preceptory at Balantrodach (A Temple in Midlothian Scotland) was the principal seat that fell under the jurisdiction at this time of the Master of the Temple in Angol-land, who summoned chapters and ceremonies attended by both Irish and Scottish preceptors.

As a shift in the balance of power, other Templar preceptories fell under the banner of the English chapter of which were endowed upon them and were seen to be controlling Templar lands in Scotland.

It could be widely argued that each preceptory south of the border was attended by a Scottish representative during key discussions that affected rule or incurred significant changes and paid token allegiance to the south.

This approach was a strategy that would pay many dividends in the years to follow as old world Briton evolved into the one we observe today; a unity and solidarity that the Brotherhood understood and an absolute necessity if the Order was to survive up through the ages.

The Knights' Templars of today have religiously stood back and watched eastern society being destroyed from within. It is clearly visible that each land segment is systemically falling apart at the seams.

The erosion of corrupt and failing governments over many years very evident as they had done consistently for hundreds of years prior to the crusades. Egypt was again in turmoil. Hebron authorities had lost control, and not for the first time in their long tenure.

The European Templar world, north of the French border, waited silently and watched as history began repeating itself as the Arab League of Nations, in this new context 'The Arab Spring', fell into yet another decline in this modern day age. Democracy or the lack of it was being challenged by the masses and the eastern world appears to have only responded with bloodshed.

Tunisia, Syria, Libya, Jordan and Egypt to name but a few, are where the Order are still forging strategic global ties and relationships to the external Brethren communities who choose to remain within their ranks and bound solid within the fabric of the Temple—a global and crucial footprint that has matured over 724 years.

As early history has unfolded, we can observe the delicate balance of power has once again shifted across the continent, stemming into middle Europe especially during the early wars of independence which enraged Scotland and the untimely death of King Alexander III during the 13ᵗʰ century circa, 1286.

There was no option and the head of the order in Scotland gave fealty to the Angol King Edward I.

> *The extent of the control Edward I. of England exercised over the Order in England, Scotland and Ireland cannot be underestimated. This, however, was in direct contravention of previous Papal Bulls in their favour as the Order had no business recognising the authority of any temporal Prince or body when they were under the direct jurisdiction of the Pope and, therefore, free from such interference, but nevertheless, they did and le Jay even seeks confirmation from Edward for a simple mandate extending authority to his officers in Scotland. Source: OSMTH public records.*

1296, September 1. Friar Brian le Jay master of the soldiery of the Temple in England has leave to appoint Friar John de Sautre and Robert de Sautre, his attorneys, in Scotland for a year from Michaelmas. Berwick-on-Tweed. OSMTH Sources 2011. Source: OSMTH archive records.

Chapter Fourteen: 'Porto — Portugal'

The small craft had been seen from two nautical miles out from the Unicorn. The Grand Master had issued each man on board the vessel with a set of personal armour including a new sword and shield. He had lined the crew up in three distinct barriers of defence—one man in front of the other in a defensive line coupled with a team deployed at each level within the bowels of the Unicorn. Below decks, eight Templar Knights remained in silence.

The Skipper then summoned Bertie, Brodie, Silky and the cook together in his cabin. Hugues De Payen gave them each a shot of neat brandy, then gave each a series of his orders, very clearly.

He then turned his attentions to his Knights and provided further instruction. The main order of the day was that if the vessel is in jeopardy, or if the Skipper was killed in the next forty-eight hours then they would have to ensure that the vessel was scuttled in the harbour area of Porto in the shallow waters, but no fire or sparks were to be permitted—they could not risk a fire on board at any cost.

This action would ensure that any chance of recovery of the artefacts could be easily undertaken by one of the remaining decoy vessels, the closest being 'The Temple Unicorn III' which was en route from La Rochelle to meet Wishart and his crew in the shallow waters on the outskirts of Porto in the next couple of days.

From Wishart's reckoning the vessel should have been in full view by now, and he had deliberately slowed his own sailing time down by one full day to ensure that they at least met in the mid-depth to shallow waters nearer the coastline. It was not long before a sighting was reported and the crew were placed on standby.

As the small vessel began to approach the Unicorn, the Captain waited until a full three cable lengths distance out, before he ordered four archers to find distance with the new weapon of the day, the short arm '**cross bow**' and fired a volley of darts towards the oncoming craft.

A single arrow shot was returned from the approaching craft with a piece of red coloured cloth attached to it; the arrow found a wooden stay beam to the aft of the vessel. Wishart ordered all his men to lie down on decks and await further orders, whilst he remained standing, taking time to confirm that only one arrow was fired and the red ensign of the Order was clearly identified.

The small craft appeared to be almost thirty foot in length and carried a crew of eight men; two of which stood upright in her midships and raised a small sheet with a cross patte emblazoned across its front.

Wishart ordered his men to stand up and make ready for the craft to come along side. The Bosun and one archer were placed in lower decks where the craft was to tie up alongside, and Brother Brodie was tasked to provide a welcome speech for the visitors.

Hugues De Payen meanwhile chose a spot near to the oak island rudder and watched on as the encounter unfolded. The small vessel came alongside and the complete crew stepped aboard The Temple Unicorn. Brother Brodie was first to greet the leader of the team and welcomed them onto the vessel then proceeded to provide each man with a mug of fresh ale and some bread.

"I have orders from La Rochelle for the Navigator," came the first words from the leader of the men. He said in a loud, commanding tone, "I am to speak with Captain Kyle Wishart, and no-one else. I am William De Souza." De Payen had stood up and watched as William made his presence known and walked between the men with an arrogant gait. He had clearly forgotten their moments meeting in the court of King Baldwin.

The Captain was also already sitting amongst the crew and was listening intently to what the visitors had to say, pondering as to whether these men were assassins from the Holy Land or just messengers of the Papacy. The visitor continued, "We are presently four miles off the coast of Portugal, Mister Wishart, we must be on our way before moon up if we are to make good speed back to our port." The crew did not offer much by way of a reply and the visitors appeared uneasy.

After a brief period of time, Kyle stood up and asked the men to follow him below decks. "I am the navigator you seek," he said, offering another mug of ale to the tallest of the group. "Captain Wishart, good day. My name is De Souza. William De Souza and I have been tasked to bring this letter to you. It appears that our original plan has changed."

Wishart smirked. "Don't they always?"

De Souza tilted his head slightly. "I was told to wait for The Temple Unicorn III to arrive, then continue my journey with her to the harbour enclosure. But since then, we have been informed that due to the events in Malta this was not now possible and the Order has requested us to stay out further afield for this rendezvous.

Forgive me if I take it, that you have not heard of the events in Malta, but we have heard that one of our vessels has been attacked. Wishart received the brief from De Souza and ordered the helmsman to make for the coast near to Porto. We will make better time if we sail closer to the coast for the next day or two. We will release your gig and your crew north of Porto Captain—if this is acceptable. That way we can take on fresh stores before we hit the prevailing winds of Biscay."

By morning time, the vessel was enshrouded in a haze of warm mist, and was sitting very quietly with little or no wind to populate her sails. Wishart had concluded that the small craft would have been stuck in the ocean with nowhere to go, and as a minimum the crew were safer on the Unicorn than sitting adrift. Throughout this complete episode De Payen had not introduced himself to De Souza, but chose to monitor his actions from a discreet distance.

De Souza and his crew were given the luxury of the spare void spaces and a cabin, and awoke to a good breakfast of eggs and bread. De Souza made his way to the upper deck and wandered amongst the extended rigging. "Bloody pea soup, I am afraid," said the Bosun, casting a fishing line over the side.

The reply was odd. "It always the same this side of the rocks," he said.

By mid-day the fog was still hovering around the ship and the three minute bell was not 'ringing'. An uneasy atmosphere was beginning to consume the vessel as vulnerability was being discussed within the crew, mainly due to the stillness of the vessel and the lack of vision that was now no more than fifty feet.

It was then that out of the heavy grey mists emerged a single huge forepeak of a rather large wooden galley ship and dispersed the layers of fog as it came into full view. The lookout guard began shouting, "Sail ahoy port midships!" And he began ringing the bell one, two, three . . . then waited.

The tall mast of the approaching vessel had cut through the mists very quickly as the darkened silhouette cast a blanket of grey over the smaller heavier galley. The dominating shadow was easily half the size again of The Temple Unicorn's displacement, and came into clear, full view and then stopped within thirty feet of the drifting ship.

Wishart had appeared on deck and ordered his crew into full armour. He was momentarily taken by surprise as he spied the huge peak of the vessel that now lay no more than twenty feet away and was drifting closer. The forrid outrigger stretching upwards like a purpose built battering ram. De Souza and his men remained silent and yet very distant.

The bell rang out. 'Buuung!' Another one, two, three rings . . . then followed by another period of intense waiting. The required response duly came back—three strikes followed instantly by another three strikes.

Then the incredible silence again. Wishart placed a hand on Bertie's shoulder. "We are getting closer to home, Garth," he said, and ordered the complete crew to decks, less for no2 Helmsman and young Brodie.

"Yes, Skipper," replied the Bosun. "If that thing had not stopped when it did, then we would have surely been visiting Davy Jones for lunch this very day. I mean look at the size of that bloody thing," he said again, and began pointing up at the huge forward end of the galley.

Wishart agreed. "It's a good job then that these seasoned Captains are excellent seafarers."

The helmsman quizzed the compass rose: it was showing SSW, and steady. "Sou sou west, Skipper!" he yelled, then fell silent waiting for the next compass point to appear.

"Aye aye!" rang out from somewhere within the mist.

The Bosun and crew had already started making ready several heaving lines with grapple hooks attached and life lines for instant use. The main deck was soon littered with twenty or so coiled ropes, each length tightly spliced with a single 'donkey's dick' at one end.

Each of the ropes had been spliced with the standard six in, and six out, and tied off with a figure of eight knot and was then hung on each of the six bolster posts available. The splices known today as the standard 'board of trade' splice—very neat and very ship shape. Albeit common practice accepts that as long as three fingers met together somewhere in the middle of the fist then the splice was apparently good.

The lashings had been fixed and the crew stood by and watched as the huge mass of the oncoming foc'sle started turning to starboard then the ship's broad side appeared with the name plate clearly coming into full view.

'The Temple Unicorn III' was clearly legible. There was a moment's excitement as the crew became elated and a few had clapped their hands in recognition and admiration whilst appearing to applaud the navigation skills of the vessel's helmsmen.

Wishart took a deep breath and stepped towards William De Souza. "How on the Lord's earth did they know we were here?" De Souza smiled and leaned forward on the handrail. "The Order knows everything, it's the problem of keeping the damn secrets—secret is where we have the problem, Captain."

Wishart gave the command to draw swords and take positions along the starboard deck, doubling his men up at the three main entry points to the vessel. De Souza appeared to be stunned by the action command just as he became aware that standing next to him was another tall, well-built man. Hugues De Payen accompanied by Andre' Montbard who had waited quietly for the vessels to be made fast.

After a display of ultimate piloting by both helmsman, the two vessels slowly came together as a 'heavy clunking' of timber-to-timber resonated across the decks. Very quickly the two ships were made fast.

Captain Wishart had sent Mr Knox and the Bosun aboard the vessel to meet and escort Captain Gordy McGregor back on board The Temple Unicorn. Wishart had issued strict orders not to say too much but to supply the visitors with bread and ale as before.

His tactic had paid off and he already had the upper hand on his peers. Wishart was happy in the knowledge that he knew who to strike should the need arise. Soon the three Skippers conversed, and then planned to continue their conversation into the wee early hours of the next morning, accompanied by the Grand Master.

Wishart, had escorted De Souza and McGregor into his cabin and opened one of the sliding panels. McGregor stared on and smirked as Wishart withdrew a couple of brown envelopes from the void and quizzed Captain McGregor.

The words 'Porto TU-III' were clearly embossed across the seal area. He then laid it reverently upon the heavy chart table top in front of him.

Meanwhile De Souza watched with great interest as Wishart and McGregor exchanged comments then sat down facing one another.

Kyle then turned to Captain MacGregor and said, "Be my guest. I have no secrets from our brethren." MacGregor took a little more time than he should and eventually picked up the envelope from the table and quizzed the quality of the paper.

There was a small 'Fleur De Lys' embossed in the top right hand corner and a Papal seal on the reverse. Kyle then filled three silver mugs of ale and toasted the memory of the ship, Temple Unicorn II, then toasted his visitor, the Captain of The Temple Unicorn III. Then turned and raised his mug to the Templar emblem above his bunk.

"To all our maritime Brothers in arms," he said out loud then tapped his goblet against the rim of his visitors' goblets then saluted Captain De Souza.

It was then that Hugues De Payen entered the Captain's cabin and introduced himself. The two visiting Captains were astounded to be in the presence of the very legend they had only heard so much about in idle conversation, but to physically meet the man and legend in the flesh was an honour—De Souza was nervous and he showed it.

McGregor copied the gesture and the four men, for the first time in a long period, had taken the opportunity to converse with one another and take stock of where the Order was strategically moving to.

McGregor explained the events that led up to the demise and burning of The Unicorn II, and went into acute detail as to how the crew had deliberately set fire to the ship whilst in port. The Knights, having spread rumours of the fictitious cargo, ironically about the same time the Infidel had already shadowed the vessel during her return voyage from the Holy Land.

From as long ago since their departure for Acre, the infidel had hatched a plan to sink the vessel at the first opportunity in the shallower waters of the Maltese Port. Then they would lay claim to the cargo as maritime spoils or booty.

Wishart recited what his crew had told him since arriving back on board the vessel after their short run ashore at the rock of Gibraltar. The intelligence chain within Europe had already reported that strange vessels had begun docking at irregular intervals in the docks but operationally had 'no cargo' for unloading or loading, and had left the busy port every three days.

It was these very vessels that had tied up directly alongside The Unicorn II in Malta, prior to the fire being discovered. Wishart pulled the wax seal from the letter and slid the knotty blob down the tying cord.

"I have never seen such seals," remarked McGregor, leaning forward watching every move Wishart was making. Kyle had already weighed up his visitor, a very inquisitive man by nature but posed no threat to the crew of his vessel. He had however not quite made up his mind about William De Souza but remembered quite vividly what the last Captain Adam Duncan had said about him: 'Slimy'.

"I must say that I should congratulate you on your navigational skills, Mr McGregor, to find us in this shitty pea soup must have taken quite a bit of time and effort."

McGregor pursed his lips then spoke. "Actually, it's not that difficult," he continued.

"I always follow the salt line out of Porto. It's where the warmer waters meet the colder. They leave a clear line of salt to and from the port, but I know that the tides are ebbing in these months, and that the small fish like the mackerel and the sardines swim nearer to surface in the warm waters, you can always tell how far from the coast you are.

However, there is a pod of dolphins or whatever you call them that swims close to us when we arrive approximately three miles out from the beach head. It is as if these maidens of the sea were guiding us back in to home port, but in essence if you don't stray too far from the North Star and the salt line then you are in a good place."

123

Andre' Montbard and Hugues De Payen had congratulated the assembled party in bringing together a very complex strategy and saluted them each explaining how the plan had been hatched twenty months prior. The execution of a clever plan that was detailed to the exact letter apart from the unscheduled death of Captain Duncan.

Wishart gave out a single splurge of ale and snot. "Well, that's pretty clear for me. Thank you very much, as I have no intention of ending up in the oggin, like our departed friend. That much is for sure and cheers."

Andre' was nodding in agreement as Kyle made a small speech. "To simply rendezvous with the vessel would have taken great strategy and understanding of weather trends, seasonal tides and these treacherous waters, let alone having to consider an exit strategy, should the vessel have to flee in these less than windy conditions. A tact that would be suicidal if any wrong doing was afoot."

Wishart had already prepared his archers with arrows for their many crossbows saturated in sheep fat and ready at the torch should things get murky, and had deployed one of his small craft waiting to be manned at the forward or focl's end of the ship with tow rope at the ready. 'Again simple measures that were necessary irrespective of who, where and what could happen,' thought Kyle, as he weighed up his counterpart again, wondering how he would prepare for such a meeting.

The 'brief' in the letter was plainly written albeit in another language. This time only too recognisable to Wishart, as it was clearly half Scottish with an old Latin influence. He read the information on the brown parchment then ripped the letter in half, passing the lower portion to Captain McGregor. The parchment appeared to have contained directions and half a schematic or map.

The Captain took the brief and quizzed its contents. "This hails from a very high source indeed," he exclaimed, patting his breast pocket having tucked the parchment into his tunic, having given it the once over. Wishart rubbed his chin then spoke.

"Yes, all of our letters appear to have originated from the top of the rank and file," replied Wishart. "I have reviewed twelve letters so far, well I should say did, and that was in the presence of my late Skipper, each letter having been destroyed after we had absorbed their secretive content. I would presume you'd do the same? Wishart shuffled slightly having acknowledged to himself that he had lied to his new found colleague, but knew it was always better to have a strategy in mind when sounding people out.

McGregor coughed then sat upright. "Not quite. I wish I had the memory retention to do such a thing. I give half my orders to my Second Officer. He cannot read as well as one would like but he is like a secure vault; his memory is almost one hundred per cent recall. He scares me sometimes, but he is a trusted Brother. Sadly, I cannot report that for all my crew, as some of them are new and required educating in the order of things. I have had to swing the cat three times this voyage alone, a tact in order to keep discipline. What about your crew, Mr Wishart? Surely twenty months underway should have driven you and your crew to acute distraction at times?"

Wishart filled the goblets to the brim again. "Actually no, but I agree with you that it would be apparent that after such a long voyage there should be signs of uneasiness or discomfort from the crew. Although the boredom of such a trip could be a concern, but I have had very little or no problems to talk or complain about. Would you like more ballast?" He snorted, offering more ale motioning toward the half empty krugs.

"Anyway, at first light I would ask that you relieve me of the burden of my human cargo and I have some relics for you to take to back to Porto. Ah! While I am at it . . ." he paused, then almost danced across the floor, then sat down on his knees in front of the not-so-secret chest.

He opened the lid gingerly. The wooden kiste had sat next to the door entrance for the complete voyage and was never disturbed. Kyle leaned into the box and slid yet another panel located on the bottom of the box to one side.

"I have two things to give you," he said, fumbling in the box. "These are from the Grand Master himself. The first item is for you personally. It is a pouch containing twenty pieces of gold coins, these are for your own personal efforts, and secondly, three important biblical scrolls that are to be housed in the Temple archives. I believe one of these two scrolls was written by Socrates himself and the other one by no other than Aristotle.

There are also four chests of trinkets and three crucifixes made of solid gold for your care. I am sure you have your own plans in order to maintain their security. I have also been apparently tasked to hand this over," he said, raising a parchment of brown vellum and a small casket in his hands. Sitting down, Wishart placed a small hexagonal box in front of his visitor. The small box appeared very insignificant at first glance as it was just a plain wooden box with a small glass panel in one side, and appeared to contain a single long ornate piece of iron.

"What's this asked McGregor?" Tapping the top of the container with his right index finger.

Wishart leaned very close to his peer and began whispering. "This, my dear Captain, is one of the trinity nails. These are the pegs that held the Lord upright on the crucifix." McGregor appeared to have turned the colour of ashen as his eyes dilated by two hundred per cent as the significance of the moment gripped his soul.

"I have an order that tells me that I have to hand this one over to you as its new custodian. It is one of three such relics. The other two will travel with the Holy rood to our next location. These are the single most important artefacts that I will bestow upon you, and I must ask, do you accept these articles of faith and to protect them with your life?"

There was another long period of silence as McGregor stared into the glass container. "Can I remove and touch it?"

Wishart smiled. "Of course you can, but only you! And no-one else. I already have. But first you must acknowledge receipt," came the warm reply. The Captain nodded in almost reverence and took the case in his hands.

"There are also eighteen pouches made of silk; each purse contains five gold pieces for each of your crew. Another drink? He offered as McGregor sat back in his chair and was perspiring profusely. "And in case you are not ready for this task allow me to introduce you gentlemen to some individuals who might motivate you a little."

It was then that the three Captains were met by Geoffrey De Saint Omer, Andre' Montbard, Gondomar, Payen of Mondidier, Roral, Godfrey, Geoffroy Bissot and Archambeau Saint Amand, as a collective group.

The men sat through part of the night each swapping tales and accounts of their many intrepid journeys. McGregor was overwhelmed by the long sea voyage and especially since he had travelled twice through the Straits of Gibraltar without encountering the Spanish fleet who scoured the waters for rich booty.

He was more at ease knowing full well that the Order's most esteemed Knights were present on the vessel and at the same time very unsure how to act. Hugues stood in the middle of the room and requested silence.

"Gentlemen down to business!" he said in an odd sort of tone; a tone that only eight other men in Christendom had heard on several previous occasions.

"We have an order of business to discuss. I wish to . . ." he stopped talking and faced Andre' Montbard directly and nodded his head. Andre' stood up and walked across the room and locked the door. Roral and the remaining Knights stood strategically around the room then turned and faced the wall, each Knight facing outwards from the circle, thus leaving the three Captains wondering what was afoot.

'Dispensing Justice on Behalf of the Order'

De Payen stood in the middle of the three Captains and drew his gold hilted Templar sword and suddenly thrust it straight into the chest cavity of William De Souza. He had struck without any warning and no quarter was given. De Souza made no attempt to fight back or run he just gargled a few incomprehensible words, then slid off the end of the sword ending up in a blood stained heap on the wooden floor.

De Payen planted the tip of his sword deep into the wooden floor near to De Souza's line of sight then bowed his head, and spoke softly with reverence, "William De Souza, you have brought shame to the house of De Souza d'el La Porta and to the Order we represent. I have been ordered to judge you for your many acts of disgrace and to serve justice on you.

This formal request hails from one William of Tyre, Israel. He reports that you serve the unholy order of the '**Grand Lodge of Cairo**' and serve Satan as his slave and executioner. You die this day—a step to end the struggle between good and evil, and may the Lord above have mercy on your cold, heartless soul."

De Payen struck another clean sword strike at the back of the neck of his victim, then spoke again. Wishart and McGregor were both dumbstruck and void of any emotions as they had never observed or encountered ritual at this level within the Order, and were both confused as to how one dangerous man from an anti-Order could get himself placed so close within their ranks, especially with such secrecy having being applied.

Hugues grabbed his sword hilt with hands. "It should also be made known to you that I serve this day as the Order's 'Whispering Swordsman' on behalf of the Knights' Templar, the Temple of St John. ***Venia (forgiveness), memoria tenere (remember), vale (goodbye).*** Amen."

Chapter Fifteen: 'Homeward Bound'

Morning came all too quickly and preparations were made ready for transferring cargo and passengers. Captain McGregor had become a somewhat happier and fresher person to be around and was making ready for departure and more than happy to continue on his quest. After a few days, the vessel had left its last international port of call and headed homeward.

The Temple Unicorn eventually entered the home strait into the wide expanse of the cold waters of the River Tay. The vessel's tall mast adorned with sail and emblazoned with the emblem of the Templar cross clearly visible; a wide banner waving high in the light easterly winds for all to see, occasionally flashing against the bright sunlight.

Wishart, turned and gazed towards the lands to the east of Fife. It was not so long ago he had ridden the beaten track with Captain Duncan to St Andrews from Dundee to receive the orders and approval for the intrepid journey. The small ferry across the river Tay was his worse fear as the unpredictable waters could catch the most seasoned mariners off guard. The ferry crossed the two mile expanse at the Old Port of Tay directly opposite the new build castle at Brocht'y.

Wishart waited a few moments and quizzed the lands before him. After picking up a known reference point, he waited and watched until his ship was aligned to the distant rocky escarpment, just visible at the mouth of the river.

As a fisherman, Wishart knew the dangers of negotiating the treacherous waters between the rock of the bell (Bell Rock) escarpment and the easterly headland, and knew any miscalculation could end the vessels existence. He knew these waters ran into a deep sandy gulley and ordered the coxswain to swing the ship hard to starboard on the helm; the huge rudder post creaked and squealed as it found its new angle as the vessel came around to almost stem the castle at Brocht'y.

A few minutes later, Wishart then ordered a sail change as the vessel lay in the lee from the winds. He remained mindful that his journey would have sparked a great deal of interest from all walks of life and skulduggery was not a new factor he had to consider. No-one was to be trusted, and soon the darkened banner of the skull and cross bones of the auld style rogue and pirate flag was clearly on display.

A notorious symbol of what is known today as the Jolly Roger or the Drapeau Jolie Rouge, flapping and blowing in the easterly wind. It was accepted that no marine vessel Captain would dare sail within ten cable lengths of her hulls, unless of course they were looking for certain death. The ensign was raised as a potential vessel that could carry a bout of 'scurvy' on board.

Captain Wishart rallied his crew around him. "Chevaliers, this is the final home run. When we hit the beach, I need every man to be on his toes. Our cargo is not to be discussed, mentioned, hinted or even thought about and certainly not shown to anyone under any circumstances until the time is right. I must warn you that any breaches will be dealt with swiftly by the sword. I know I should not have to have this conversation but we have been through much. Am I clear gentlemen?"

The crew all nodded in unison. I require eight Knights at all times to remain on board the vessel until nightfall or until we can relocate our precious stores to the castle keep. Helmsman, make for the Broch'ty Castle, and don't get too close to the rocks. Master Bosun, make ready the wee boat and some fresh provisions for the shore party. We will go ashore at the beachhead at Broch'ty and march the last couple of miles towards the town. This will ensure that no surprises await us when we reach the town's east port gate."

Wishart opened a large box and furnished each Knight with a new white mantle. "Gentlemen, be proud of what we have achieved, we are now part of history, and will remain in obscurity until the powers that be inform the wider world that our religious beliefs and treasures are in safe hands, and these mantles are promotion and your acceptance into the global Order of the Knights' Templar of Scotland."

Chapter Sixteen: 'The Nine Trades of Dundee'

In Dundee's wide harbour, many inlets could easily have been identified for dropping anchor and heading ashore. Three inlets were considered: the Broch'ty Ferry inlet but that was too congested with fishing boats, and an almost certainty that the vessel would be boarded in the wee small hours and looted of her precious cargo. Or further towards Dundee, nearer the vicinity of the Stannergate or the sewer gate, and perhaps not the most hygienic of options as the old water stream contaminated with bodily waste converged on the river.

The third inlet was not too far away, but close to the local population, and could make an impact on the inhabitants for all the wrong reasons. One of which could prompt the city people to think that the city is about to be sacked again and they could become aggressive—but perhaps a safer option as far as the cargo was concerned. The third inlet was also the deepest and the easiest to embark in haste should the need arise. This is where the modern Port of Dundee is housed today.

The tall half wooden and stone construction scaffold of the St Mary's 160 foot tower dominated the distant skyline as it rose almost twice as high above most of the other buildings in the vicinity. Her two hundred and eighty-nine stairs to the top of the tower were a certain nightmare for the many masons and labourers who toiled to build the structure which was eventually finished in the 1480's and dedicated to St Mary by Earl David himself having endured an horrendous sea journey and exposure to the wrath of Mother Nature's awesome force.

The City's castle was aptly situated on the Castle Street rise as the darkened silhouette stood out against the light blue sky. The main tower keep itself was located to the middle of the city and was overshadowed by the huge mass of volcanic rock of Law Hill which dominated the hinter ground and stretched eastwards towards Scone and Northwards to Coupar Angus. In the far distance the trio of hills known locally as the Sidlaws, clearly added a solid and defensive backdrop to the middle grounds of Angus's fertile lands.

Dundee, Dei Donum, boasts nine main commercial industrial trades, and these nine crafts are as significant today as they were many years ago. Celebrated up until the mid-17th century then faded away into obscurity. The city played a major role in the commercial world in early times by transporting a wide range of goods to distant continents and back again as the collective city of weavers, hammermen, fleshers, bonnet makers, tailors, glovers, bakers, cordiners or shoemakers and dyers lay their commercial seeds of industry for the future growth of both the city and the country.

The secret society, or crafts as they were locally dubbed, came together in varying guises and often secret societies as single units and assembled at secret locations dotted across the city. They had lodgings in pubs, clubs, hotels, stables and churches and closed shop premises and other locations which can still be found today if one looks closely enough at the detail of the city.

It is a known fact that the 16th century cemetery, donated to the townsfolk by Mary Queen of Scots, is one such meeting place. History has continued to repeat itself as we observe obedience to what was is deemed auld, extinct 'ritual' towards the old Dundee trades, and regular meetings across various locations in the city of discovery Dundee are still evident today.

One significant location in the centre of city, is called Barrack Street due to its relationship with early Military dominance, and mentioned in previous paragraphs which, as the name implies was an earlier military garrison settlement of which was co-located and controlled by the Grey Friar Monks and early Augustinians in the Middle Ages.

The lands were split between Dudhope Castle and the old city clergy, until Her Majesty Mary Queen of Scots gifted the old Greyfriars land to the city in the early 1600's. The land that once belonged to the army, was passed to the townsfolk through an initiative designed for better purpose as the local cemeteries were quickly filling up as death took its unrelenting toll.

The land was destined to become a more significant inner city burial ground, which did not appease the military order of the day with favour, and after much negotiation the land was declared sacred. As a direct consequence, the trade's masters continued holding their secret meetings in the 'Howff' and other cemeteries within the city. A spot was designated and was normally the grave of a previous Grand Master, where the assembled party would enact the ritual of their rule.

The marker stones of such rituals can be found if one looks carefully enough—small stone columns with little or no inscriptions and near to the green man. The tradition of ritual is still practised and the central cemetery located in the old Barrack Street plays host to many old world ways, especially as these 'free men' and masons of the Royal Burgh continue with tradition as they have always done.

The Temple Unicorn's small work boat eased her way up against the old, wooden timber quayside nearer to the first shallow inlet. The jetty appeared to be somewhat distressed and would not support the mass of the Knights should they use it. The boat was steered on a beeline for the shallow waters nearer to the beach.

One of the Knights jumped into the water and grabbed the lead line then pulled the craft the final ten feet towards the beach. The crew had furled the single sail and the rudder was lashed to her lee side.

Two miles east of the Castle of Brocht'y, four of the crew dressed in their full Templar Scottish Knights' attire had made their way to the wooden quayside and watched as the tall galley ship slowly sailed into full view. Nearby many people were scurrying to the shore side, mostly pointing at the emblem they recognised as an 'indicator' of death, then furiously searched for a safe haven away from the reach of their uninvited guests.

The vessel eventually came to a steady but controlled halt approximately thirty feet away from the protruding jetty, then, on the command of the Skipper, "Trebuchet," echoed out across the harbour area, followed by a volley of three equal lengths of heavy, hemp rope whistling in the wind as they made their way over the wooden gunnels, eventually landing on the wooden decking, some distance away. Within a few seconds, three Templars had seized the ropes and had secured them against the various wooden 'bits' of the upright timbers and the vessel was made fast.

Wishart and Hugues De Payen stood and watched the complete docking operation—Wishart with one foot resting on the forward wooden backstay; the backstay beam being the long strut that fitted nicely across the forward deck to one side of the ship, sitting just proud above the ship's figurehead, denoted in this case by an effigy of the colourful unicorn. Then he took a few deep breaths.

Hugues retained a more dominant pose, one of an Officer observing the battle field; after all it was his first visit into Scotland since childhood and he amused himself by taking deep breaths of fresh air one breath after the other whilst absorbing the beauty of the land.

The crew had assembled in one straight line along the length of the Unicorn's decks, the mass of white robes clearly visible, and an awesome sight of terror to bestow on anyone who knew or had heard of the many exploits, fights, battles and wars these champion soldiers had endured whilst in the Holy Land

The quayside had almost cleared of people and just a couple of large, feral, black cats stared on; the felines waiting for any rich pickings of fish scraps or meat that could be had from the visiting vessel. Sadly, on this occasion, the cats were very much disappointed.

To the eastern gate towards the Arch of the Wishart, a few clergy had assembled with a select few of the town's dignitaries. They were contemplating and debating in how to deal with what they would determine as another potential sacking of their city, but this time with a force that would simply win outright.

Kyle Wishart waited and watched as the Lord Provost and his entourage approached his vessel—only recognising the Provost by the large gold chain of office that was crudely draped around his neck, and the fact that everyone else was walking behind him.

Wishart stood upright and faced the visitors, raised his hands then, said three things very loudly, "Jute, jam and quietness!" He had requested sufficient jute sacking to make satchels and bags for the many riches that had to be transported across the open countryside, and jam for the taste of the fresh fruit and honey that only the Carse of Gowrie could provide. A unique taste made famous even in antiquity as the human taste buds never really changed and finally a demand for quietness with little or no interruptions to allow his crew to get on with making ready for sailing further up the river. Hugues wholly agreed and nodded in agreement after Kyle's quick demands and descended to talk to his Knights.

The town's people, on the other hand, were very inquisitive and asked many questions, but soon the sight of fifteen, silver Damascus steel sword blades suddenly flashing in the sun light quenched their thirst for answers, and the assembled group of high ranking officials fell silent and quickly agreed on the request of the Grand Master.

After a short period of unhealthy debate, the council walked away in a flurry of confused discussion and deliberation. Within three hours of the Provost's departure, a guard of twelve soldiers had appeared at the rudimentary entrance to the quayside, armed with clear instructions that no-one was permitted entry unless authorisation was presented up front from his office.

Hugues had despatched Andre' Montbard and Geoffrey Bissot and three of his trusted Knights to travel by foot to the town. Between them they were carrying a single, two foot long, gold encrusted cross wrapped up in a white linen shroud. The artefact was to be presented to the Church Deacon of Balmerino Abbey.

The Deacon just happened to be conducting a presentation of the new order's ideas to the local town's folk and was reported to be nearby in the town during the unannounced arrival of The Temple Unicorn. The gift from Acre was to be located for evermore in the city's main church.

After a lengthy presentation, the Deacon returned with the crew and sailed with The Temple Unicorn and the holy cargo up the river to the abbey at Balmerino, a small inlet and building that lay some five miles up the southern side of the Tay, heading Westwards towards the town of Perth. It was here at Balmerino that various riches and artefacts were offloaded and hidden within the Abbey grounds for safe keeping.

Many relics that were eventually transported across Scotland to their final destinations had been secreted in many graveyards across Scotland, each artefact being interred and hidden out of sight from the many brigands or marauding intruders; others items were placed in the many new Castles and kirks, structures that had been recently acquired or built in the Kingdom. The more holiest of artefacts were hidden not too far away at either of the churches of greater importance such as Kilmartin and Ros'lyn in the middle Kingdom of fife.

Wishart watched and waited as The Temple Unicorn quietly slid through the cold waters. Then out of the blue he ordered the helmsman to make a few adjustments to the rudder angle by a few notches. His aim was to swing the ship to port. Almost instantly the vessel veered left into the headland just as many small, lit candles came into full view; the flickering of nearly a hundred candles provided a welcoming path for the vessel as it approached the beach head.

De Payen watched eagerly and pulled his robes together. The vessel was almost within a hundred and fifty feet away from the water's edge just as the clear waters below permitted sporadic viewings of the muddy sludge on the river bed below. "How beautiful against this light," remarked Wishart, spying the many candles.

Hugues De Payen watched on as a small figure emerged at the Abbey's modest doorway on the outcrop, then followed by another single figure, which appeared to be beckoning several monks to the shore side by waving his arms and swinging a single candle. After a few more minutes, Wishart observed a hive of activity on the shore side, and then ordered the Bosun to assemble the crew together.

The candle was still swaying from left to right in the distant doorway then . . . nothing: it had been extinguished. 'Maybe deliberately extinguished,' thought Wishart, just catching the signal in his peripheral vision and he commanded his crew to stop and wait. It seemed like an eternity as three or four small bats began flying in and around the vessel, momentarily disturbed by the visitors. Then, as if on cue, a lone hoot from a distant owl echoed from somewhere deep in the forest and made him laugh a little. The hoot startled the three men as they waited to jump ship and join the Monks.

"Bloody birds give me the creeps," whispered Wishart drawing his sword. The Abbot turned and faced the Captain. De Payen's sword already drawn and was at the ready.

"No! No! No! Mr Wishart, there is no need for swords, my dear friends. This is only our signalling process, once the candle is relit, all will be clear, trust me, you will see, we have done this many times before." De Payen was nodding and Wishart relaxed his poise.

The candle, as promised, was re-illuminated and started swaying from left to right again. The Monk with the candle then beckoned the crew ashore again.

Wishart placed his big hands on Mr Bertie's shoulders then spoke in his soft broad Scottish overtone. "One whiff of any shit, Mr Bertie, and you get yer arse out of here and take my ship with you. I canna be doin wi losing good sailors like you and Willie."

The Bosun smiled and nodded in appreciation. "Aye Skipper, dinna worry we are on it a'ready."

Within a few minutes the small, coral shaped boat was slowly making its way to the makeshift jetty with four Templar souls. The Cistercians had done a good job of constructing the small but functional one craft jetty and had even supplied candles with leather covers for night time operations. A single rope line was passed and tied to the small craft which was pulled to and from the vessel to assist crew embarkation.

The visitors were eventually met at the beach by a few other senior monks who had stepped into the icy, cold waters to ensure that no guests had prematurely ended up in the water. The single figure had grown into four figures then to six, and soon a mass of grey habits dominated the small doorway to the chapel, each staring outwards to witness the visit form the infamous crew of The Temple Unicorn.

De Payen was reluctant to the leave vessel, given the nature of her godly cargo, but knew he had to satisfy himself that the Abbey was free from intruders and that the Visigoths had not intercepted the building or were lying in wait for their arrival. Especially as he carried direct orders to leave the 'chalice of Christ' in the custody of the Cistercians.

"Pax vobisum, father," came a soft tone from the Arch Deacon, as Hugues stepped into the House of God. I am Deacon Brodie we have been waiting for you." Hugues appeared to be cold and distant; he had a hunch that something was not right and had quiet discussion with Captain Wishart.

De Payen viewed the layout of the Abbey and from what he could see would swear he saw many shadows pass by the southern windows then disappear; conversely, he also thought he could make out other shadows of people lurking in the treeline. He then decided it was the night light playing tricks on his mind and turned his attentions to the crew and the vessel.

The tall, grey spire of the Balmerino Abbey (Balmerinach) was clearly visible, silhouetted against the grey clouds and the moonlight. The overall structure had been built during the period of St Regulus's lifetime in the early years of Christendom and was situated in the middle of the wide eastern estuary of the River Tay. The tower and Abbey itself situated centrally within a small grey drystane dyke (dry stone wall) that ran the full circumference of the yard and set within a small copse of trees keeping the community in a tight and orderly manner.

The wall was nice but functional and formed a clear boundary with small interruptions inset every ten feet or so; each of the interruptions consisting of a series of small recesses in the brickwork enhanced with small gothic grey gargoyle figures and tropical fruits, each sitting on the many ledges. At night time these would normally be substituted with candles.

At the leading edge to the small cemetery, a single wooden gate silently swung in the night time breeze, a single yew tree creaked slightly and dominated the middle ground extending its long limbs toward the out buildings.

To the south side of the Nave a single young Spanish chestnut tree was reaching outwards and stretching out across the doorway of the small outhouse. The Nave stretched some forty-six feet or so into the nearby tree line and was also captured under the overhanging limbs of the many sycamore and oak trees that formed a natural outer perimeter barrier, each tree of life caressing the house of the lord from above. De Payen suddenly felt uneasy as he spied too much activity for his liking.

This house of Melrose was very much obscured by foliage. De Payen turned to Wishart and spoke softly. "I think we may be in for some surprises my friend, keep your wits about you, we are back on terra firma."

Wishart and his team stepped off the small boat and entered the first building, once inside the entrance way they stood and observed. De Payens was first to speak. "How long has that been like that Arch Deacon?" he said, pointing to the slab of grey stone, then drew his sword again.

The central walkway of the small church Ermingarde's tomb appeared to have been recently disturbed and the Deacon was quizzed about the tiles underfoot. "We have recently placed a few gold trinkets in her tomb; we have heard the Visogoth's were scouring the land, and that they will stop at nothing in their drive for greed," retorted one of the Priests, casting his hand across the altar top.

Wishart stopped and gazed across the small room, then spoke. "We will do a quick search, just to be sure." Then he sent his crew to search the outbuildings for any signs of intruders.

140

"Are these artefacts safe here?" asked De Payen, "Or do you wish our Order to take them on our journey northwards?" The Deacon declined the offer and motioned the Grand Master into the refectory house with a little more haste to avoid any further conversation about his Order's holy trinkets.

The Deacon appeared to be humbled by the fact that this mercenary was prepared to place his life on the line for another religious Order's artefacts, knowing full well the penalty if he was to fail in their protection.

A short time later, Hugues De Payen and his full team of Knights had placed themselves in and around the Abbey; each Knight taking time to walk the many passage ways and out buildings to ensure that it was indeed a safe place to be.

"All good," remarked Andre' and Roral removing their swords and handed them to one of the junior Monks for safe keeping. The young monk could hardly lift the sword, let alone run off with it, and placed the steel up against the wooden pew that was now employed by eight of the largest men the community had ever met let alone seen.

The Abbot was mesmerised as the assembled Knights took time to pray before breaking bread and saluted their efforts as an example of striking unity and trust. Wishart glanced out of the small window to his left and spied several Cistercians making their way in and out of the Abbot's cellar with several brown bottles of ale, each clutched in their collective robes.

Then he spoke directly to the Deacon. "You appear to have everything here one could wish for Arch Deacon," he said, paying more direct attention to his host. "You are to be commended for your efforts and of that and your Order." The Deacon nodded and drank a sip of wine.

"Father, are you and your flock without visitations from the Visigoths?" he asked.

Brother Brodie stared on, and then responded in quick reply. "Indeed we are free my Brother, these Visigoths were seen in the area about a fortnight past, and have already departed without any issues. They were given bread and ale for the night and they moved westwards, heading for the Kinnoul Monastery towards Coupar Angus, I believe."

"We have no visitors now, as we have been waiting for the Unicorn for several weeks, and you can trust me when I say that not a mention of your arrival was discussed, and it was only yesterday that the fisherman informed us that your ship was approaching the open waters towards Dei Donum harbour."

Hugues rubbed his chin. "Are you aware of the condition that you and your six Brothers are to accompany us to the island of Iona, Father? Your services are required as protectors and scribes for the wider Order."

The Deacon stopped and gazed upon a known face, whilst acknowledging the comments of the Grand Master. The young face belonged to a white-robed Templar Knight. "I see you have found my son, Captain Wishart," he said. The Skipper froze and smiled. "A worthy protector of God's trinkets don't you think?" De Payen watched in silence.

Deacon Brodie smiled and placed a single page of parchment in Wishart's hands; the Captain viewed the parchment then passed it straight over to Hugues De Payen who recognised his own handwriting.

It was a simple few scribbles and a four letter word with the inscription INRI and a few other words written in gothic Latin script. De Payen took a deep breath and smiled. It was the very same parchment he had passed to Captain McGregor with orders to despatch by horseman to Scotland a few weeks' past.

The messenger had done his job and alerted the St Andrew's Diocese and Abbey staff that The Temple Unicorn was safe and making for Dei Donum (God's Gift) the township of Dundee. The message was twofold: the first instructions were word of mouth and secondly the parchment was tangible evidence and notice to assure the Order that the message had been passed correctly, and that all preparations were in good order.

After an hour or so, the troop had taken time to relax and move around the Abbey with relative freedom. "Wine, Brother?" asked Brodie, pointing to the refectory.

"Great idea," replied Wishart, drawing his sword from his side sheath and placed it in his shoulder scabbard.

After a few drinks of apple wine, Wishart and Brodie took time alone and started slowly making their way through the open courtyard towards the crypt. "The Deacon is your father then?" he asked. "And you never thought to mention it?" Brodie, thought for a moment, although quite young he had a mature head on his shoulders.

He answered very carefully having harboured his secret. "I prefer the sea to the Monastery, what about you?" Wishart did not answer but knew what the young man meant.

"It is not an issue I find it amusing that your loyalty has been unblemished and yet you still serve the Church, good on you," remarked Wishart, and walked back into the Abbey leaving Brodie to ponder on his thoughts.

Meanwhile, The Temple Unicorn sat in darkness just a cable length's distance off the headland waiting for her departure to Iona. As she sat in the shallow waters of the mightiest river in Britain, the River Tay, the tide had begun to turn.

The river itself runs for twenty-two miles towards Perth, and consists of many deep regions of shifting sand banks and a certain nightmare if any mariner fails to respect the ever changing tides.

Cargo—Scotland

In the eyes of the Order, only one piece of cargo remained sacred above all others and that was the skeletal remains of Mary Magdalene. In her lifetime, Mary had travelled to and from the Holy Land in many guises, but her final resting place is rumoured to be somewhere in the Temple's global footprint. In her death, she had travelled further afield, and now it was time for her journeys to end.

The Temple Unicorn was bound for the northern islands off the north of Scotland and a single cross was marked on an older cartograph in black ink. Ironically, the location was indeed marked with a large black X. The symbol of the X lay between two significant points on the map between a series of numbers as northings and eastings. The X marked a point set slightly higher on a hill—if the map's detail was to be believed.

Wishart turned and locked his cabin door and opened the chest where he kept most of his belongings. Ironically, this chest was never locked and his crew would often ask the Skipper if they could hide an item or two for safe keeping.

Wishart would often say. "Throw whatever it is in that box over there, and fetch it when you need it." Explaining that it was not that secure but safe enough for personal things for a short time. By his reckoning, half the crew knew that this was the worst kept secret on the vessel. Wishart lifted a few items from the kiste, then slid another single panel that was secreted at its bottom off to one side again.

He then removed a series of linen 'sail' fabric parchments and placed them in a row on the chart table. The fragments had been taken as sample pieces from a much larger series of parchments that were stored deep in the bowels of the Unicorn and resembled a series of breast pieces for a costume.

Wishart made some notes then placed the parchments back in the box then proceeded below decks. As he stepped below the first t'ween deck bulkhead, he encountered Roral who was standing staring at one of the internal storage chamber doorways.

"What is wrong?" the Captain asked. Roral pointed towards one of the doors indicating a feint glow that appeared to be pulsing from within; a visible stream of blue and yellow lights were emanating from under the woodwork.

"Come with me, Mr Roral," ordered Wishart. "We have a job to do." He explained and removed a set of industrial size keys from his tunic. "You my young friend are about to be educated. Wishart unlocked the door and both men entered the room. I hear you have taken to accounting for the rule of the great order; well I have been tasked by Hugues De Payen to ensure that some alterations are made to some rather sensitive tapestries. Don't worry Hugues will join us shortly."

Wishart pointed to a huge tapestry that had been hung between two of the wooden beams that supported the deck head. "This tapestry was almost eighteen foot long and five foot six wide and had been folded enough to accommodate its length within the cabin space, and you can observe, young man, that it contains a secret that no man has ever fully deciphered. This blanket captures many maps and ciphers that have been strategically woven into its fabric.

Many scholars have tried to work out the hidden secrets of both the Scandinavian and Egyptian knowledge whilst attempting to locate secret treasures perhaps. But for us, my dear, young Mr Roral . . . guess what? I have the code.

This is an ancient scroll and will be delivered to the Orcadians in the Orkney islands but first we have to ensure that some symbols are added before we give it to the islanders. I am sure that St Magnus of the islands will look after it—even from his far off spirit world."

Roral stroked the edge of the cloth. "Does it really lead to hidden treasures, Captain?" he asked, still stroking the fine linen criss cross pattern.

"To be honest, young Roral, I wish I really knew. What I am doing is unpicking these seven symbols here and there. As I have said, I am adding and taking away some symbols," he said, again pointing to the relevant areas of the carpet. I am doing this because I have been ordered to, and to leave the work in perfect condition. It has taken me nearly six weeks so far to remove just five symbols, and I am nearly finished! But I need someone to see that I have actually completed it—should something sinister or dreadful happen to me. Do you understand young man?" Roral nodded in acknowledgement as Wishart explained this blanket of mystery.

"The tapestry apparently contains symbols of a hierarchy of succession; it shows how to ascend the levels within King Solomon's rank and file, but more importantly details of an ancient Arabic culture of ascension as opposed to Turkish or Cypriot influence. If you look here, and here, you will see symbols that have no order of significance at all, but they do have meaning. Did you notice the tattoo on the Deacon of Balmerino's left arm earlier? It was this symbol here, look, the one with the lamb."

Roral shook his head. "No, I did not notice," he remarked and walked towards the Ark with an odd expression on his fresh, inquisitive face.

Wishart watched and waited, then spoke out just above normal talking volume and with a tone of certain authority. "Don't go near that, do not take another step!"

Wishart placed a hand on the young man's shoulder and pulled him backwards away from the tools of God. He then picked up a gold coin from the table top and looked directly at the young man and said, "Watch this." Then he tossed the coin at one of the upright golden cherubs that was partially obscured by the red linen cloth.

Momentarily, just as the coin almost touched the cherub, a series of blue sparks arced outwards from the Ark and the coin instantly disappeared in a fizz of light and a puff of white smoke.

Roral, was a beast of man and had acquired a lot of knowledge over the past few months, having spent a long time talking about the signature pieces of God but no one person was permitted to touch any singular pieces at any time. He sat down staring back at the Ark. "That's awesome!" he exclaimed, pulling his robes tighter together. For a moment he contemplated falling into a quick prayer.

Wishart stopped him. "No time for prayer my friend: work now, pray later, you'll thank me for it. If you lift that linen cloth there," said Wishart, pointing to a small parcel that sat near to the desk. "you may well get an even bigger surprise." He said no more. Roral was momentarily bemused then lifted the lower corner of the red linen cloth and took a glance at what lay underneath.

Staring back at him was a white skull, encased in glass and captured in a ribbed golden framework. The Skipper caught the young man before he fell onto the hard decking with fright. The Knight then stared a lot longer at the object than he should have.

"The Skull belongs to one Mister John the Baptist, so please don't touch it, it might bite you," remarked Wishart, as he began playing with his pieces of linen again just as Roral placed the cloth back over the skull's golden and crystal case.

Wishart and Roral smiled at one another then continued in their visit with the shrine in transit. There was a sudden shuffling of footsteps just outside the cabin door. The two were instantly alerted and drew their swords. Five seconds later Hugues De Payen entered the room.

"Roral, Mr Wishart, have you conducted business? Time is of the essence?" Both men nodded in unison. De Payen stared at Roral, then spoke again, "You are now the custodian." Then he turned and faced Wishart. "Thank you, Captain, the Order is eternally grateful."

'The Voyage North'

The Temple Unicorn had silently slipped out of the Tay estuary and was heading northwards up the Scottish coastline. The crew had planned to break off at the most northerly point, heading for the outer islands towards the inlet of Kirkwall which was to be her next destination. Her task was to deliver a series of manuscripts, gold trinkets and the huge scroll.

Having departed Balmerino and sailed past Dundee event free, all was going rather well. Her silent departure was executed perfectly, even the Monks at the Abbey had no idea the vessel had sailed and was making best headway with an easterly wind driving her bulk northwards; that was until around 07:22 hours when a single sail was spotted on the distant horizon followed by what appeared to be several multi-masted vessels of similar design.

Captain Wishart commanded all hands to the main deck and made ready for a race against time and Mother Nature. His aim was to reach his next waypoint in order to head west across the top of the isle.

By his reckoning, a huge storm was brewing and he had spoken with his new crew of Knights. He explained that he could feel that this thunderstorm was going to be a monster. De Payen or Captain Wishart had no intention of stopping to fight any thieves or even contemplate losing their precious cargo. They were so close to home, especially now, with the crew having dedicated their lives thus far. Sadly, at this time, the Holy Order may not be as potent as it once was—if rumours were to be believed.

Wishart grabbed the Bosun and whispered something in his ear. Mr Bertie suddenly made off below decks and soon the crew began to assemble on the aft of the vessel. It was not long before The Temple Unicorn had swung hard to port and began making her way along the most northerly rugged and dangerous coastline.

The plan as far as Wishart was concerned was to sail The Temple Unicorn around the top of Scotland then head north to Kirkwall, but now she was somehow southbound, heading towards Ireland and the Island of Iona. The Captain announced a sudden change of plan and a hail of rigging changes followed and deck activity ensued.

It was a straightforward plan and a route that neither of the mariners had undertaken. Wishart had sailed many times between the Emerald Isle and his homeland under the direct wishes of the Lord of the Isles and had often found him too often sheltering in a cosy cove or sprinting between known land points.

Wishart had explained to the Grand Master that did not like unchartered waters and this was the challenge that he rose to in the name of the Lord when accepting the mission. He had heard of waves that were much larger than any he had conceived. The waves were rumoured to be almost two or three miles across, their height could reach several hundred feet high.

Often a series of five waves could stem to the distant horizon miles off and take minutes to catch you unawares.

The harsh waters between Stornoway and Tiree were any mariner's worse nightmare. Wishart had spent time on the islands of Uist and had traversed the westerly waters of the outer Hebridean Islands, and would have never considered running the gauntlet across the top of Scotland especially in gale force winds, let alone navigate the sound of Mull.

Hugues spoke softly, "Well, Kyle, we all have to face our demons sometime, and trust me I have faced many, but the burdens of belief lie on our shoulders. We are part of something far greater than any one man can imagine. I have no doubts that you will deliver us safely." Then he left the Captain alone to contemplate his next move.

Wishart took a long look at the skies and wiped his brow. Then shouted at the darkened skies, "Lord, I have twenty men to fight your cause and twenty men to protect your holiest of relics. These are the heavy burdens you mark my soul with, your precious cargo and the lives of these men who have given their all for you. I swear. Should I have to dump the cargo overboard, and then I will, if such actions preserve the lives of your dedicated servants of Christendom then so be it. I now, this day, pray for your divine assistance. And now Lord this is definitely the time."

A short burst of lightning shot across the distant horizon as the wind and rains intensified. De Payen watched and smiled then gathered his Knights for a final pre-hurricane briefing.

The crew above decks watched in amazement and listened to their Captain. The Bosun clasped his hands and placed one of his heavy hands on the shoulder of the galley rat. "Leave him be, go make some spuds or something we must eat." The cook turned and smiled one of his toothless grins then scurried below decks.

Bertie then stepped over the coiled ropes on the deck then stood adjacent to Wishart. "I see your faith is running low, Skipper?" he said, and stared towards the approaching masts.

"Mister Bertie, I . . ."

The Bosun cut him short. "Captain, you know that these men will die for you, and so will I, but I have not ventured all this way to die for stupidity? The Grand Master is right, you are a far better Skipper than Mr Duncan ever was, rest his soul. We will be fine, you will be fine, the Lord has protected us thus far. Why would he want to give up on us now?" he remarked, and walked off leaving the Captain to ponder on his few well-chosen words.

The larger of the two masted vessels appeared to be getting closer. Wishart was anxious. He had navigated the Bay of Biscay with relative ease, and had negotiated the Straits of Gibraltar as any professional seasoned mariner could, and had managed to drop off fifty per cent of God's treasures at many hostile locations. But somehow the final leg north was appearing to be her most vulnerable hour.

The helmsman shouted, "Sou sou east, steady . . ."

"Aye aye," came the ever responsive answer from nowhere.

The Ballaster had appeared on decks and found the Skipper. "Captain, we appear to be carrying more cargo than I had anticipated. We could shed some of the dry stores and boxes of old meat. We could make three or four more knots if we jettisoned the lot, Skipper?"

The Skipper turned and yelled at the top of his voice, "Half hands below decks, and Mister Knox take the helm if you will. Mr Brodie get this deck ship shape. I want to have a clear pathway from that hatch there to that star observation board there. Get on with it, please."

"Aye Cap'n," came the quick reply. "Consider it done."

The vessel atmosphere geared up a notch as the crew scurried over decks dumping anything that was useless or took up extra weight. The pathway was cleared and the coxswain was fighting with the helm as the ballast was being thrown across the deck into disarray.

Wishart was too pre-occupied to notice that they had been pushed well beyond the inlet to Thurso and before he realised his error, they had missed their pre-determined waypoint and he was unable to swing around against the prevailing winds for Kirkwall. He took the decision to take a wider swing and was edging towards cresting along the wave tops to keep the galley both safe and stable, but the helm was somehow locked.

The Captain turned towards Brodie and stared for a full twenty seconds, then spoke out in his commanding tone. "Do not try and crest, Mr Brodie. No point in fighting with Poseidon, leave her be. We will ride this storm out, then return when this 'hoolie' disappears. In the meantime, keep your keen eyes on those masts and head for the horizon. We can't win against a vessel with so many sails, but we can out manoeuvre them if need be, and, Mr Brodie, the helm will feel as if it is locked at this speed."

Wishart had kept his final set of commands up his sleeve to the very last moment and started to form a game plan in his head, just as he felt the forward end of the ship raise out of the water and was offering a fair degree of freeboard. By his reckoning, it was a good full fifty inches at the peak. He then took a good deep breath of fresh air.

Wishart was impressed. He tapped his temple with his hand and stared across at the rudder column then spoke out. "Ballasters worth their bloody weight in anyone's gold," he muttered, then took a peak over the side of the vessel.

Wishart turned to the crew and smiled a smile of gratitude; the many faces of the crew equally responded and waited in anticipation for his next bout of orders. He gathered his thoughts and removed his sword from its sheath, and then at the top of his voice he commanded the crew to stop what they were doing and listen. "Gentlemen, I have been blessed with a fine body of men and I owe a great deal of gratitude and my life to each and all. We are about to head westwards and the winds up here are unprecedented. It is rumoured that ship's masts can be simply ripped off their mounts, even under normal sailing conditions.

If you think Biscay was a harsh and brutal voyage, then brace yourself for the mother of storms, and trust me when I say she is heading our way, and we will be taking her full forrid on. If we are not crushed on the rocks of the ragged coastline then we will surely perish at the hands of the infidel, who, as you can see are not too far away. I want to deploy all sails and spinnakers, mid-sheets and spare sheets, and make full sail towards the far off coastline. It is a huge risk that we must take to survive. As you are aware, we carry a cargo that will change the face of mankind for the future years to come and cannot be permitted to change hands now.

We are fifteen cable lengths off the coastline of our homeland, but we have to come in closer to the rocks. The worst outcome is that we die for our Lord as a team, or best, is that we live for our Lord having swum ashore with none of the relics intact—those articles of faith that we have sworn to protect." It was then that all the Knights had assembled collectively having left their posts on the vessel.

The Grand Master, Hugues De Payen, raised his sword aloft for all to see; he then cast it across the complete crew and shouted. "With this steel, I Knight one and all. With this sword, I appoint you all as Ship's Officers and Knights and it is with this sword I pledge you all my life. Brothers: Knox, Bosun, Berie, Brodie and Captain Wishart, make full sail. We have little time."

Wishart exploded into a hail of commands and standing orders as the crew began climbing the mast to the masthead in order to cut away the tie downs. The wind had caught the sails instantly and the huge mass pitched downwards then shot up. Then it rolled port and starboard with a series of pitches and yaws then took a final huge surge as her bows protruded out of the water almost twelve feet.

Wishart and the deck crew, supported by the Knights, grabbed what was to be grasped and waited until the bulk of the craft settled. It was then that the cook flicked open a small deck hatch and passed a plate of hot potatoes to the Skipper. Wishart wiped a single tear from his eye, "You too Cookie, Officer of the fire and Knight of the Order."

The Temple Unicorn was in full flight; her many ropes and lines were flapping in the wind along with the loose wind sheets that beat the air in futility. The untied ropes were left to the elements, as all concentration was being applied to the mainsail rigging.

A few minutes and the 'hoolie' took bight of the full mainsail. There was a series of cracks as several, smaller yard arms split their mountings and fell to decks, and were quickly pushed aside by the crew. The huge foc'sle was being battered with heavy waves as they beat against the forward beam. Clear signs of damage were beginning to occur as ton, upon tons of sea water whipped the forward decks.

There was debris everywhere and minor backstay posts lay strewn over the uprights. The ship's loose items had taken flight overboard, but in essence the ship remained eighty per cent intact. Albeit, the vessel was making good headway and Kyle was becoming concerned for his crew. He knew they could not maintain this level of intensity for too long and he had succumbed to the fact that his final efforts could be misconstrued as suicide or even negligence towards his crew.

Something broke his concentration again. It was Brodie. He had reported back to the Captain after three hours to inform him that they had turned by the most northerly outcrop and the strong winds had ripped the top mizzen mast and destroyed a few backstay and bolstrop lines.

He was also quick to inform the Skipper that the approaching vessels appeared to have given up their hasty chase and had observed several main sheets being lowered to mid-mast indicating that it was too treacherous to give chase, as the winds increased.

Wishart passed comment that the local Masters were obviously opportunists and knew the dangers that lurked in these unchartered waters between the isles. But he said something odd that triggered Wishart's sense of duty. He had alluded that the first vessel had failed to lower her wind sheets and would swear that he had momentarily observed the Templar Emblem on her main sail for a short period. The winds had eventually settled to a blistering gale and the rain beat the frail flesh of Mr Brodie who was trying to assist the Bosun in packing ropes into the scupper holes. De Payen gave a quick glance and thanked Wishart.

"Mr De Payen?" came a voice from the Bosun. "What would happen to the Unicorn's riches if we lost her now?" he asked, just as De Payen pulled the sword out of its scabbard and placed it on top of the wooden rudder post.

"Well, Mr Wishart, the riches would be sold to the highest bidder and more false prophets would emerge with relics that were not in the order of things. As for the marine vessel 'The Temple Unicorn' she would most probably be stripped and broken down into artefacts and relics and sold on to the masses as biblical treasures."

It was a few minutes later when the vessel took an almighty thump and crunch to her port midships. The crew were instantly thrown across all areas of the heaving vessel and soon discovered that a single rock had struck the underbelly of the vessel, ripping out two great chunks of planking from her outer hull. The Captain feared the worst and headed for the Steering Island.

There was another series of crunches as The Temple Unicorn started to almost flounder on the many rocks that lay below the shallow surface. The lookout could see no water lapping the surface and could not determine the way in which the confused swell was going to throw them around.

He stared at the Captain who seemed to both acknowledge the predicament and simultaneously send a comforting message. Wishart shouted, "Don't panic, Mr Bertie, do your best; we are not through this big beastie yet."

Wishart grabbed De Payen and they both quickly ventured below decks. Kyle was shouting his orders between the wind and the heavy battering of wind and waves that the vessel was being subjected to. "Grand Master, we need to jettison the stone coffins and some other artefacts or we are as good as dead. Firstly, I want you to push that end of the . . ." Wishart and De Payen were stopped in their tracks; ten feet before them they could observe a huge crack beginning to appear and it was running the length of the inner bulkhead from forrid to aft.

Kyle grabbed De Payen's tunic and splurged a set of orders. "We need to get every member of the crew into the inner cargo void spaces; no-one on deck and no-one in the galley, and do it now!" he screamed, searching for a piece of wood to support the now collapsing outer bulkhead. The water was nearing knee height and was cascading into the ship at every conceivable opportunity as the cracks widened with every uncontrollable heave of the vessel.

Wishart watched and held the wooden beam by placing his back against the stay in order to flatten the planks together, and then he yelled another series of inaudible orders as the crew started filtering into the small cargo hold.

A few minutes later and the huge crack had split open as tons of sea water started to ingress the inner void, just as De Payen hurriedly pulled the door shut then locked it. The crew gazed at the Grand Master totally mesmerised by his actions and perhaps thought the Grand Master had lost his sea marbles. His Knights collectively placing their lives at his disposal yet again. Captain Wishart had barely made it into the void.

There was a deadly silence in the cargo hold as the vessel pitched to port then to starboard. Then was followed by an encore of ear piercing squeals and screeches as the outer skin of the vessel was ripped and torn completely apart—each plank separating from the main keel bracing. There were a few more unidentifiable noises and creaks mixed in with the back drop of the hurricane. Then, as if by magic, it went very quiet.

"No, no!" cried Captain Wishart. "There is more to come! By the Saint of Magdalene and the will of God should we survive, I will eat my hat!" It was then that another bout of tossing and turning on the high seas took place. The crew inside the ship were suffering severely as the vessel began to list to port then was violently swung back the opposite way, then another series of tosses and turns throwing the crew into complete disarray.

The many bodies within the void were being thrown around the inner cargo void like childrens' rag dolls; each scrambling to latch onto to some strong point or solid object in their midst. Conversely, the mass tonnage of the ship was no different to a small cork in the proverbial glass bottle, being bounced around at will.

Wishart was thrown a full ten feet across the decks and landed on the flat of his back, almost spread eagled, facing upwards and splayed across the top of the Ark. He coughed, spluttered then flinched as his head made contact with one of the golden cherubs as it stared back at him. He was expectant of the Ark to incinerate him there and then, but, it did not. He instantly rolled off the Ark and landed on the decks on his knees.

Meanwhile, De Payen and another crew member had been launched forward simultaneously as the second bout of waves hurled the bulk of The Temple Unicorn up onto the rocks. De Payen's sword had broken in half and the rugged edge had ripped clean through his white tabard. Sadly, it had landed on the breast plate of the young Brodie as they clashed, piercing his skin, Brodie was momentarily bounced off the stone coffin top and cascaded on to his rear end towards the rear of the cabin, ending in the upright position and unconscious.

The remaining sarcophagus had inadvertently shifted and had trapped Cookie against the bulkhead, leaving the unfortunate chef's lifeless body also in the upright position affixed against the golden crucifix, almost in the same manner as St Andrews had been crucified, but on this occasion Mother Nature was to be accused.

The remaining crew members had begun grasping and clinging on to the deck head beams and had begun lashing themselves to each of the uprights, using their sword straps as tie downs. Roral had found a spot at the corner of the sarcophagus and was clenching the small effigy as Andre' Montbard had grasped his belt straps and was hanging onto his dearest friend for his life.

Wishart took a quick stock of his crew and started counting, "One, two . . . four . . . nine . . . fourteen in situ and the unfortunate chef making fifteen. At least Davy Jones gets us as a complete crew," he yelled, as a sudden darkness engulfed the complete cabin as the vessel started spinning and corkscrewing in the cold, deep waters of the cruel and unrelenting Atlantic Sea.

The storm had continued to batter the vulnerable hulk of The Temple Unicorn for another eighteen hours. Her keel had been ripped, battered and shredded into pieces and huge chunks were very evidently missing from her structure. Mother Nature had been eating the vessel piece by piece by commanding the powers of the wind and waves.

The Temple Unicorn had been propelled across an unprecedented distance and had managed to pass between several islands and shores without hindrance. She had been directed through both deep and shallow waters, caught up in an unprecedented mother of all storms. As the bulk of the ship sat quietly on the beach embedded in the sand and sitting amongst a myriad of ship's debris that had been washed up and strewn across the beach, all was relatively quiet.

Thousands of tiny fragments of the vessel lay in abandonment. The ship's wheel was neatly stuck in the wet mud up to mid-axle level, and the mass of the huge, oak island rudder was almost gone. All that remained was the wooden, oak base plate that once housed the actual rudder; a chunk of oak that now lay in two pieces, split nicely down the middle.

Further up the beach, a few hundred feet away, lay another carcass of a shipwrecked vessel. Only thirty per cent of her hull had survived the storm, and just a few uprights were visible. She looked like a dead beast as its huge rib cage reached up toward the skies.

A single backstay beam had been wrapped up in rope and a piece of the sheet sail had covered part of the ship's bell and retained it from being released into the murky depths of the sea. The sun's rays momentarily peaked over the horizon sending a shower of intense light across the beach, and a single ray of light caught the shiny bell and appeared to be sending another single beam of beautiful colour into the guts of the distant Temple Unicorn.

The mass of the Unicorn lay in the sand, almost sixty feet from the water's edge. Her solid spine and back were completely broken. Although she was still recognisable as a ship, but alas the outer skin of the once awesome ship had been totally ripped away leaving the internal skeletal framework intact exposing only the void that had saved their many lives.

A single body rolled off the top of the sarcophagus and gave out a series of disturbing coughs and splurts as mucus, mixed seawater which spoiled the colours of the Templar's tabard. Wishart stood up and bumped his head against an overhead beam that had inconveniently made its way uninvited into the cargo void.

There was a flurry of activity in the small void as several of the crew members awoke from their induced sleep. He spied the cabin and watched Wishart and Brodie move, and almost come alive. Cookie had somehow managed to find himself sharing the stone coffin with the remains of a well-known skeleton named Pilate and soon found his second wind realising where he was, and began exiting the tomb. The Bosun had broken his arm but was nevertheless in good fettle.

The majority of the artefacts were readily identifiable as they lay in close proximity to the many cases and broken boxes that had found their final resting places. The Ark was intact. To Hugues De Payen it appeared that of all of God's pieces, this single artefact had not be touched or had moved from its original stow location. He spied the many urns and vases which had been smashed and the contents were clearly sparkling in the sunlight.

A welcome sight to his eye line was that most of the crew were mobile and were in the process of either fighting to stand up or recovering from whatever awkward contortion their bodies had endured—each man helping the other.

Apart from a few bumps and scrapes, they were all very much alive. The confines of the internal second skinned compartment had saved their many lives, thanks to the pragmatism of the ship's foremost informed designers.

Brodie stood up, and looked at his blood-ridden tabard. His wounds had somehow been cleaned and made good. Although heavily blood stained, his mantle was undamaged. In spite of what was transpiring, De Payen still appeared to be pre-occupied as he gazed into the void of nothingness.

Chapter Seventeen: 'The Knights' Templar Order Move in Mysterious Ways'

De Payens stepped down from inside the hulk of the carcass, almost tripping whilst negotiating his way towards a huge, gaping hole that once resembled a doorway—the entrance-way once located somewhere in the mid-ships of the vessel. The North and Atlantic seas had indeed been ruthless and had tortured the hull of the wooden ship to almost disintegration. The many wooden uprights barely holding together as the floor planks began shifting under his weight.

After a few seconds, he stood at the hole, his head almost reaching and touching a single beam that had extended downwards. With his eyes almost glazed over, he stared aimlessly into the desert of brown, salty sand that was spread out in front of him. He could hear shuffling close by. He did not turn; he still gazed on.

"We are lucky to be alive my friend," said Wishart, wiping the sand from his face, then began falling into a bout of uncontrolled coughing to an almost violent spew, attempting to continue in his dialogue. De Payens had paid little attention to anything until that point and turned and stared again at Kyle Wishart.

"The design of this awesome ship has definitely saved us my friend. Not just design, but your sea skills and a great belief in what we are protecting." Kyle spurted out another range of incomprehensible syllables again, struggling to speak between his mixed vowels with seawater and slime.

The Grand Master slapped his big, broad back then took a very deep breath himself, then looked deep into the eyes of Wishart as he stood up. The big man was momentarily disturbed as he observed a copious amount of tears rolling down Hugues De Payens' face.

De Payen looked down again and then pointed to the tracks that led away from the wreck of The Temple Unicorn, waving his free hand in the process, his other hand still gripping his broken sword hilt firmly.

He then traced the footsteps and hoof prints up the beach towards the church spire a few hundred feet from the water's edge. He could see two distinctive wheel tracks that clearly lay in the wet and dry brown patches of sand, and then disappeared as they ran through a small curtain wall of seaweed and pebbles.

"Look," he said, pointing to the tracks in the sand. "We have had visitors. It looks like our good lady has brought us home." He smiled and lowered his head in reverence, just as the sun continued to send its rays across the sand. The crew of The Temple Unicorn, meanwhile, had gathered together and were hugging one another with great admiration. Each man was just happy to be alive.

A few feet away, stuck in the sand, was the ship's wooden name plate:

'Di Templi Unikorn' with a small Fleur De Lys carved at one end.

The End.

The Lords Prayer

Latin

Sancti spiritus adsit nobis gratia. Maria, Stella maris, perducat nos ad portam salutis. Amen.

Domine, Jesu Christe, sancte pater, aeterne Deus, omnipotens, sapiens creator, largitor, administrator benignus, et carissimus amator, pius et humilis redemptor, clemens, misericors salvator, Domine, te deprecor humiliter et exoro ut illumines me, liberes et conserves fratres Templi, et omnem populum tuum chistianum turbatum.

Tu, Domine, qui scis nos esse innocentes, facias liberari, ut vota nostra et mandata tua in humilitate teneamus, et tuum sanctum servitium et voluntatem faciamus ; contumelias iniquas, non veras, contra nos oppositas per graves oppositiones, et malas tribulationes et tentationes, quas passi fuimus, et pati ulterius non possumus.

Omnipotens, aeterne Deus, qui beatum Joannem evangelistam et apostolum tuum valde diligis, qui super pectus tuum in caena recubuit, et cui secreta caeli revelavis et demonstravis, et stante in ligno sanctae crucis, pro redemptione nostra, sanctissimam matrem tuam virginem commendavis, in cujus honore gloriose fuit facta, et fundata religio ; pro tua sancta misericordia liberes et conserves, prout tu scis nos esse innocentes a criminibus contra nos oppositis, et operas possideamus, per quas ad gaudia paradisi perducamur, per Christum dominum nostrum. Amen.

Translation

All Thy Christian people, troubled as they are.

May the grace of the Holy Spirit be present with us. May Mary, Star of the Sea, leed us to the harbor of salvation. Amen. Lord

Jesus Christ, Holy Father, eternal God, omnipotent, omniscient Creator, Bestower, kind Ruler and most tender lover, pious and humble Redeemer; gentle, merciful Savior, Lord! I humbly beseech, Thee and implore Thee that Thou may enlighten me, free me and preserve the brothers of the Temple and Thou, O Lord, who knowest that we are innocent, set us free that we may keep our vows and your commandments in humility, and serve Thee and act according to Thy will.

(Dispel) all those unjust reproaches, far from the truth, heaped upon us by the means of tough adversities great tribulations and temptations, which we have endured,
But can endure no longer.

Omnipotent, eternal God, who hast so loved the blessed John the Evangelist and Apostle, that he reclined upon Thy bosom at the Last Supper, and to whom Thou revealed and showed the Mysteries of Heaven, and to whom, while suspended on the Holy Cross, for the sake of our redemption, Thou commended.

Thy most Holy Mother and Virgin, and in whose honour (our) Order was created and instituted; through Thy Holy mercifulness, deliver us and preserve us, as Thou knowest that we are innocent of the crimes that we are accused of, so that we may take possession of the works, by which we may be guided to the joys of Paradise, through Jesus Christ our Lord. Amen.

Amen—Andrew David Doyle.

The American Way
Vis-à-Vis The School

by

William J. Goins

Note for Librarians: A cataloguing record for this book is available from Library
and Archives Canada at www.collectionscanada.ca/amicus/index-e.html

Printed in Victoria, BC, Canada.

ISBN: 978-1-4251-8689-0 (sc)

*We at Trafford believe that it is the responsibility of us all, as both individuals and corporations,
to make choices that are environmentally and socially sound. You, in turn, are supporting this
responsible conduct each time you purchase a Trafford book, or make use of our publishing services.
To find out how you are helping, please visit www.trafford.com/responsiblepublishing.html*

*Our mission is to efficiently provide the world's finest, most comprehensive book publishing
service, enabling every author to experience success. To find out how to publish your book, your
way, and have it available worldwide, visit us online at www.trafford.com*

Trafford rev. 7/6/2009

 www.trafford.com

North America & international
toll-free: 1 888 232 4444 (USA & Canada)
phone: 250 383 6864 ♦ fax: 250 383 6804 ♦ email: info@trafford.com

The United Kingdom & Europe
phone: +44 (0)1865 487 395 ♦ local rate: 0845 230 9601
facsimile: +44 (0)1865 481 507 ♦ email: info.uk@trafford.com

Contents

Introduction

THIS BOOK is based on my experiences as an indelible American and 40+ years of teaching in the Chicago Public School system—specifically the neighborhood ghetto school. It addresses the plight of millions of so-called cursed Americans who are engorged, flailing, floundering, in the "belly of the tiger," searching, groping and hoping to find some way or ways of maneuvering through the labyrinth of intestines, to find a more suitable environment. Further an attempt is made to critically examine the deceptions, myths, bigotries, racial intolerances and hypocrisies entrenched in our not-so-equal society—vis-à-vis the school. The school is charged, as other American institutions, to instilling, imparting, protecting, reinforcing and ensuring those behaviors remain intact and permanent.

I borrowed the term nice/nasty, the title of the book, from my grandmother. She used the term to describe people who were two-faced—talking out of both sides of their mouths; people who pretend to be what they are not; people who were religious hypocrites and people in general who were delphic. Nice/nasty, then, is all of the hypocrisies, debaucheries, chicaneries, contradictions, mendacious and bigotries practices entrenched in U.S. society. They are so pervasive, so natural; they have been accepted as a "correct" way of life.

Listed are a few patented examples: war is necessary to have peace, destroying a country, its people, its cultural institution to make them free, whites readily accepting blacks in their homes to cook and help with child-rearing and have apoplexy at the thought of black children attending the public school with their children; granting blacks unenforceable legal and civil rights and deviously plotting to ensure their status in society remain "fixed," giving indigenous people western style Christianity, a promise of brotherhood and taking their valuable resources, proclaiming only Christians can qualify for heaven, all others are doomed. Nice/nasties are constant reminders of U.S. deceit, amoral practices and institutionalized myths that keep the "American Way" flourishing. America's false consciousness is her "Achilles heel."

Teaching was not my vocational choice. A traumatic happening steered me into that profession. I really wanted to be a lawyer. The Communist mania of the Cold War era dramatically altered my plans. I was chosen to be one of many victims charred at the stake in the resurrected New Salem – America.

Witch hunting was an elaborate scheme by decision-makers to contain the spread of Communism, to protect America's image abroad as the "Savior" of the free world and to enact legislation for defense spending, military build-up and to convince Americans such were vital for America's survival.

The plan was set in motion and orchestrated by the noblest of witch hunters, the venerable J. McCarthy. Under his guidance and tutelage he and his henchmen launched relentless, brutal and unscrupulous attacks on all persons who were labeled communist, communist sympathizers and persons who knew or associated with so-called communists. Those persons were considered anti-Americans and their sole objective was to overthrow the government and to undermine the American way of life. Xenophobia became more than an obsession. Those suspect, disloyal persons were summoned for loyalty hearings, found guilty, fired from their respective jobs, labeled, branded and ostracized. Big Brother was working overtime. The enforcers were given carte blanche. The Attorney-General compiled a "hit" list and targeted supposedly subversive organizations.

As a student at a local university I belonged or joined one of those organizations—really a club. I had three loyalty hearings and finally was charged with being a wayward traveler, a poor security risk—throwing letters in a pigeon hole at a U.S. Post Office! Of course I was fired—just another statistic.

Statistics are excellent for what they do, but they cannot or could not possibly fathom the ensuing emotional upheavals they generate. I lost my job, my wife; the thought of her being married to a Communist wrecked her world and nearly destroyed mine. Moreover, being a wounded veteran—WWII—made finding a job extremely difficult. Nevertheless, not all was lost. Fortunately for me I had an astute advisor. He advised me to take educational courses in addition to prerequisite ones necessary for law school. I had enough education courses to qualify for teaching in the public school. So my attorney strongly suggested that I apply for a job as teacher in the public school system. There he felt confident that I would have union support. I really thought my attorney was off his rocker. I took his advice and was hired.

My first assignment was to teach history and civics in a high school. Fired from a job throwing letters in a pigeon-hole at a post office for being "a poor security risk"; hired to teach history and civics was mind boggling. That encounter really "opened my eyes" to see how deeply ingrained hypocrisies, irresponsibilities, and deceptions are embedded in the U.S. society. That was my induction into the teaching ranks.

I do not have definitive answers; rather, constructive criticisms. My issues are topical. My intent is not to rewrite the history of American institutions but to explore the ambivalence of the American Way. I have combined specific historical facts, personal experiences, philosophical, economical, political, religious legacies, and honest and reasonable marketplace opinions. Further, I borrowed the term "Bitch Goddess of Success" from *Lady Chatterley's Lovers*. My aim is to arouse all Americans out of mental stupor, Charley McCarthy constructs to incite them to think for themselves, have them to realize how their ineptness, apathy, nonchalance and undying faith in irresponsive, irresponsible, unscrupulous leaders who owe fealty only to the Bitch Goddess of Success—money and power, have forced them to negate their natural rights, civil and moral commitments. Such behaviors have made the label of "Ugly Americans" more ugly and permanent.

My approach is rooted in the muckraking concept. I am not about mindless rabble-rousing, agitating, tampering with or modifying American institutions nor plotting to overthrow the government. I repeat, I am deeply concerned with finding a plan, a method, a philosophy to guide lesser-breed Americans through the maze of inequalities, to escape from their apparently defined status, to for once retire the ageless, tireless opiate, hope and ultimately to find an acceptable alternative to the mythical American Dream.

In addition, the book sets forth a series of interrelated truths. We do not live in an egalitarian society—some people are more equal than others. The American assumption is regardless of race, creed, will, station or subcultures and associative problems all inhabitants culturally speaking will become White-Anglo Saxon Protestants; all institutions reflect that mission. American society is belied in the American Dream delusion, "unlimited horizons" psychology, the "melting pot" simile, the Prodigal Son allegory, rugged individualism myth, ordained white paternalism and a host of anti-egalitarian philosophies. Indelibility is to many an object of disgust and a divine curse. Americans are money junkies and will do whatever it takes to appease that addiction; they have "hocked" their souls to the Bitch Goddess of Success in pursuit of that "drug." Americans rely too heavily on authorities, experts, apathetic leaders and controlled media hype for guidance. The chosen, the "fraternity of whiteness," with its divine entitlements, and prophecy is fulfilling its divine, destined mission—the redemption of mankind.

Religion, racism, poverty and war are the mainstay of the American Way. Those divine, indivisible, irremediable, partial institutions have an involuntary tendency to favor some groups of people over others and set the stage for the American dreams. In spite of their powerful influence and position, they are not autonomous. Their actions or reactions are dependent on the political, social and economic climates of the times. The school is no exception. Therefore, it can be no better or worse than the society it is sworn to protect. We delude ourselves in believing the school can change the status quo. Even if that fact were possible, our needs for jobs, money and our reverence for money would not welcome the change. For example, if the school were to develop, pinpoint, and exploit the creative talents and intellectual abilities in a warm supportive environment a countless number of people would be out of work. Public education is a mega-million dollar enterprise. As such, it creates a myriad of specialized and service jobs. The byproduct of change, in the main, is seen in our country as a loss of jobs. Therefore, reform is fraught with the fear of job losses. There are too many people depending on public education for their livelihood. The other delusion, lesser-breed Americans think moral persuasion tactics can change the American mindset. The challenge, then, for lesser-breed Americans is to stop trying to change the system; instead to focus collectively on finding ways and means to live in a harmonious, safe and secure community within the system.

Chapter I

RELIGION

I   T WOULD be unwitting to think, suggest or hint that Christianity as
     perceived by our uprooted ancestors played no part in their lives
     in the New World. How much of a role would be pure conjecture
on my part. However, it is believable their concept of Christianity
gave them hope. The late Weldon Johnson in his book *The Book of
Negro Spirituals* had this to say:

> The Negro slave far from his native land and customs,
> despised by those with whom he lived, experiencing the
> pang of separation of love ones on the auction blocks,
> knowing the hard task masters, feeling the lash, the Negro
> seized Christianity, the religion of compensation in the
> life to come for the ills suffered which implied hope that
> in the next world there would be a reversal of conditions
> of rich man and poor man, of proud and meek, of master
> and slave . . . regardless of the vast differences between
> Christianity preached to the Negro and the Christianity
> preached by those who preached it.[1]

That legacy still impacts the present black community. Those who
preached Christianity sanctioned the black inferiority myth—blacks
were cursed by God. To support that myth a book was written in 1900
entitled *The Negro Beast*. The author asserted:

---

1   Johnson, James Wheldon. *The Book of Negro Spirituals*. New York: Viking Press.
     1925, pp. 20-21.

> If this book were considered in an intelligent and prayerful manner, that it will be in the minds of Americans like unto the voice of God from the clouds appealing to Paul on the way to Damascus. In order that the American people might be convinced of the scientific nature of the Bible printed in this book. The author included a picture of God and an idealized picture of the white man in order to prove that white people were made in the image of God as stated in the Bible, and a caricature of the Negro showing that he could not have been made in the image of God ... That the Negro was not the son of Ham or even the descendent of Adam and Eve, but simply a beast without a soul.[2]

Western Christians see themselves and their religion superior to all others and are obliged to take care of the rest of the world because some people, mostly of darker skin, are not able to handle their own affairs.[3] Further, they fervently believe it is God's purpose made manifest in the instincts of our race whose present is our personal profit, but whose far-off end is the redemption of the world and the Christianization of mankind.[4]

None-whites challenged such arrogance and hypocrisy. Outspoken was Mahatma Gandhi of India. He wanted to know how or why was it that only Christians could go to heaven and attain salvation. Further, Gandhi observed the corruption, wars, violence, hypocrisies in the West, and how these behaviors triumphed over true Christian morals led him to believe "much of what passes as Christianity in the West was a negation of the Sermon on the Mount; when Christianity went to the west it became disfigured, it became the religion of kings.[5]

General Omar N. Bradley, Chairman of the Joint Chiefs of Staff of the U.S. Armed Forces in a speech in Boston on November 10, 1948:

> We have too many men of science, too few men of God. We have grasped the mystery of the atom and rejected the Sermon on the Mount. Ours is a world of nuclear grants and ethical infants. We know more about killing than we know about living.[6]

---

2   Frazier, E. Franklin. *Black Bourgeoisie.* New York: Simon & Shuster. 1962, p. 144.
3   Baker, Hayes, Straus. *The American Way.* Chicago: Willett, Clark & Co. 1936, p. 58.
4   Leckie, Robert. *The Wars of America*, Vol. II. New York: Harper and Row, p. 43.
5   Fisher, Louis. *Gandhi.* New York: Mentor Books, 1954, p. 131.
6   Fisher. Ibid., p. 131.

How a people who claimed to be followers of Jesus have a moral commitment to the brotherhood of man can condone racism, inequalities, wage immoral and unjust wars, sanction greed, poverty, inhumane practices, justify such behaviors under the banner of Christianity is a gross and vulgar misrepresentation of true Christian principles. The principle of the Sermon on the Mount have been brutalized, sabotaged and made a mockery to appease and satisfy the cravings of the Bitch Goddess of Success—money, wealth, power and greed. A well-known "man of the cloth" on national television can suggest that the U.S. should assassinate a sovereign leader of a country can attest to that fact. Western Christianity is a giant business conglomerate; therefore, it is in the business of making money; accepts and justifies the illicit behaviors that accompany it. As a result amoral practices have preempted moral values.

America is bullish on Christianity. Many men of the cloth apparently have sold their souls to and committed to serving, appeasing and worshiping the Bitch Goddess of Success—wealth and power. To prove that accusation, one only has to visit their websites, publishing companies, TV contracts, economic holdings and net worth. Western Christianity as applied is simply a patented, sanctioned and institutionalized nice/nasty. What is puzzling is how brilliant, creative blacks believe and trust American Christians' moral interpretation and practices.

People "who use Christianity for redemption and are not concerned with the Sermon on the Mount rather that Jesus was a divine spirit who died for their sins, to accept him as a savior is to be saved and pursuit of that salvation is paramount, not to live by his principles and practices.[7] Tragically, a countless number of naïve, ingratiating blacks have lost their directions and lives trying to persuade Christian America to honor its moral commitment to the brotherhood of man by marching, climbing, singing, hoping and praying.

For years, blacks have never wanted to accept the fact that American Christians owe their allegiance to the Bitch Goddess of Success and fealty to the "divine fraternity of whiteness." Perennially "Blacks are seen as sub-humans, amoral beings never spiritually equal to whites, regardless of their commitments and sacrifices.[8] Hypocrisies and

---

7   Schimke, David, "Heaven Can't Wait." *UTNE*, March-April 2005, pp. 56-60.
8   Tannenbaum, Frank. *Slave and Citizen*. New York: Random House. 1946, pp. 114-15.

contradictions have been on the American scene for centuries and are likely to remain for centuries to come. The Honorable Minister Louis Farrakhan has pointed out for years until the church overcomes its religious hypocrisies, recognizes and addresses its pervasive contradictions, the problems will multiply and will forever remain to plague American society.

The church has failed miserably in its efforts and attempts to build moral character in individuals. Its failure, perhaps, may be to its practices of reinforcing the same inhumane, vulgar and hypocritical practices it is sworn to extinguish. The late Prof. Henry Overstreet stated, "The church needs a complete overhauling. It needs to start with its religious teachings." He believed religious teaching, as well as preaching have been unpsychological. It has not taken into account the way individuals think and the laws of human behavior. Further, many "men of the cloth" have taken adult conceptions and tried to teach them to children. Such concepts do belong in the child's world. Adults, he felt, have false notions of what religion is and what it means.[9] Religious education must, using the principle from the Sermon on the Mount as a model, set, develop, keep and maintain moral values.

It is imperative for black ministers to modify their teaching and preaching registers. They must become more creative in their teaching techniques. You seemingly have been so busy developing the scriptures and preparing a place for people after death and ignoring the conditions of the living. You have done a superb job at heavenly architecturing and building magnificent churches, but what about the homeless, the wretched, the poor, the hungry, declining neighborhoods, moral decadence, violence, fear and interwoven miseries of black life. People want out of the "belly of the tiger" as well as the "good book.' I applaud your energy levels. Is it sacrilegious to be genuinely and actively concerned with the deplorable economic, social and political upheavals in the black community? Accolades to those of you who are actively addressing those issues and are still fighting to raise the responsibility levels in the community.

Unfortunately, your religious teachings have created all sorts of fears, insecurity and guilt in children. They have a very difficult time trying to understand, digest, cope and apply the principles of Western Christianity, a religion that is shrouded in contradictions and hypocrisies. As a result many are driven away from the church. For

---

9   Baker, Hayes, Straus, op. cit. pp. 56-7.

example, as a youngster I had to rid myself of sin. I wondered what sin I had and where I got it. At length I repented, got some religion and was baptized. I guessed I was no longer sin riddled. Confusion, fear, dread, feeling of impending doom and my shame dominated my childhood. Moreover, the conflict between the will of God and the actions of people remained surreptitious. I spent countless hours trying to figure out why the Almighty seemingly loved whites and hated blacks—whites had everything. I could not understand why my mother was taken away (died) from me at such a tender age. I knew her but never got the chance to know her. My grief was supposed to be lessened by the aphorism, "everything happens for the best."

I dare not get angry with the Almighty. The fear of his wrath added to my frustration. Disenchantment, fear, confusion and bewilderment reigned supreme. Such conditions can lead to instability in a child's world. Such a state over an extended period of time must have sent many a child into hibernation and eventually to the mental hygienist's couch.[10] I cited my experiences because I feel many adults do not have a clue as to how much guilt, fears, and anxieties a child experiences in the cause of religion. Regrettably, my experiences were not unique.

Church, you must mend your differences. You have the responsibility for clinical teaching of religion. How you interpret, model and teach religious concepts will determine the outcomes—successes or failures. You are charged, in the main, for developing moral character in individuals, to work closely with the home, the school, and the community. Obviously, this mission cannot be accomplished using Western-style Christianity. Again, Western Christianity thrives on hypocrisy, debauchery, Phariseeism, arrogance, treachery, greed and racism.

> They who believe in the brotherhood of man that transcend all differences of blood and race must live in terms of it. It is impossible for those who profess to believe—which belief in God involves to establish that brotherhood to social order if they are unable to practice it among themselves.[11]

Christianity as practiced in America is just another institutionalized nice/nasty.

---

10   Crow, Lester D., Crow, Alice. *Child Development and Adjustment.* New York: The McMillan Co. 1962, pp. 227-32, 240-50, 417-21.
11   Baker, Hayes, Straus, op. cit, p. 15.

Chapter II

Racism

Racism, the second exalted member of the destined, divine quarter grips Americans like a gigantic vice and has a domino effect. It makes the U.S. a vast wasteland of human talents and aspirations. It postulates some people are more equal than others. The gap between the "haves" and the "have nots" progressively widens; some are destined to be poor, others wealthy; some of color are supposedly divinely cursed; still others are blessed with destined divine whiteness. Those chosen people are endowed with divine entitlements, manifest destinies, whose sacred mission is to redeem, democratize and Christianize all mankind.[12] Racism is deeply rooted in these myths.

The federal Constitution provides framework and structure of the United States government. 'It was written, conceived, defended and glorified by white, Anglo-Saxon Protestants. It has explicit and implicit behaviors. It does not deal with mutual moral considerations or the guaranteeing of moral acceptance of minorities."[13] Cruse recognized that the melting pot metaphor and the American Dream allegory were gross representations of American society. He observed that American society is composed of groups, the dominant group being White-Anglo-Saxon

---

12   Leckie, op. cit., p. 43.
13   Cruse, Harold. *The Crisis of the Negro Intellectual.* New York: New York Review of Books, 1967, p. 394.

Protestants and Northern Europeans.[14] The Constitution embraces the implied social benefits of that group, the constitutional celebration of the sanctity of the individual means that some people are more equal than others.[15] It is unwitting, then, to think the U.S. Constitution can eliminate racism and guarantee moral acceptance of indelible Americans.

Take for example, according to Cruse:

If you, as an individual derived the WASP – Northern European ethnic, you have more constitutional rights than other lesser breed. You have more economic, political, cultural and educational privileges. You have property rights. In fact, you practically have an ethnic title to the lion's share of the nation's national, industrial and natural resources and its all upheld, defended and ratified . . . . It depends on which ethnic group h olds power in the American hierarchy. Naturally, Negroes, Indians and some other "colored" are the very lowest on the totem pole. There will be a selected sprinkling of Negro individuals who will "make it" by integration, in as much as the Constitution upholds the rights, privileges, and pursuits of some individuals in addition to certain others, all in due time.[16]

Moreover, justice is not equal for all. Justice is tilted by the lesser breed syndrome. Laws have always been passed to insure the rights of the chosen, not the cursed. History will verify that accusation. America makes concerted efforts to address racism only of necessity, never from a moral commitment. Even then, those efforts are designed to protect her image at home and abroad.

The U.S. proudly projects itself as the citadel of democracy and professed leader of the free world. It has to act, although in most instances superficially, to fulfill that mission. Moreover how can a nation be a beacon, model for the world if itself practiced brutal discrimination within its own borders."[17] It then is imperative to extinguish deceptions, contradictions and negative thoughts in the international community that would

---

14   Ibid., p. 394.
15   Ibid., p. 395.
16   Ibid., pp. 394-5.
17   Dudziak, Mary L. *Cold War Civil Rights*. New Jersey: Princeton University Press. 2000, pp. 10-48.

tarnish and jeopardize America's leadership claim.[18]

On the home front, civil rights legislation was passed for similar · reasons. The laws were enacted and made void according to the political climates of the times and expediency—to wit, forty acres and a mule, integration and affirmative action. All laws are passed to serve decision-makers' interests and are nullified for the same reasons.

America's divine mission from its inception was steered into three directions: (1) a total commitment to the Bitch Goddess of Success – wealth, power and dominance; (2) to become and emulate ancient Rome; (3) the redemption of mankind, democratize and Christianizing the world.[19] Racism and social injustices are not priorities and are superficially and hypocritically addressed. Only laws that are essential to her mission are important.

Racism will be part of the American way for a very, very long time. Families, churches, schools and other institutions are in place to ensure its permanence.

---

18   Ibid., pp. 10-48.
19   Leckie, op. cit., p. 45.

Chapter III

POVERTY

THE THIRD member of that divine, hydra-like group is poverty. Poverty denies millions the means to provide the essentials of life—good, clothing, shelter, productive schools and health care.[20] Poverty as the other members of the divine, destined institutionalized groups plays a significant role in the American schemata. It is shrouded in the following institutionalized myths and theories: (1) Poverty is self-imposed and voluntary. (2) All a person has to do is keep at work; if he is not making it, it's because he is not working hard enough. (3) It is a will of God that some people are rich and others are poor.[21] Such myths perpetuates the theories of predestined inequality—Calvinism, Puritanism, Social Darwinism, psychology, rugged individualism and unlimited horizons.[22] Those untruths have been perpetuated and made poverty permanent. According to the U.S. census, there are some 37 million Americans who lack the means for providing the essentials of life—living with frustrations and agonies.

---

20   http://en.wikipedia.org/wiki/Poverty_in_the_United_States
21   Tawney, R. H. *Religion and the Rise of Capitalism*. New York: Harcourt, brace & Co., 1926, pp. 81-115.
22   Gottschalk, Louis. *Transformation of Modern Europe*. Chicago: Scott, Foresman & Co. 1954, p. 402.

2003

On August 26, 2004, the U.S. Census Bureau published its poverty report for 2003. The official poverty rate was up to 12.5 percent from 12.1 percent in 2002, since 2002 the total of people below the poverty line increased by about 5 million.

2005

On August 20, 2005, the Bureau published its poverty report for 2004. The official rate rose from 12.5 percent in 2004. This puts the number of people in America at 37 million.[23]

When people usually think of welfare, they automatically associate it with the poor. What is not talked about is the fact that welfare for the wealthy cost American taxpayers 350 percent more than welfare for the poor. Spending for corporate welfare programs amount to $161 billion a year, compared to $51.7 billion for low income programs. In fact, over 90 percent of budget cuts passed by Congress in 1994 and thereafter cut spending for the poor. If poverty is progressively increasing, it follows the gap between rich and welfare of the poor is progressively widening.[24] Welfare for the wealthy is embedded in tax breaks, subsidies, and legal loopholes, political, social and economic clout.[25]

According to the noted sociologist Herbert Gans, poverty and inequality serve the wealthy and middle classes. Poverty creates a myriad of jobs and has a rippling effect. A countless number of jobs would be eliminated without poverty: social workers, mental hygienists, teachers, soldiers; and businesses would suffer greatly. Pharmaceutical companies would have to cut back on the production of drugs. The justice system, law enforcement, and prison construction would be placed on hold. Many middle class persons would be forced to join the ranks of the poor. The country would be at economic impasse.

There are millions who depend on poverty for their livelihood. As a result those depended persons are committed to finding ways of

---

23   *Federal Register*, Vol. 70, NO. 33 (February 18, 2005), pp. 8373-75.
24   http://www.angelfire.com/ca3/jphuck_216_html_pp1-5.
25   Mintz, Morton, Cohen, Jerry S. Power Inc.

ensuring that poverty persists. They care about their jobs and their full bellies rather than the bent-backs and empty bellies of the poor. Further, poverty serves as a measuring rod for other classes to gauge their movements up and down the stratification hierarchy. The poor does society's dirty jobs. Being poor and politically powerless they can be forced to absorb the cost of change and growth in American society.[26] Therefore, all means in the divine, destined quartet arsenal will be used to en sure that poverty persists. An excellent example is its quaint way of flaunting America's supposed opportunities, plenty, ecstasies, and camouflaging the unequal opportunities, pains and suffering. The truth of the matter is a land of opportunity for a few; for the many agony and frustrations.

Why should money be spent on the shiftless parasitical, ignorant and unproductive poor? They were and still are destined to be pawns. Therefore decision-makers will continue to "whittle away at the money for social programs to bolster the military-industrial complex.[27]

---

26   Gans, Herbert J. *The Uses of Poverty, the Poor Pays, Social Policy.* New York: Random House. 1974, pp. 78-86. Roper, Richard, *A Persistent Poverty, Dream Turned Nightmare.* New York: Pheen Press. 1991, p. 4.

27   Fitzgerald, op. cit. pp. 75-77.

Chapter IV

WAR

W AR, THE last but certainly not the least, member of the divine, destined, quartet equally impacts every facet of American society. "The idea of war or threat of war is the ultimate stimulus for the economic survival of the United States is deeply rooted in the American economic history.[28] War is an essential part of the American social, political and economic institutions.[29]

The Depression of the 1920's left the country in dire straits— politically, socially and economically. The country was literally shut down. The Hoover Administration offered no solution for recovery. The Roosevelt regime, influenced by the British economist John Keynes, applied his theories, pulled the country out of the quagmire—social unrest, financial chaos and political upheavals—out of the Depression. Under his New Deal programs prosperity was at an all-time high, employment was at the highest level in history, personal incomes by July 1953 rose to a record of $288,000,000 for the entire country and the nation was at peace.[30] The power-elite military militarists hypothesized that prosperity was due primarily to WWII. How to

---

28   Fitzgerald, Michael. "The Permanent War Militarism and the American Way of Life," Utne. (March-April), 2005, p. 75.
29   Mills, Wright C., *The Power Elite*. New York: Oxford University Press, 1956, p. 275.
30   Gottschalk, Lach, Donald. *T he Transformation of Modern Europe*. Chicago: Scott, Foresman & Co., 1954, pp. 78-9; pp. 932-8.

test that hypothesis presented a problem—how to establish a military-industrial complex in the time of peace and prosperity.[31]

In 1946, the militarists got the "break" they needed. George F. Kennan, the American charge d' affaires to Moscow sent his "long telegram" to President Truman portraying the Soviet Union as a villainous ogre whose primary goal was to "gobble up" the non-communist world and destroy its social, political and economic institutions.[32] The communist ideology was often taken out of context; nevertheless, it made the U.S. and the west susceptible to that threat. Fear of communist domination galvanized the west as such and democratic capitalism could never co-exist.[33] The long telegram not only gave birth to the cold war but also polarized the differences between the Soviet Union and the free world vis-à-vis the west.[34] According to Fakiolas in his analysis of Kennan's long telegram and NSC-(68) state the cold war was really designed to prevent the spread of and contain communism. To that end, the National Security Council was given unlimited powers. It made war a necessity and called for America's intervention into world politics. More importantly, it proclaimed and mandated that the U.S. take the responsibility of world leadership, to remake the world in its own image, and to coerce the non-freedom countries to comply with its wishes.[35]

> What is markedly interesting in NSC-68 was its thesis that even if there were no Soviet Union we would face the great problem of a free society [. . .], of reconciling order, security, and the need for participation with the requirements for freedom. We would face the fact that in a shrinking world the absence of order among nations is becoming less tolerable. In this sense, it would be a very useful enterprise to connect this debate with the model of American Hegemonic stability theory.[36]

Therefore, the U.S. as the mandated leader of the "free world" cannot and must not, using all means at its disposal to allow the lack of oil, the United Nations or irresponsible non-democratic regimes to experiment or dabble in atomic programs regardless of the intent. The West will

---

31 Fitzgerald op. cit., pp. 74-76.
32 Ibid. p. 74.
33 Fakiolas, Efstathios T. "Kennan's Long Telegram and NSC-68. A Comparative Analysis." *East European Quarterly*, Vol. 31, No. 4 (January 1995), p. 6.
34 Ibid., pp. 5-6.
35 Ibid., p. 6.
36 Ibid., p. 10.

not tolerate any philosophy, behaviors, principles, or practices to disrupt the homology of the free world.[37]

Such a mission has led the U.S. to attack Korea, invade Vietnam, Cambodia, Granada, Panama, smother Cuba, break up the Soviet Union, create havoc in Eastern Europe, Central America, Haiti and make a mockery of the United Nations.[38] Moreover, it has crypto-legal justification for all kinds of nefarious intrigues, secrecies, lies, deceptions, CIA initiated coups and assassinations; flagrant disregard for the integrities of non-Western countries, use bounty hunters. Further, create hysteria at home and abroad, continue to rape the country, ignore human rights and domestic problems, all to secure the integrity and vitality of the so-called free world.[39]

History has shown that people will fight to preserve their properties, institutions and culture, "war, even a so-called peaceful one." ____ Shuster from his chapter lessons from other land in the book *The American Way* stated:

> We learned we cannot repress a proud, strong people and expect them always to play the underdog in international affairs without letting loose economic and political storms which will trouble the world. We learned that nations so treated suffer emotional disturbances and become psychopathic just as individuals do, and are therefore disturbing and dangerous influences in the world. We learned how easy it is under such circumstances for a people who feel put upon and frustrated to seek ways out which under ordinary circumstances would not deign to accept.[40]

Non-Westerners have known for centuries that the West's idea of peace, humanness and brotherly love were mere fragments of its disguised mendacity and contrived verbiage. The West really wants wealth, power and control. It has no problem disrespecting the sovereignty and territorial integrity of non-Western countries. They understand your true mission is to tap their natural resources, supplant their cultures and thrust upon them your distorted

---

37   Ibid., pp. 8-10.
38   Mintz, Morton, Cohen, Jerry. *Power Inc.* New York: Viking Press, pp. 72-3, 328, 393, 562, 487-8, 457.
39   Elan, Gilboa. "The Panama Invasion Revisited – Lessons for the Use of Force in the Cold War Era," *Political Science Quarterly*, Vol. 10, p. 539.
40   Baker, Hayes, Straus, op.cit., p.20.

concepts of your Christianity and democracy all to perpetuate your extravagant amoral styles at their expense—the ways of the West. That awareness and your present behaviors have reinforced the seeds of distrust, suspicions and a pervasive fear of cultural extraction have polarized concerted drastic actions against you. You have vilified their institutions; continue to flaunt your superiority, arrogance and disparaged their lifestyles. All avenues for redress have been aborted. You have usurped and negated the authority of the United Nations, made a mockery of international laws and stymied legitimate voices by the threat of economic sanctions, retaliatory tactics assassinated and incarcerations. To put it succinctly, people will use any and all means at their disposal to fight, forever if necessary, to protect and preserve theirs. Terrorism is a prime example. Terrorists are made not born!

Terrorism, the newly created war is divided into two camps. The West to fulfill its divine mission, entitlements and manifest destinies; the other to protect its culture, its right to live, from the ravages of intruders. Both are sworn to protect their respective homologies.

> By now, it's a familiar and hackneyed war story. A jarring event rouses a dormant people. Diplomacy fails, conflict erupts. The modern mechanized nation overpowers the atavistic feudal regime. The victors send soldiers, consultants and contractors to free the oppressed, rebuild vital resources and territory, and put their own society that will emerge. In the midst of this benevolence loose woven network of terror, gangs stage dogged acts of sabotage, kidnapping, assassination, and graphic that demoralizes the occupiers. The victors are gradually forced to compromise those principles to whose name they first fought; or to withdraw.[41]

Cold war, real war, or war on terrorist creates jobs and huge profits for the military- industrial complex. It is no secret that the military-industrial complex represents one of the most powerful in America's economic, social and political life.[42] According to Fitzgerald what is less talked about is just how dependent on the war machine we have become. Approximately six percent of the U.S. work force is employed or supported directly by companies or governmental agencies in the

---

41   Shulman, Ken. "The Soul of Resistance – Civil War parallels in U.S. and Iraq." *Christian Science Monitor (commentary- opinions)*, August 25, 2005.

42   Brody, Dan. *The Iron Triangle*. New Jersey: John Wiley & Sons Inc.

business of preparing for war—as soldiers, civilian professionals, factory workers and military retirees; that is to say nothing of the countless other supporters indirectly by that juggernaut in restaurants, retail stores, schools and other services in communities across the country.[43] War, then, will be on the American scene for a very, very long time. There are millions of Americans who depend on war for their livelihood.

> War is structural and built into the American way of life. War or the threat of war is the ultimate economic stimulus. It's capitalism on steroids. Prolonged use creates unprecedented growth but the upside isn't worth the risk. The steroid metaphor is essentially apt.—side effects include euphoria, confusion, pathological anxiety, paranoia, hallucinations and even violent criminal behaviors—and users can easily become addicted. Let's face it, we're addicted to money.[44]

Moreover, the love of money transcends humanness and creates an "anything goes" mindset. To get it Americans are dedicated and owe fealty to the Bitch Goddess of Success—money and power—not to moral commitments or responsibilities. Therefore, the likelihood of living without war is many light years away.

---

43   Fitzgerald, op. cit.
44   Ibid., p. 275.

Chapter V

The American Ethos

According to Carey and Quirk I their article "The Mythos of Electronic Revolution" in the *American Scholar* (Summer 1971) Vol. 3:

> The American character from its inception has been pulled into two directions and has not been able to commit itself to either. The first direction is to the dream of the American sublime, to a virgin land and a life of peace, serenity and community. The second direction is to the Faustian and rapacious—the desire for power, wealth, productivity and universal knowledge; the urge to dominate nature and remake the world. In many ways, the American tragedy is that we want both things and never seem to respect he contradiction between them.[45]

Americans are held captive by the same forces they swear by to free them:

> You call your thousand material devices labor-saving machinery. Yet you are busy multiplying your machinery. You grow increasing fatigue, anxious, nervous, and

---

45   Carey, James W., Quirk, John J. "The Mythos of the Electronic Revolution." *American Scholar*, 39 (Summer 1970), p. 420.

dissatisfied. Whatever you have you want more and wherever you are, you want to go some place else . . . Your devices are neither time-saving nor soul-saving machinery. There are so many sharp spurs which urge you to invent more machinery and to do more business.[46]

Your commitment to buying the newest, biggest, and the best capsulate your lifestyle:

Americans are carried about in mechanical vehicles, earning their living by waiting on machines, listening much of their working day to canned music, watching packaged movie entertainment and encapsulated news . . . It would take an exceptional degree of awareness to be anything but a supine consumer. Society begins to take on the character of a well-kept woman. Each day brings its addition of silks, trinkets and shiny gadgets, new pleasures, techniques and new pills for pep and painlessness.[47]

America produces a society of frenzied, confused and harried people.[48]   It is shrouded in a Faustian syndrome and exerts tremendous pressure on individuals and families trying to chase the elusive, mythical American Dream. Such pressure forces Americans to abort their moral responsibilities. Americans when describing freedom, democracy and themselves exhibit behaviors that resemble those of the Blind Men of Indo-Stan. America has not strayed from the contradictions that have engulfed it from the beginning. Non-Americans describe you as ugly, arrogant and vulgar. Kirk in his book *Defeat of Presidential Powers and National Character* corroborates that description:

You have always been ugly. Only a people infatuated with their own moral virtue, their own superiority, exempted from ordinary laws of history and of morality could so critically embrace a double standard of morality

46   Abraham, Mitrie, Ribbany. *Wise Men From the East and West*. New York: ;Houghton Mifflin Co., 1922, p. 21.

47   Carey; Quirk, op. cit, p. 400.

48   Wurmser , Leon. "Drug Abuse: Nemesis of Psychiatry. "*The American Scholar* (Summer 1972), Vol. 41, No. 3, p. 395.

as the American people.[49]

You have been so busy basking in your powerless laizzey-faire freedom, paying homage and serving the "Bitch Goddess of Success"—money, money and more money—you have hocked your morality, sense of decency and negated your God-given rights. Any and all sorts of amoral behaviors are accepted. As a result you have become a disconnected people; Christianity from the Sermon on the Mount, off-springs from parents, people from people, spouses from commitments and vows; men of the cloth from their congregations; students from teachers; teachers from parents and students; politicians from their constituents; heads of state from the electorate; and intellectuals from society. Apparently, discontinuity has become the model for relationships. Moreover, your obsession for the "almighty" dollar has forced you to "farm-out" your civic, moral responsibilities and accountabilities at every level to persons in authority. As a consequence, you cannot hold any one accountable or responsible for his actions, good or bad. Government nor law enforcement agencies cannot be panacea for your ineptitude. Accountabilities and responsibilities are heralded as the pillars of a "true democracy." Yet they are flagrantly disused. John Stewart Mills in his *Dissertations* succinctly stated:

> The idea of national democracy is not that the people themselves are the government but have security for good government. This security cannot have any other means than by retaining in their own hands the ultimate control. If they renounced this, they give themselves up to tyranny. A government class not accountable to the people is sure, in the main, to sacrifice the people in the pursuit of separate interest and inclinations of their own.[50]

Understandingly, you have been constantly bombarded by contrived, controlled media hype and administrative verbiage. Without a doubt your perceptual systems have been short-circuited by those mounds and mounds of extorted, extraneous, mendacious practices. Such practices apparently have sent you wavering and floundering

---

49   Kirk, John. *Defeat of Presidential Powers and National Character*. New York: Simon and Shuster, 1974, pp. 46-7.

50   Mills, John Stuart. *Dissertations*. Discussions Political, Philosophical and Historical I. New York: Haskill House, 1975, p. 475.

with behaviors similar to those of a drowning person. Perhaps your frenzied condition explains your undying faith, loyalty and trust in governmental officials and your giving them carte blanche to continue to do what they do best—lying, arrogance, mendaciousness, never realizing such hypocrisies and contradictions are germane to America's social, political and economical institutions.

Voting, a mainstay for democratic behaviors seemingly has become a travesty. For example, presidential elections like leap years come every four years. [You are now swarmed by controlled media hype, campaign rhetoric, political verbiage and shallow debates every four years.] You are now swamped by controlled media hype, campaign rhetoric, political verbiage and shallow debates. Everywhere you turn candidates and their euphoric, empty promises are discussed. Excitement now fills the air. Candidates have now become visible. They present their spills everywhere to an uninformed electorate. Candidates are well aware that images to Americans are extremely important for winning elections. Therefore, little is left to chance. A whole host of specialists gets the candidates ready. Writers prepare and edit their speeches, make-up artists take care of their appearances. Mental hygienists coach them on the content and their deliveries to ensure the greatest impact on the victims. Statisticians via their polls inform the bamboozled voters as to what candidate or candidates are behind or ahead and who will win long before the actual voting takes place.

The controlled deception is over. Time to exercise your God-given democratic right. Now one witnesses the "American way" in action. SWAT teams are deployed to keep order. C.P.A.'s are needed to do the tallying of ballots to prevent frauds. Even so, some ballots are counted, some lost, some destroyed, some found, some never found, as in the 2000 election—the Florida fiasco—the rest is history.

The gamut of deceptions has subsided; time for the acknowledgements or recognitions. There has to be some reason or reasons for the candidate's victory or defeat. If he is the loser, hapless and helpless voters are the blame; they either did not vote or too ignorant to make wise choices. The winner's victory was due to his down-to-earth demeanors, disguised or camouflaged intellectualisms, and/or his straightforward approach, not on issues, domestic or foreign. You seemingly are not motivated by intelligent, honest, moral commitments or responsible leadership. For example, "The present head of state and his conclave have made it crystal clear that" he believes [American] freedom is God's gift to all mankind and God obliges the United States to spread it into countries where it is denied. That belief has transformed our present leader from a foolish, sanctimonious do-gooder at home to military aggressive crusader abroad. For that he and his band of zealots should be exorcised from American political power."[51] Such a position you have overwhelmingly accepted as a necessity for America's destined manifest destiny and divine mission—to remake the world in America's vis-à-vis the West's image.

Obviously, the brilliant future you and your divine endowed leaders have visualized for the non-Christian, and so-called non-freedom world is but a figment of your imagination. Your divine clairvoyance and divine entitlements are tantamount to Western sainthood. In reality your diviness is an anathema to natural rights and humanness everywhere, including your own. The future of your home country is suspect, anything but brilliant. Scape-goating, political demagoguery, domestic spying, paranoid actions, amoral practices, staggering unemployment, rampant criminal behaviors at all levels; platitudes, hidden agendas, social unrest, public apathy are examples of your brilliant future? Openness, accountability and responsibility must have been delegated to the Bitch Goddess of Success.

Control of mass communication is essential to the destined, divine quartet. Through its carte-blanche, all authorities of every description, experts, authorities, statisticians, loyal researchers interpret and explain all information and values. As a result, quite a few of you have convinced yourselves that you are hapless, helpless and stupid. Frustrated with your respective lots and mistrust of your own intellect, you have become comfortable with your self-induced status. You are told how and what to think, how to rear your children, how to choose your mate, what to wear, what to eat, what pill to take for every pain, real or imagined—in-grown toe nails, high and low cholesterol, obesity, impotency and mental aberration and depression. Moreover, your dream-chasing lethargy, undying faith in myths and Charley McCarthy mentality, you have allowed yourselves to become people who sit on ventriloquists' knees, content on allowing the thoughts of others to control your thinking.[52]

---

51   Leonard Sullivan, Jr., U.S. Assistant Secretary of Defense (1974-76). *Time* "Letters," July 12, 2004.

52   Mills, C. Wright. *Power Elite*. New York: Oxford University Press, 1956, pp. 303-

"Rugged individualism" is a prime example of your blind faith in myths. Individualism prevents you from knowing, talking to or helping each other. That proclaimed panacea for successful living has made unity extinct. According to Dr. Steiner in his Scripts states:

> Individualism gives the impression that when (people) they achieve something it is on their own and without the influence of others. Belief in the value of individualism obscures any understanding of the way in which human beings affect each other in both good and bad ways, thus it mystified both oppression and cooperation. Individualism results in the isolation of human beings from each other, so that they cannot bond together, to organize against the forces that oppress them. Individualism makes people easily targeted when they step out of line and fight their oppression without support from others, when people are unhappy or dissatisfied. Individualism keeps them isolated instead of finding each other and cooperating to remedy their oppressive condition; people wind up individually defeated, each person in his or her separate impotent paranoid system.[53]

Individualism serves the needs of the Divine, Destined Quartet. Are there any options? Yes, hypothetically. If the United States were to abort its divine, destined mission; if the myths of predestined inequality; false consciousness; divine entitlements; rescind the carte blanche of the divine, destined quartet; if Americans were to by a heavenly vision realize that decision-makers are not divine, destined or collectively blessed, instead a collection of persons whose sole purpose is to control and maintain their sweet life. Back to reality.

In spite of America's ambivalent character she has not veered from her proclaimed manifest destiny to democratize, Christianize, infidels—non-Christians and non-democrats, and to save them from themselves. America's paternalism is a moral obligation. More especially, the assumption is the only way to enjoy life to the fullest is the ways of the West. Therefore, the U.S. as the leader of the West—the free world—cannot allow anything to abort its mission. Oil, the United Nations, irresponsible non-Westerners, non-democratic

---

324.
53   Steiner, Claude. *Scripts People Live*. New York: Grove Press, 1974, pp. 156-7.

regimes to develop, experiment, research or dabble, for whatever reason or reasons in atomic programs. It matters not that Western countries and Israel have atomic programs. America apparently suffering from acute selective amnesia has conveniently forgotten she was the only power to drop the A-bomb on humans. The bombs were dropped on the Japanese. There were no military targets involved. The intent was to serve notice to the non-white world that divine whiteness must be recognized, respected, accepted, revered and never, ever violated.

Chapter VI

THE DYNAMICS OF COLOR

COLOR PLAYS an essential role in the American scheme and its influences are all encompassing. From a historical perspective, it was herald the panacea for controlling the slaves in America. The designer of such a plan was Willie Lynch. Lynch was a slave-owner from the West Indies, who was invited by the U.S. slave-owners to share his method for slave control without torturing, maiming or killing their valuable property. Color and age were paramount. Simply, pitch the old black males against the young black males, use dark-skinned blacks against light-skinned blacks, females vs. males, and males vs. females, use only white overseers, distrust all blacks; it is necessary that slaves trust and depend only on us. He vowed if they followed his plan religiously their slaves would be under their control for at least a century or longer, and your slaves will be perpetually obedient. That prophesy is still hovering over the American horizon and has become a meandering necessity that impacts every facet of the American way. It is a political, economic and social package that solidifies, perpetuates myths and fixed statuses in the U.S. It is used to attract and unify some people; repel and alienate others. Moreover, it breeds and fosters the myths, some people are more equal than others due to their color. As a result, the color white has evolved into a symbol of the chosen, destined, divine people with special privileges, unlimited entitlements with divine carte blanche to make the world in its own image. Further, it is catalyst that brings, so to speak, all whites under one roof, regardless of languages, boundaries, cultures, station or position in the hierarchy of whiteness. For example, all are shrouded in blessedness; some of lesser degree than others, i.e., some are "lace curtain"; some "shanty': some just plain "trashy." The fact the majority will never reach "lace-curtain" status does not create any major problem. The symbol of whiteness is far more important than in-house statuses; no matter what they are, where they live or have been, what they say or do, their whiteness prevents them from being at the bottom rung of the national and global social ladder.[54]

The color black, unlike your white counterparts has not been a unifying or gratifying experience. The legacies of inferiority have smitten, blemished, blinded your glorious past, and left you in dire straits. You have been led down a blocked path. How the color black impacts colored society will be discussed at length in later paragraphs.

---

54   Bell, Derrick. *Silent Covenant*. New York: Oxford University Press, 2004, pp.

Chapter VII

BLACK SOCIETY

B
LACK AMERICANS, unlike your white counterparts, your coming
to America was not voluntary in quest of a better life. Yours
was "involuntary, compulsory and unavoidable." You were,
according to Daniel Boorstin, "a black immigrant unassimilable by
definition. You were never accorded the status of an immigrant either by the official census or by the historiography of American im-
migration; for to do so would have to acknowledge you as a candidate
for graduation from that status, a potential assimilable and that has
been denied you. You are so to speak hyphenate."[55] To paraphrase
Tannenbaum's statement from his book *Slave and Citizen*: "In spite of
your adaptability, your willingness, your competence and your complete identification with the mores of the U.S. you are still excluded
and denied your graduation. It has served to deny the very things
that are greatest value among 'real Americans'—equality for growth
and development as men among men."[56]

Without a doubt, your mission, since your arrival in the New
World has been to gain full acceptance in mainstream America. That
goal has dominated, molded your character and mental construct.
It was relatively easy for your forefathers to be ecstatic, hogtied,
mesmerized and hoodwinked by the claims, promises and ideals of

---

55   Schlesinger, Arthur; Boostin, Daniel. "The United States of America—in These
      Times." www.inthesetimes.com/article/3094.
56   Tanenbaum, Frank. *Slave and Citizen*. New York: Random House, 1946.

America. Many saw integration as the only way for their redemption—graduation. Their vision was limited. They could not see the future. Moreover, they could not visualize or believe the claims, promises, the moral commitment to the brotherhood of man, and the American Dream were delusions, myths, empty, shrouded in hypocrisies, pendulous political, economic, social and continuous euphonious verbiage. Nor were they privy to the knowledge there were many well-conceived, designed stumbling blocks in place to abort their acceptance. Integration, then, was their mainstay. As a consequence, each generation leaves for the next the same legacy; chances are you will continue passing the baton of integration via hope. Nothing has changed. Since time immemorial you have stacked hope on top of hope, never realizing all you live for is hope. Will hope forever be your perennial haven that will house your frustration, your sorrows, your impressions, private thoughts and aspirations?

Tragically, the legacies of inferiority have smitten, blemished and blinded your glorious past, clouded vision and left you in dire straits. An assassin's bullet has ended mountain views. Racial integration nailed to the cross; the idea of separation unwitting., the Bakke and other cases have derailed affirmative actions, and driven a stake through the heart of "the spook who sat by the door." Moreover, you have gained precious little from moral persuasion tactics and international pressures. You have been given unenforceable civil rights and vehemently denied moral acceptance. Further, you are supposedly suffering from the sins of your ancient father. As a result of that curse, you are supposedly destined never to be men among men; never to march and receive your coveted diploma.

In reality, your curse parallels the curse of Sisyphus. According to Greek mythology, Sisyphus, the King of Corinth, was condemned forever to roll a heavy stone up a steep hill in Hades, only to have it always roll down when he reached the top. As soon as you think you are prepared and going to graduate, you are always demoted to the hope and dream levels. Your obsession with racial integration your only plan—faith in the promise of integration—is your curse. Moreover, historical truths have not, in the least, diminished your trust, zest, zeal and hope for integration. One is led to believe that "neo-siren" has become your mainstay. You apparently see no need for change. Your faith in that plan has negated the proverb, "God bless the child that got his own." Having your own has been misconstrued and interpreted as being disloyal, irresponsible, inflexible, injurious, diabolical and sacrilegious. That mindset has placed you light years behind other minorities in the U.S.

Other minorities have their own sub-cultural institutions which do not clash with the dominant culture. They are quite comfortable being WASPs. What ever happens their national cultural families are in place to sustain them. They are not bamboozled by or totally dependent of the dominant culture for their survival. Their working relations are not seen as threats or culturally demeaning. They see no need for revolts, rebellions or "burn-baby-burn" tactics, antics or the ingratiation of middle class manners, assumptions as a necessity.

On the other side of the minority register, everything you get or will get is dependent climates, whims and pendulous behaviors of governmental bodies. You have no cultural haven for support. In sum, you are at the not quite stage—not quite human, not quite a citizen, and not quite moral. Little do you realize you are a "permanent hyphenate" no closer to graduation than your predecessors. That situation is not to say many legitimate, visual blacks do not reach the senior level, and are awarded GED certificates, not diplomas. Those certificated blacks—political figures, Miss America's, Oscar winners, coaches, many recipients of awards and prizes—have acquired a miniaturized slice of the American pie. It would be unwitting not to recognize their accomplishments, their hard work and many sacrifices have benefited themselves and inspired others. The issue here is not individuality, rather individualism.

Individuality is God's gift to mankind; individualism is a nice/nasty folkway shrouded in the divide and conquer syndrome. It would be equally unwitting to believe citing a few certificated blacks, their accomplishments and successes as emblematic of social justice in the U.S. society. In spite of their successes and accomplishments, they are still denied real citizenship. That condition gives credence to the melting pot myth—all colored people are poured into the black mold—and are seen collectively.

All legacies have their roots in history. The legacies of inferiority fall in that category. However, the legacies of inferiority for blacks are debilitating obstacles and obstructions that bar or impede their progress toward graduation to "real" citizenship. Moreover, some are institutionalized, some folkways and some self-imposed. One such impediment is color. According to E. Franklin Frazier in his *Black Bourgeoisie*:

Since the Negro's black skin was a sign of the curse of

God and of his inferiority to the white man, therefore a light complexion resulting from racial mixture raises a mulatto above the level of the unmixed Negro. Although mulattoes were not always treated better than the blacks, as a rule they were taken into the household or were apprenticed to a skilled artisan. Partly because of the differential treatment accorded the mulattoes, but more especially because of the general degradation of the Negro as human being, the Negro of mixed ancestry thought of himself as being superior to the unmixed Negro. His light complexion became his most precious possession.[57]

That mindset has been a catalyst for whites; an asphyxiate for blacks. More importantly the color black has evolved as a symbol that consolidates all manner of vile, contemptible, amoral, inhumane behaviors. As a result that "symbol of evil" has forced "certificated blacks" to distant themselves from "non-certificated blacks"—the masses—creating a neo-caste of untouchables. Moreover, it was crucial for "certificated blacks" to disconnect themselves from the masses. The masses were seen as a threat to their graduation.

In order to graduate they felt it was a must to get as close to the white middle class as possible. Therefore, in their ingratiation role, they, too, revered middle class assumptions.[58] Those assumptions are riveted to destined theories of inequality, social Darwinism, rugged individualism and "unlimited horizons." More especially, the assumptions made the masses scapegoat for their disconnection. To illustrate, the assumptions have maliciously, viciously, by design, labeled, branded, and discredited a community of people as lazy, inept, insipid, irresponsible, cognitive deficient and parasitical, unaccountable, amoral, vulgar and scapegrace people. Middle class assumptions are patented nice/nasties veiled in a contrived inequality theme. They have effectively, and efficiently negated natural rights, civil rights and made the disconnection between blacks a seemingly insurmountable barrier.

The color obsession, as other legacies of inferiority, is still tormenting black life. So much so, getting as close to the dominant cultural traits are/was paramount to graduation. Therefore,

---

57 Frazier, op.cit. p. 135.
58 Couse, op. cit. p. 11.

integrating of middle class traits became the mainstay of "certified black."[59] After distancing themselves from the masses, denying their birthright, were still not accepted in the divine fraternity of whiteness. After being blackballed the "certificated blacks' were left alone in their solitude and sanctuary.[60] As a result of their crushed egos and tarnished pride they devised a segregated system resembling that of the dominant culture, to give them a feeling of self-worth, contrived superior and inferior statuses and an established pecking order. The system was not designed for control and dominance, rather sublimation and wannabeeism. Moreover, their system was based on facial features, jobs, social position of families and schooling.[61] To illustrate: blacks who had light complexion, almost white with straight or "good" hair, and "good breeding" were the top of hierarchy, next, browned skinned, fairly "good hair," less negroid features; at the bottom rung were the "non-certificates" with dark skinned, "kinky,' "curly" or "nappy" hair and stereotyped negroid features.

That system became a measuring rod to gauge the black stratification and movements up and down in black elite circles. Not too surprising, churches, schools, newspapers, magazines, fraternities, sororities and "anybody who was somebody" reflected that system.[62]

Black Americans your construct is far from immaculate and is couched in nice/nasties galore. Abandoning your moral responsibilities, rewarding oppositional and deviant behaviors—gangsterism, hoodlumism, errant parenting, "getting over on the man" mystic, contrived self-righteousness, blaming, self-indulgence, have and continue to undermine the integrity of your community. More especially those behaviors are reinforced, approved and modeled. Too little has been done to make you aware of your base actions and behaviors. Rick Henry in his thought-provoking commentary in the *Afro-American Chronicle*:

> We need to stop lying to ourselves. It's time for us in
> the Afro-American community to take a good look in the
> mirror; even that might not work because often what we
> see in the mirror we do not want to accept. (Too bad,
> we do not have magic mirrors to give us honest, sincere

59   Ibid., pp. 458-75.
60   Frazier, op. cit., p. 112.
61   Ibid., pp. 82-5; pp. 192-4; pp. 195-208.
62   Harris, William J. "The Militant Separatists in the White Academy." *The Ameri-can School*, Vol. 41 (Summer 1972).

feedback.) For instance, fat people look in the mirror and say "I'm not fat"; a drug addict looks in the mirror and says "I have it under control"; black politicians look in the mirror and say, "We are doing a great job." To extend the analogy: black parents look in the mirror and say, "We give our children everything they need"; black men of the cloth look in the mirror and say, "We are doing an excellent job preparing people to make sound moral judgments"; black intellectuals look in the mirror and say, "We have for too many years trying to reach and help a hapless people"; black teachers look in the mirror and ask "What do these people want for their children." Rick disagrees with their respective mirror readings. He doesn't care what neighborhood you live in, what job you hold, and what title you carry, you have the responsibility as black Americans to do something . . . . . . African males are dying at faster rates, as if the community was using firing squads, dying at the hands of Afro-American children. The biggest problem, it's nobody's business but our own . . . . . believe it, if we don't do something, it won't be long before the knock on your door will come and say your son is dead, your wife has been carjacked, and your daughter has been raped.[63]

Your own genocidal practices, lauding, accepting amoral practices and behaviors may be becoming detrimental to the Ku Klux Klan's survival. To paraphrase Cook's "The Last KKK Meeting" in N'Digo, August 1, 2006, you are forcing the Klan to abandon its overt racial actions against blacks. The Exalted Imperial Grand Wizard's speech at a convention:

Fellow members, we are going out of business. Niggers are doing a better job of getting rid of themselves than we did. So we are no longer needed. Their rap music says more vulgar, vile and degrading things about black women than we ever thought of. Their women write books and songs that demean their black men than any speech we ever did. Their children mirror the manners and behaviors of prison inmates. Their children are killing each other and innocent bystanders with their drive-by shootings. They are afraid of their own children.

---

63   \Henry, Rick. "Stop Lying to Ourselves," *Afro-American Chronicle* (Commentary) March 4, 1994.

> Their leaders disown their own kind. They show no
> respect for each other. So, you see, we cannot compete
> with them. Besides what they are doing to themselves
> is not against the law. In closing, as they say, "we are
> through booking."

Your pious demeanor belied in Phariseeism is astounding. Your newly acquired blessedness has replaced "I'm black and I'm proud, with I'm blessed and saved." What is extremely puzzling about the last aphorism, is how a people living in a perpetual state of fear, violence, apathy, indifference, hunger and unemployment is so blessed. The writer witnessed some revealing, troublesome and disturbing behaviors that led him to believe your blessedness and piety are suspect. You have a quaint way of putting all your problems in God's hand and throwing "bricks" and hiding your own.

In two cities, Saginaw and Chicago, many of you in both cities lined up four-abreast, many blocks long, creating huge traffic jams, in the rain, to eulogize and pay homage to their fallen "magnificent" drug king-pins and posthumously award badges honoring their philanthropy. In spite of the fact those celebrated gentlemen through their drug-trafficking made addicts of your children, prostitutes of your daughters, and created all kinds of pathological problems, anxieties, criminal behaviors, destroyed and continue to render your families dysfunctional. Tragically, those persons, along with other camouflaged gangsters and hoodlums were and are still seen as modern "Robin Hoods," have exerted a tremendous impact on manners and moral behaviors in your community. Such "angels" made and still make huge financial contributions to religious, political and social organizations. Moreover, they help people of lesser means to open taverns and other small businesses, loan them money, contribute to the needy around the holidays, establish drug operation "centers" and other questionable jobs.[64] Those "benevolent" benefactors are seen as "beaters of the System" and "getting over on the man" behaviors. You have obviously hooked your souls to and declared your fealty to the cult of underworld.

Blaming is a classic example of your futility. You blame "no-good' white folk for everything that happens to you, your children and your community. You even blame sport figures and other celebrities

---

64   \Frazier, op. cit., pp. 108-9.

for not being role models for your children, for not putting you on your feet financially. You put all of the blame on the school for your children's educational problems. You blame the police for not arresting lawbreakers and blame them for arresting the wrong-doers. Do you really believe you can blame away your problems? Apparently blaming has become your security blanket. Are you so blessed you have divine immunity against moral responsibilities? Perhaps your blaming has caused a defect in your visionary organs. No-good white folk did not install your segregated system in your community that rivals that of South Africa, flood your community with apathy and indifference, initiate drive-by shootings or perpetuate black on black crimes. What benefits, if any, can come from blaming? How is it possible for you to hold no-good white folks answerable for your faults? Should you the blamer bear the blame for your own mistakes? You make the call.

Chapter VIII

THE SCHOOL

IT WOULD be of little value to approach the school without understanding its place in the institutional hierarchy. The school, like other American institutions is not autonomous. They all are influenced, pressured and forced to abide by the dictates of political, economic and social climates of the times. These basic institutions are irremediable and stationary. Therefore, the likelihood of changing the school is extremely remote. What appear as changes are only the reactions and reflections of those pressures. Moreover, as purveyors of culture, the school is charged with the all en compassing mission of imparity, imprinting, reinforcing, interpreting and protecting the American way.

The writer's paramount concern is the inner-city neighborhood school. The school that certificated black abandoned. Blacks, who in their patented role of ingratiating white middle class assumptions without any pangs of conscious, negated their moral responsibility, fled and followed their white counterparts to suburbia to circumvent forced integration and bussing. That move widened the gap and completely isolated non-certificated blacks, leaving the community and the school without any real guidance. They were forced to fend for themselves, creating a virtual topsy-turvy zone. The aim is to take a closer look at the principles, procedures, practices and behaviors that have rendered the school ineffective in meeting the needs of those abandoned parents and their off-springs. The approach is not to rehash the tons of educational philosophies, psychologies and purposes; rather, those seemingly non-important placated tokenism, hidden agendas that have been skirted, ignored, never sincerely addressed, vigorously pursued, exposed or dealt with, and the lack of creative plans and methods to meet the need of those children of the damned.

The school is a reflection of the total society. The problems that plague society also impact the school. For example: racism, middle class assumptions, myths, war, poverty, religion, contradictions, frustrations, decision-makers omnipotence, media hype, forced integration, contrived research—interpretations and misconceptions— parents and students' haplessness, teacher attitudes, euphonious rhetoric, blaming, out of sync curriculum are seen in the school. How all of those factors act and interact in the school environment within that framework will provide the key to understanding the "ghetto" school. According to Ross in his book *A Ghetto Principal Speaks Out*:

> To be either a teacher, or administrator, or a student in
> the average city school of America is to be a participant
> in a war, a war against poverty, against ignorance
> [apathy], against an establishment that couldn't care less,
> an establishment asking only that schools maintain the
> status quo of middle class respectability.[65]

Teachers represent and reinforce middle class attitudes, manners and skills.[66] All behaviors are predicated and approached from that perspective. As a result of those all-inclusive, encompassing middle class assumptions have rendered a whole host of people null and void. In that context, parents and their off-springs see the school as a cold, closed, hostile, arrogant and snobbish place run by "wannabees," who use their children to support their frustrated, discontented and disenchanted lifestyles.[67] Many indelible teachers are seen as status-seekers rather than having social or moral consciousness. They believe by flaunting their contempt for the "null and void" would boost their chances of being accepted into mainstream America. Human values are heralded as virtues, however, acquiring the latest,

---

65   Ross, James I. *A Ghetto Principal Speaks Out*. Detroit: Wayne University Press, p. 314.

66   Mills, C. Wright. *White Collar: The American Middle Class*. New York: Oxford University, 1951, p. 265.

67   Gold, Stephen, F. "School-Community Relations in Urban Ghettos." *Teacher College Record*, LXIX (November 1967), pp. 145-50.

biggest and best—accumulation—is the goal. "Teachers have little interest in 'making men' but are concerned primarily with teaching to maintain middle class standards and participate in Negro society."[68]

Equally significant, indelible teachers, in their maintaining role, have been saddled with a perplexing eternal dilemma. On one hand, they are mandated to defend and perpetuate a static, unchangeable system which has perennially denied them moral status equal to their white counterparts. On the other hand, they are obligated to help all children help themselves and to work with their parents, people they see as their inferiors. Are there any options? Can the two prevailing commitments be reconciled? How teachers deal with the contradictions and hypocrisies will greatly influence their teaching registers and mental constructs.

It is no easy task trying to get the children of damned hooked into the school system. To discover the "why," one has to search through mounds of nice/nasties, hidden agendas, myths, bias research and a combination of factors. Children learn very early to distrust, disrespect, and demean authority figures outside of their domain. They have been well-schooled in the art of blaming and the necessity for secrecy. They have bought into the disadvantaged and culturally deprived myths by design. Those myths add to their futility concept and justify their inept demeanor.

Those children have been sacrificed to further economic, political and social gains; forced integration and bussing are classic examples. They have been taught to lie, cheat and spy; used as assassins, drug peddlers, and forced to accept sexual abuses by their "uncles," in many instances, the abuses are known. Moreover, many significant others' refuse to act for fear of destroying the family's "good" name. The prodigal son allegory has led many to believe the good has to be bad to get needed attention. DCFS mandated hot-line has given children carte-blanche in reporting all alleged, suspect, real or imagined practices of abuse. Such a ploy has prompted widespread usurpation of authority and authority figures' controls. Unwitting parents and significant others have added undue pressure by telling them they have to be twice as good as their white counterparts to be a success.

Children's role models seemingly have shifted from "being like Mike" to idolizing incarcerated wrong-doers and alumni from like

---

68   Frazier, op. cit., pp. 82-5.

institutions, wearing their pants at half-mast, exposing their rears and undergarments is a classical example. Mooning has become an appropriate behavior. Moreover, they have been exposed and witnessed, on a daily basis, murder, rape, sexual abuses and other human exploitations. Small wonder positive human values are fraught with danger and fear. Further, they have grown up in an anti-intellectual atmosphere. The impact of movies has contributed to anti-intellectualism in the school. Nerd movies have influenced children to believe if they are smart, make the honor roll, dean's or principal's list, they are labeled social misfits. All of those negative, deviant practices, harrowing experiences hinder their social, emotional adjustments and their overall school performance. To what extent, no one seems genuinely concerned.

In sum, an un psychological rewarding system shrouded in the Prodigal son allegory, anti-intellectualism glamorized nerd movies, granting carte-blanche to middle class assumptions riveted to destined inequality, unsavory class groupings based on statistical significance—bell curve, age appropriate, cognition—have created formidable barriers for the children of the "doomed."

The school's plan for dealing with such issues, and to fulfill its avowed mission, is through its curriculum. The late Professor Hofstader observed:

By means of exclusive bookish curriculum, false ideas of culture are developed. The child was never conceived as a mind to be developed but as a citizen to be trained by the school.[69]

In general, class materials for teaching the academic skills are provided by textbooks. Textbooks come with teacher manuals giving detailed instructions on how to present and teach the specific subject materials. Moreover, the books are designed for the average and above child of a specific statistical, age-appropriate level; not for the atypical-student below the norm. In that system success is measured by time spent, in or on, each subject area, i.e., 350 minutes in Language Arts, 250 minutes in arithmetic, 250 minutes in social studies, and so on, not necessarily on the mastery of the skills. That time allotment and others are fanatically obeyed. Standard practices, policies and procedures are based not on the needs of students, rather local and state boards of education, state laws and curriculum-makers

---

69   Hofstader, Richard. *Anti-Intellectualism in American Life*. New York: Vantage Books, 1963, pp. 334-5.

omnipotence. Therefore, decision-makers believe the primary mission of the school, other than maintaining the culture and associative skills, is to develop the kinds of intelligence—IQ, cognitive and bell curve assumption purports to measure.

The school tends to ignore the other factors that have as much or more influence on success than the standard IQ. "There are at least 120 different factors of intellectual abilities which at least 80 or more are known."[70] It continues to reward individualism—competition and devaluate cooperation—cooperativeness. A practice that Dr. Steiner states is a gross misconception and creates a false concept of human relationships; it fosters rivalry, strife, superior and inferior peeking orders, compound the pressures on children who are already anxiety riddled. Human beings are created equal but are not endowed with the same constructs. Each human being, then, is unique with his own learning style, maturation cycle and idiosyncratic behaviors. Yet "it is characteristic of the school to have children compete with each other even if they do not have similar abilities, experiences and accomplishments. Such practices ensure failure. To be successful in that setting without individualized plans and instructions for the less able will leave and have left long-term emotional scars."[71] When a student does not succeed in that environment, he is labeled and branded cognitive delayed. The intent here is not to ignore individual efforts and accomplishments, only to draw attention to the fact the school continues to pay "lip service" to the idea of individualized instructions, in reality measures and compares the individual to/with some statistical age appropriate norm. Unfortunately the negative aspects of pitting competition against cooperation, by the school, ignores the fact that instilling in children and teaching them to manage their emotions, resolving conflicts non-violently and respect individual differences are an important as teaching the academic skills. Perhaps such a move might lessen in-school violence.

The school, as other huge institutions, relies heavily on research and statistical data. Statistical analyses are useful in compiling many kinds of useful information. Nevertheless, in many instances biased interpretations compound and disguise many real problems. To illustrate, let us focus on Jim and Johnny, two victims of the school's

---

70   Guilford, J. P. *The Nature of Intelligence.* New York: McGraw-Hill, 1967, p. 63 and Wachel, Paul L. *Race in the Mind of America.* New York: Routledge, 1996, pp. 87-93.

71   Crow and Crow, op. cit., p. 318.

folly in addressing the needs of atypical students as they make their trek through an average "ghetto school." If the two survive the onslaught of gangs, they have a 50-50 chance for physical survival, if they survive the neighborhood. They are emotionally battered and bruised by the school. If they are fortunate and get by the school, they are sure to be entrapped by unemployment and become easy prey for the armed forces.

Jim and Johnny have average intelligence. Yet researchers have written them off as failures long before they entered the school system. More importantly, their "shortcomings" have been declared irremediable. Therefore, only a minimum effort and time were allotted to address their chronic needs. Both students have a history of failures victimized by social promotions, apathy, indifference, inadequate screening practices and unrealistic remedial plans. Nevertheless, the students do not give up. The harder they try, the more they become aware of t heir problems. To protect its image the school makes them scape-goats for their lack of success. Jim has started to react to the school's planned ignoring. He is now belligerent, profane and exhibits all sorts of act-up and out behaviors.

The school, reacting to Jim's aggressive behaviors, declares it is time to transfer Jim to a school where his needs could be addressed. He is transferred to an alternate school. At the new school, Jim thinks he will finally get some "real" help; to no avail. He quickly discovers "here," he is simply given "watered-down" materials presented in the same or similar format he had experienced in his former school. The only change was the campus. Jim began to realize how far he had lagged behind the students in his original class. His spirit demolished, he sees no way out. He takes his damaged pride, crushed ego, and fragile self concept and leaves. Away from school for a while, he realized dropping out was not the answer. He tried to re-enroll. He found his former school did not want or accept him. According to the *North/West/South Gazette*:

> School will not readily take drop-outs back for safety reasons—gangs and the likes. The schools lack accelerated programs—they are too far behind. If the returnees are 19 years of age, they need to graduate by 21. As a result there are some 70,000 to 80,000 children on the street at any given time.[72]

Johnny does not drop out, although his problems and school

---

72 "Problems with 'Drop-Outs.'" *North/West/South Gazette*, Vol. 2d, No. 12, p. 13.

experiences parallel Jim's. His temperament is different. He is described as a personable, likeable young man, slow but not belligerent or displays disruptive behaviors. Students describe him as a "loner." As a result, he is allowed to remain at the school. In reality, he has no options. He has to continue in an academic high school, his skills are too low to be accepted at a vocational high school. He is still without a viable, realistic individualized program. Therefore, he is still saddled with his fears, long-term failures frustrations, anxieties and extremely poor self-concept. He progressively regresses. Nevertheless, he continues solely on his dogged determination. He finally graduates; gets his diploma. He has graduated with no marketable skills. He is now a licensed drop-out.

Chapter IX

ASSESSMENT

A SSESSMENT IS a process of collecting data for the purpose of making decisions about individuals and groups and involves far more than tests.[73]   Schools need to know what students have learned or have not learned, and where they should be skill-wise. No one can deny the importance of quantitative measures for meaningful evaluations. However, problems arise not from the collection of data, rather on how the information is interpreted, how it is used and what it is used for.[74] If the data collected is used to justify superior and inferior racial myths, solely used to prevent some students from attending a certain college or university; to justify withholding or misusing funds for remedial programs is a vile nice/nasty—the usual. According to Dr. Janet Lerner:

> Diagnosis and teaching should be interrelated parts of a continuous process trying to understand the child and help the child to learn the institutional program that consists merely of routine teaching of skills or blind use of materials, the diagnostic information about the unique problems of the child may not only be a waste of time and effort but also prove detrimental to the child.[75]

---

73   Salvia, John; Ysseldyke, James E. *Assessment.* Boston: Houghton Mifflin Co., 1998, pp. 5-10.
74   Ibid., pp. 5-10.
75   Lerner, op.cit., p. 72.

Testing is extremely essential to school systems. Mega-millions are spent on all kinds of tests—criterion-reference, PSAT, ISAT, ITBS, ACT, SAT and many more. Why? Data from tests, more especially reading, determines money amounts and other grants given to schools by local, state and federal governments. If mandated reading levels are not met, funds are withheld, specific schools reprimanded, placed on probation or closed.

Successful reading programs lessen political and social pressure and determine the schools' "worth." Nevertheless, if the data does not give clues or insights as to why students are, or are not achieving, what is the value? In this area one witnesses some good and some unusual testing practices at the elementary and high school levels. To illustrate: in reading and math students were given pre- and post-tests, an excellent practice. What seemed a bit strange, students were not tested at their functional levels, rather given standardized tests for specific age appropriate skills. How useful are the test results for below grade level students? Such testing for atypical students in that instance is stressful, painful, frustrating, anxiety riddled and self-defeating.

High school testing parallels the elementary school practice. However, at this level tests require a far more important personal goal. The student who does not record a certain score on the ACT and/or SAT puts his college or university chances in jeopardy. Here a strange, haunting paradox surfaces. The regular school's aim is to prepare its students for institutions of higher learning. For generations, parents, teachers, communities, the media and the armed forces have drilled into youngsters, "to be somebody one must go to college."

A college degree is heralded the panacea for all of their problems. They will make more money; more apt to be employed, socially, economically and politically accepted—a perpetual nice/nasty. If the student is not accepted, admitted into the "Hallowed Halls of Ivy," then what? Who is held accountable? Is the student solely responsible? Moreover, no one seems remotely concerned about the emotional impact of not being accepted. If the school does not and cannot prepare students for admittance into those institutions, pass the ACT and/or SAT tests, what does twelve years of schooling and a diploma mean?

Chapter X

THE FUTURE OF THE PUBLIC SCHOOL MIRRORS THE MISTAKES OF THE PAST

I F HISTORICAL perspective has any validity, it is to allow people to critically examine their mistakes and make plans to extinguish them. By so doing people will be less prone to reinforcing and making previous mistakes permanent. The school has apparently ignored or dismissed the relevance. Therefore, the more it purports changes the more it remains the same. For many decades educators have been searching for remedies not cures for the ills of the school. "In the day," there were all kinds of real and unreal plans and schools for school reform. There were schools without walls, school parks, humanist, community, non-graded and performing arts schools; access to excellence, performance contracting and continuous progress programs. Those plans and programs have been scrapped due to political climates and the lack of money.

The new redeemer, reinforced by law, is/was forced integration and bussing. Forced integration triggered all kinds of emotional and social upheavals. Fear, panic, isolation and related problems did irreparable harm to the inner-city schools. To circumvent integration and bussing laws and to preserve their whiteness, whites orchestrated mass exodus to suburbia. Legitimate or certificated blacks followed suit to keep hope alive. Schools were left in dire straits.

Teachers were/are upset for many reasons. Teachers were

randomly transferred to schools to meet mandated federal guidelines for integration. Regular transfers were granted only if they enhanced integration. As a result, many teachers were uprooted from schools where they had been working for years. Many had to travel miles to get to work. Traveling such distances prevented them from participating in, and developing realistic teacher-parent-community relationships. Still others were frustrated by their lack of teaching experience in the "ghetto" schools and had problems maintaining control.

Such practices and problems were not atypical. In the southern public educational systems, black schools were closed. Principals, teachers and auxiliary staff were left jobless. Black school's cultural traditions and accomplishments were lost in the shuffle. Parents in northern cities were upset and frightened with the idea of bussing their children into unwanted, hostile communities. Blacks in the southern sector were constantly threatened, harassed, murdered, jobless, loss of properties, businesses and suffered untold atrocities.[76] Children were subjected to all kinds of inhumane, emotional and physical abuses. They were even denied proms, warm supportive environments and the usual school fanfares. The sad truth is Americans on both sides of the "color curtain" have squandered years perpetuating rather than dispelling and reinforcing planned contradictions, contrived research and folkways. By so doing children are befuddled, distracted, confused and shackled with mounds of nice/nasties—contradictions and negative behaviors.

To illustrate, two recipients of the integration fiasco, Nora, a black student from the south and her white counterpart, Jeremy representing the north—their experiences:

Nora

Myself, like many children have been victimized by the dream-chasing of our parents. Looking for quick fixes and their obsession with the promise of integration, little or no thought was given to the kind of abuses we had to face on a daily basis, by exposing, nudging and goading us to attend the citadels of racism, hatred, callous discrimination and recrimination. I realized parents and leaders were groping for a better way of life. I began to wonder if those sort of sacrifices were necessary for living and working in America.

---

76   Bell, op. cit., pp. 97-107.

I vividly recall the first day that I entered the all-white school. My world was literally turned upside down. I thought about my parents, friends and longed for companionship. Each day I left home was like revving up for a kind of impending doom. I had watched TV and had witnessed how the first wave of black children were treated. Still I pretended not to be afraid. My parents tried to assure me that God is/was on our side; I would eventually be accepted as an equal and get a quality education. Such a belief about equality never surfaced. I had no friends. In my solitude, my concentration gave way to day-dreaming. There were many days I felt I was "losing it." The pressures and rigors of the school seemed insurmountable. In my reverie, I vividly recalled marching and singing "We Shall Overcome." I secretly wondered from what!

No one here or there seemed interested in my personal problems or the way I felt about things. My opinions were ignored and only compounded my plight. I never tried again. It seemed the stakes were too high. I don't really recall when I realized that things were not going to get better for me. Nevertheless, my thoughts now focused on the condition of my best friend. She had to withdraw from school. She had developed serious mental problems and had to have psychological help. I was determined not to let that miserable environment get the best of me.

I truly believe some of my white classmates wanted to become friendly but didn't know how. I found myself in the same bind. My trials and tribulations held fast. Moreover, one thing was in my favor, I was now a senior. My change of status bought time for me. I graduated. I was not overly concerned with competing with my white counterparts. My sole mission was to graduate from high school and "be the best I could be."

Although I lived through the ordeal, I tried to find something meaningful beyond the diploma. Still there are/were days when I wake up thinking, what was it all about? It should be no surprise that experience left some deep-rooted emotional scars. The irony apparently is lost in antiquity. After years of poverty, inequality, apathy, sacrifices and indifference still remain. Where is the pride? Where is the joy? Where is the victory? What is next now that the contrived torch of equality has lost its glow and has been expeditiously extinguished?

Jeremy

I grew up in a stable neighborhood during the midst of integration and bussing—racial upheaval. At that time I was ten years old, an age when parents and significant others could do no wrong. As a result I clung to every word they said. I even quoted their sayings and mimicked their attitudes and behaviors when I had no idea of their implications, motives, thinking, actions and negative attitudes toward black Americans. In retrospect my behaviors seemed automatic without thinking or understanding the reasons for the negative attitudes.

Bussing and integration brought with them and left in their wake many disturbing and depressing problems for me. I had to attend classes with so-called thieves, lazy, inept, shiftless, amoral inhumans with low aspirations and sloven work ethics. Such labels and conversation I witnessed and heard a countless number of times, at the dinner table, churches, community centers, barber shops, YMCA, on the playgrounds and throughout the neighborhood. Problem two, I was terribly confused. I found many black children clean, honest, intelligent and had similar values my mom and dad had instilled in me.

In school, I was assigned to Group 1, the highest reading group in my class with two blacks. In addition, I was on the inter-mural basketball team with several blacks. Mind you, I had been drilled and given strict instructions never to fraternize with inferior blacks, regardless of situations or circumstances. Problem three, now I was torn between satisfying my desire to fraternize and to play on a team with them or disobey my parents. My anguish mounted. If I continued t associate with my classmates, and if my parents found out I would be disobedient and downright defiant. Each time we played a game or assembled in the reading group, I felt guilty. At that point, I began to wonder what it was that pushed my parents, significant others, and the community to hate blacks. My biggest problem now was not having anyone to share my concerns, or just talk about problems; certainly not my parents.

Moreover, my anxieties, frustrations and guilt proved to be a formidable barrier to my overall school adjustment. I was no longer interested in making the honor roll or school period. I never found solutions to my problems. My parents finally transferred me to a private school—a blessing in disguise for me. There I gradually lessened my guilt and cleared my conscious and graduated. Of course my parents blamed integration and blacks for my "planned" regression. My experiences were not unique. I firmly believe there are many children like myself who have been "caught up" in a double-bind moral struggle.

I never found any resolutions for my thoughts. I decided to go to the source and ask blacks about their unique situations. I wanted to know why they were so obsessed with and relying on integration as the only way to solve their problems. I wondered why they couldn't develop realistic and rational plans for their own redemption. How could they expect others to respect and accept them if they don't respect and accept themselves? I got no definitive answers.

> It is futile to suppose that children will develop right mental attitudes toward those of other groups merely by [associating] living with them. They need to understand the cultural and historical backgrounds of others to appreciate their best qualities.[77]

In sum, "dream-chasing" at the expense of damaging wholesome emotional and social development of your off-springs is/was disgusting and depressing. Hocking your moral responsibilities and your children's "right to be children" in pursuit of a mystical dream; blindly following leaders whose sole purpose for living is to be accepted as a frat-brother in the divine fraternity of whiteness seems unwitting and detrimental to your emotional constructs. Today the never ending search for school redemption continues. There are probationary schools, clusters, college prep, military academies, vocational schools, the voucher and no child left behind controversies.

The most recent redeemer is Renaissance 2010. This plan claims it was designed to improve student performance. It calls for eliminating or restoring 75 percent of non-producing = probationary schools – where students are functioning well-below federal guidelines and grade levels determined by the ISAT. Those schools will be replaced with 100 new schools over a period of five years. Structurally the plan will consist of three main schools—charter, contract and CPS. Students will be placed in each school depending on achievement. There are currently seven charter and 10 Renaissance schools. Charter and contract schools will have their own school board or sub-constructed management organizations. Are they to be autonomous? Such being the case, who will or what body will they be accountable

---

77   Hayes, Baker, Straus, op. cit., pp. 78-9.

and/or responsible to? In other words, who will do the watching? What will be the status of teachers from the closed schools? Will they be rehired or will they join the unemployed ranks? Obviously such a plan will cost a good deal of money. Who stands to profit from the plan, the students or the "money-givers" or both?

Funding will come from local, state and federal governments and a slew of private investors. Without a doubt Renaissance has created a bonanza. Religious organizations, financial, political and private investors are all vying and bidding for a piece of the action. Money now is no object. Funds are readily available at a time when churches are closing their schools and parishes, governments raising taxes, balancing budgets, cutting back on services and programs, businesses downsizing and laying off employees; now suddenly monies are there for the asking. Something "big" appears to be on the horizon. Perhaps school financing and reconstruction parallels city construction—urban renewal. Perhaps within the next five years or more, urban renewal will have accomplished its clandestine mission—enticing, preparing, inviting and goading the reentry of "real" Americans back to the city. There will be no pressing need or pressures to spend additional monies and "wasted" efforts on the "damned Americans" and their off-springs. After the reentry has been completed, there will be so few left in the city they can easily be absorbed in the system. "No child will be left behind"; most will be matriculating in suburbia.

Proclaiming school reform reminds me of the nice/nasty putting on clean and pretty clothes without taking a bath. One is clean and pretty on the outside, and underneath ugly and dirty. That comparison seems appropriate for describing school reform in the inner city. The astute policy of destroying schools and building new ones will guarantee quality education parallels an equally astute national policy "destroying a country to make it free." Cosmetics, along with euphonious verbiage may appease and fortify the American way but have little value in problem-solving. Schools cannot change the social order; however, they change the way the cultural dogma is presented. Moreover, reform cannot take place using the usual as a guide, model or framework. Realistic reform requires resourcefulness, imagination, innovations, and creativity, not relying on the usual way of doing things.

Chapter XI

TEACHING AGENTS AND OTHER AGENCIES IMPACT THE SCHOOL

PARENTS AND teachers as prime teaching agents your jobs are too important to be left to chance. Parents, knowingly or unknowingly, insure that many of the negative behaviors your children exhibit will remain in tact. It should not surprise you that your children mimic your behaviors—good or bad---parrot your attitudes, manners and opinions. Therefore, as premiere teaching agents it is crucial for you to model appropriate behaviors. You set the stage, their tone, and wholesome developments. Further, you seemingly have wasted too much time and energy looking outside of yourselves for role models for your children. Ready or not, you is it!

It seems to the writer, if you are to help yourselves and your children you should try the following: (1) Analyze, understand and seriously review the reason or reasons you chose to have children. (2) Know yourselves and your children. (3) Now, as parents, critically examine how your parents reared you. You will be able to incorporate, add those experiences to your own parenting registers. Use what is workable for you and discard the rest. (4) Know your strengths and weaknesses, your expectations, value system, tolerance levels, your biases and your unique specialized actions and behaviors. You will now, hopefully, be able to critically examine and evaluate your own parenting and to isolate chance. There will be no need to "throw the baby out with the bath water." Far too many of your children have been lost to gangs, drugs, drug-dealing, murdered, and self-style gangsterism. Too many are matriculating at the "Shallowed Halls" of prisons. Unwitting parenting, contradictions, hypocrisies, lauding deviant behaviors have been detrimental to positive development of your children.

You get to know your children by developing positive relationships with them, spending time with them and being there for them. You owe yourselves and your off-springs, regardless of social conditions, to be the best you can be. You must provide a safe, secure, warm, caring, loving, supportive environment for yourselves and allow your children to be children. To do otherwise is amoral, vile and vulgar.

Teachers, like your parent counterparts, your role is extremely important, you are the main purveyors of American culture. You have the mission of instilling, imparting and imprinting the culture in the minds of the nation's most valuable resources, the children— yet you are not honored, trusted, respected or even considered real, qualified professionals.

According to the late professor Richard Hofstader, you are haunted by the ghost of anti-intellectualism in American society. You have been saddled and hogtied with earlier ideas about teachers and teaching. They were given extremely low salaries, branded shiftless, incompetent and unprofessional. Moreover, able candidates were steered from teaching to more rewarding fields, creating a kind of self-perpetuating system of second-rate professionals. Teachers' pay was commensurate to society's perception of their worth. Therefore, ordinary laborers were paid more than people who were responsible for keeping the American way in tact.[78]

Little has changed. Displayed values, pervasive anti-intellectualism continue to flourish, contribute and perpetuate the degradation of teachers. "They remain at the bottom of the professional hierarchy and are the proletariats of the professionals, especially those in the public schools."[79] Moreover, the Bitch Goddess of Success—money and power—defines and selects priorities. Teachers do not make enough money to demand or command respect. Money determines worth.

As a retired teachers, the writer understands you do not make

---

78   Hofstader, op. cit., pp. 309-12.
79   Mills, C. Wright, op. cit., p. 329.

educational policies, decisions nor involved in curriculum making or planning. Such policies are made without your input and are based primarily on decisions made by experts, educational authorities, and decision-makers' infallibility. Nevertheless, you are charged with their contrived narcissus, arrogance and overall blunders.

It is extremely difficult for you to form in-house alliances, find meaningful support or realistic avenues for redress. Such efforts are discouraged, considered anti-authority, insubordination, and fraught with fear. Many administrators with whom you worked, came up through the ranks, understand the problems from their teaching experiences, have distanced themselves from you. Moreover, now they have been "moved up," see you as incompetent, slovenly, inept and ineffective. They can no longer empathize with you; they have aligned with their own wise "fellows." When problems and issues surface, they are resolved by the "wise fellows." Those resolutions, more than likely, are of little or no value to you. Only you can save you. Your mental health and overall adjustment depend on your helping each other; your understanding that the schools cannot change the social order. However, you can circumvent many of the amoral, unwitting, racial myths and practices and make a difference for all of your clients.

All teaching agents, more especially you understand the kind of teaching agent a child has will determine in a great measure whether his school experiences will foster his development, or simply increase his difficulties and frustrations. You cannot help others manage their frustrations until you have yours under control.[80] The more knowledgeable you are about yourselves the better you will be able to minimize your frustrations, strengthen your egos, boost your self-concepts and do the job of your choice. For example: you must critically examine or analyze your reason or reasons for choosing the teaching profession; understand your strengths and weaknesses, be acutely aware of your own biases, expectations, teaching goals, concept of social problems, tolerance and intolerance levels. Your role demands such understanding for you and your clients' survival. "You must be able to empathize with your client, enter into his world in a way that will enable him to manage anxiety, overcome frustrations,

---

80   Crow and Crow, op. cit., pp. 423-29.

become self-confident, overcome adversities, independent and be successful."[81]

It seems appropriate to distinguish between the general welfare system and DCFS—Department of Children and Family Services. The difference, basically, is not its mission, rather its function. Both are concerned with keeping the family together and the children safe. Nevertheless, DCFS, inadvertently, your mission to protect has initiated serious distractions, disconnections and misunderstandings between teaching agents and legitimate authority figures via your mandated hot-line practices and procedures. Moreover, they have driven a wedge between children and authority figures. To illuminate: children have been, with or without your knowledge or purpose, instructed, coached, coaxed, goaded to spy on authority figures and report any alleged child abuse, real or imagined, via your mandated hot-line. They are instructed to use their discretion in reporting such case—suspect or real. Further, their carte-blanche has triggered frustrations, fear, traumas, and mixed messages in the home, school, courts and throughout the community.

Children are master manipulators. They have used their unlimited, legislated powers to threaten, blackmail parents, teachers and other authority figures when they are not allowed to do as they please. In fact "don't touch me; I'll get your job" has reached the panic stage. Fear of being sued, summoned before a magistrate, loss of jobs and aid grants have caused a collapse of control and moral responsibilities.

Caring and concerned parents have been adamant, making it known and clear to all concerned, their children will obey, abide by their rules and will be disciplined. They have challenged you, schools and the courts by simply stating, "If you are going to usurp our authority, if we are not allowed to rear and discipline our children, then you feed, clothe and take care of them." Everyone agrees that children must be protected against all forms of abuse. How to carry out that mission has become ugly and needs revamping.

It is now time to take an uncommon look at the controversial, emotional evoking men in blue, who wear badges, carry firearms, whose sworn duty is to preserve and protect; not to teach or preach. Like teachers, policemen are not honored, respected or considered real professionals. Many Americans feel that many became policemen because they lacked the savvy or moxie to "make it" in

---

81   Ibid., pp. 482-5.

other professions. As a result, they are paid low salaries; many supplement their salaries by working part-time. Their pay, apparently, is commensurate with society's perception of them and their worth. That image has placed them "in between a rock and a hard place." Therefore, they often work in extremely hostile environments. As civilian "grubs" they have to deal with the good, the bad, the ugly, beauty and the beast. Unfortunately, they are not equipped with the uncanny sense of "The Shadow." They do not know what evils or goods lurk in the minds and hearts of men so it is extremely difficult to distinguish friend from foe.

The following are excerpts on Dick Gregory's views of the police from his book *The Shadow That Scares Me*:

> Imagine the mental pressure a cop must live under daily in the ordinary line of duty. He sees daily the horrors we read about in the newspaper, or see on TV. We read about a three-year-old been sexually molested and murdered. The cop sees it for himself. He walks into an apartment minutes after a man has gone berserk and chopped up his wife and mutilated his kids. Perhaps he has little kids of his own waiting for him to come home. What does such a gruesome sight do to a man's mind? How does it affect a man mentally to daily smell and touch dead human beings? It is the cop's job to live in an atmosphere of death—to see dead kids, to hear people moaning, groaning and crying for help. Society expects the cop to experience such sickening horror and take it in his stride. He is expected to forget what he has seen and walk back on the street without holding a grudge. Have we done enough research to find out what such an occupation does to a cop as a man? Without such basic research, he cannot be adequately trained to deal with the conditions which his job imposes upon him. The cop's daily work is certain to affect him mentally. One cannot witness daily the horrible reminders of the worst that man can do without developing a low evaluation of humanity. Just and proper training for the cop must take this inevitable reaction into account.[82]

If you can stretch your imagination a mite further, suppose you are

---

82 Decker, Randall E. *Pattern of Exposition* (Editor's excerpt); "The Ghetto Cop," from Dick Gregory's book *The Shadow that Scares Me*. New York: Little, Brown and CO., 1966, pp. 26-35.

a black policeman, in addition to the other problems, you are entangled and hogtied with the mental anguish of serving and protecting a system that has perennially denied moral acceptance equal to your white counterparts. You are committed to your role, your job. You respect the rights and dignities of all human beings. You are not apathetic, vindictive, callous or indifferent. You understand you cannot change the social order. What are your options? When will Americans learn that only when all Americans are equal in the eyes of the law, morally accepted as equal to privileged Americans, will they have communities where people respect each other, the laws, the police and enjoy positive relationships with the "police" as well as other institutions?

The American way creates an anxiety-riddled way of life. The coveted goal for food and good living is money. The reverence for money is a virtue. Without money a person is a non-entity. That mindset continues to provide motivation for all kinds of deviant, anti-social practices and behaviors by people seeking to become somebody. More especially people who don't have it, it's their fault. Moreover, such people are caught in a vicious mental bind, producing shattered self-concept, crushed egos, wounded self-worth, pride, mesmerized by the mystical concept of individualism, and left in their solitude. Dr. Claude Steiner in his *Scripts People Live* had this to say about the individualism trap:

> Individualism gives people the impression that when they achieve something it is on their own and without the help of others, and when they fail it is, once again, on their own without the influence of others. Belief in the value of individualism obscures any understanding of the way in which human beings affect each other, in both good and bad ways; thus it mystifies both oppression and competition. Individualism results in the isolation of human beings from each other so they cannot bond together to organize against the forces that oppress them. Individualism makes people easily influenced and also easily targeted when they step out of line and fight their oppression without the support of others. When people are unhappy and dissatisfied individualism keeps them isolated. Instead of finding each other and cooperating to remedy their oppressive conditions, people wind up individually defeated, each person in his or her separate

impotent paranoid system.[83]

People who are "making it" in the system are used as measuring rods to evaluate those who are not. Their failure, then, is not the system, rather their lack of motivation, tact, good work ethics. Many do not rationalize their assumed status. They merely seek and find refuge on "cloud nine." Others are overcome by unwitting behaviors, going "underground" to get over on the man or system. Still others never lose the faith, truly believe with reverence if they don't make it their off-springs will.

---

83   Steiner, op. cit., pp. 156-7.

Chapter XII

AN INTERVIEW WITH THE INDELIBLE MAGI

Asked the magi from the black sectors his views on the American.

Q: What are America's greatest assets?

A: Racism, eclecticism, installment plans, arrogance and avariciousness.

Q: How do you view America?

A: As gigantic cesspool and its populace gorged on its contents.

Q: What is Black America's Achilles ' heel?

A: Its undying faith in believing the power elite is going to relinquish any of its power to satisfy or appease some moral code or promised commitment.

Q: How do you see the Bush Administration?

A: As an overseer and expander of the cesspool.

Q: Do you like Condi Rice?

A: Yes, Edgar Bergen's Charlie McCarthy, Lucrezia Borgia and Edith
      Sampson, too!

Q: What do you think of Clarence Thomas?

A: Who? Oh! The invisible Judge. Well, he is the "Tyler" of the U. S.
      Supreme Court.

Q: What is the role of the Armed Forces?

A: To protect the cesspool and to be oblivious to its contents.

Q: What do you see as the ultimate mission of the global community
      concept?

A: To spread the contents of the cesspool and paraphernalia for
      disguising and disquieting its contents.

Q: What is the "real" role of blacks in the cesspool?

A: Dedicated and magnificent scavengers shrouded in the Lazarus
      and Job syndromes and riveted to its contents.

Q: What is the difference between Rock Stars and Evangelists?

A: Only their themes.

Q: Give me your honest opinion of Western-style Christianity. What
      do you really think?

A: When a high ranking "man of the cloth" gets on national TV
      and advocates the assassination of a sovereign head of state, for
      whatever reason, you make the call!

Q: How in your opinion will the Bush Administration be
      remembered?

A: T he President with his visible cohorts—Cheney, Rice, Tenet,
      Powell, Rumsfeld and Wolforitz will be remembered as having
      posthumously eulogized past dictators throughout the world

and causing Machiavelli's Price to become agitated in his resting place.

Q: Sir, What about the United Nations?

A: What about it? It has been baptized in the American cesspool.

Q   Do you believe parents play a pivotal role in perpetuating racism?

A: Yes, children are not born with racial prejudices. It is a learned behavior. Women, more especially, as premiere socializing agents fix or imprint the attitudes and mindsets of their children.

Q: Are there any further comments on Powell and Thomas?

A: Yes. If a squirrel were to scamper up the legs of either of those distinguished gentlemen, it would starve to death.

Q: The final question, sir. How would you compare the present Head to State and the Ancient Roman Emperor Nero?

A: That is an apt question, since America's divine, manifest destiny is to become the neo-Rome. Both had/has a unique way of handling crisis situations, one wades and the latter fiddled.

Chapter XIII

Honest, Reasonable, Marketplace Ideas, Thoughts, Attitudes And Opinions

IN THIS section, the worker can finally shed his muckraking, discard objectivity and trade the "you" for the "we" and "us." First and foremost, I am not a "money junkie." I am not a racist nor anti-America; however, I have serious issues with the American way. I am not a goody-two-shoe, and I do not hate. I found hate to be self-destructive, irrational and nebulous. One cannot pinpoint persons, things or objects hated. To hate humans and you are supposedly human, you must, without any choice, hate yourself. The same axiom applies to racists. I am a Christian; not a Western-style Christian. I follow the precepts set forth in The Sermon on the Mount. In fact, I find it difficult to understand, if a people cannot go to heaven while they are living, how can they go when they die?

I have searched the mounds and mounds of nice/nasties, even traveled the Yellow Brick Road, met the "Wizard," no comment necessary. In my searching, I stumbled upon my niche. My travels have sent me all over, around and under marketplaces; anywhere I could listen and hear thoughts and ideas of non-certificated Americans—the left-out-ones—in bars, barber shops, pool halls, alleys and wherever.

Sometime ago, while sitting in my favorite bar to unwind from the rigors of Friday, I met an entertaining and interesting "brother."

We exchanged pleasantries. Sitting directly behind us were some persons loudly discussing freedom. We had no choice but to listen. At length, the "brother" stated people have no real concept of freedom and wondered how can a people who have never been free, know when they are free; how can people find what they are looking for, when they have no idea of what it is they are trying to find? Then he came up with a mind-boggling statement, most people, he said, fight, die, march, sing, scamper, grapple for "it," to be free without a clue. He was trying his best to escape from freedom. Continuing, at every funeral he recalled the minister would say, sister or brother 'so and so' is finally free; no more trials, tribulations, no more pain, sorrow, aches or pain. He was convinced only when people catch the "heavenly-bounded bus" are they free. Further, he used *Roots'* Fiddler as a prime example; for the first time in his life he was able to play the music he felt and loved, only when he was to board that "bus." So the brother declared he was very busy trying to escape from freedom and is perfectly content with being "un free."

Ever since that chance meeting our Friday get together became a must. Other patrons joined. Still others followed, making our discussion site and discussing in the style of the classic marketplace.

The following week discussion of freedom again became the focus, this time from a different perspective and a different patron. He began by saying we as a people have been focusing on the wrong issue, i.e., equality and freedom. In reality, they never enter the picture on either side of the "color curtain." They are not understood nor do people give a hoot about them. We all are more concerned and preoccupied with material possession—beautiful homes, cars, clothes, trinkets and gadgets—accumulation—the middle class concept of the good life. We exist not to fulfill or satisfy human and moral needs, rather with keeping up with the buying trends and styles. The problems arise when we do not have the means to buy or acquire those material things. Rather than deceiving ourselves trying to eliminate racial prejudices, becoming equal to whom, free from what or to do what; we should concentrate on breaking down equality and freedom in their component parts. By so doing it might give us a better understanding and a clearer picture of those rights and possibly organize, discipline ourselves to put those ideals in available and attainable forms. Then we could focus all our energies, strategies, approaches and collectively help each other reach his potential, respect and help each other attain the same rights. Regrettably, there are no guidelines, models or standards for establishing or evaluating how those rights could be reached, or administered.

At our gathering, my self-declared role has been to listen, hear, and absorb their thought and ideas. "To listen to another is honor and respect him as a worthy person. The art of listening, even though it seems to contain no action, oftentimes liberates others to act and to move on with their lives."[84] Irrespective of my role, I realized, sooner or later, I would be expected to share openly my thoughts, ideas and opinions.

My turn came sooner than I anticipated. I was asked to share my views, attitudes, pet-peeve in a subject of my choice. I chose, "I'm just doing my job" syndrome. Of course one has to do his job. The question, how one is doing his job. The concern here is not with the policymakers, rather those important line-personnel who are charged with executing the policies and procedures. For example, teachers have little choice in the materials they present; however, they can see each student as a unique, precious human being with feelings, emotions, attitudes, idiosyncratic construct, and modify the materials to fit the specific interest, skill levels, capacity and needs.

Policemen cannot change the Department. They can become more humane, civil and legal in performing their duties. Social workers can become more people-oriented, less arrogant, more understanding and show some humanness. Lay people, you cannot change the American way; you can, however, overhaul your disposition, superficial, pious, self-pity, blinded arrogance, eliminate blaming and stylized scape-goating. Politicians, you occupy the best bargaining and compromising positions. You can enhance bargaining position by listening to, and working with our constituents to build a political base in the community. Men-of-the cloth, as pillars of the community you can, irrespective or your denominations, come together with a unity of purpose; as a unit expand, cement the moral fibers and fabrics of the community. Intellectuals, you can lessen your ingratiation of the white middle class, deal with realities so you can focus your efforts and energies on the values of music, art, ethic, culture, policies, working collectively, charting the course for developing a national cultural family where we all can find fulfillment in American society.

84   Stephen Post, Jill Neimark. "Listen with your Heart." *Ladies Home Journal* (May 2007), pp. 18-12.

There are too many people suffering from the byproducts of the American way. People who do not care about themselves, their jobs, people, and are miserable performing their duties. They cannot hide their frustrations and negative demeanors. Such attitudes compound the problems for sincere, honest people who care about themselves, people oriented, care about their jobs, responsible and accountable. Therefore, the line-personnel and other "have-nots" for their mental health must develop a viable, workable plan, a plan that would, without risks, threats, pressure free, reprisals or penalties. To make the plan a reality, each person has to have a thorough knowledge of himself, his biases, weaknesses and strengths and his capacity to distort. He must critically examine his values and have a clear perception of his status in the American scheme. The ultimate goal is to get all persons regardless of occupations and statuses come together as a unit to lessen anxiety, fear, apprehension, vindictiveness; develop a unity of purpose, love, and work in a caring, supportive, harmonious environment.

Perennially, the barbershop has been an ideal place for a challenging game of checkers, superb haircuts, local gossip and the lively art of conversation, often heated, never violent. Below are some accounts of those conversations. One of the self-proclaimed checker champs thoroughly thrashed, lost his usual bragging rights, somewhat agitated, and initiated the present discussion. He stated the other day that he heard something that made his blood boil: black folk are not loyal Americans; white folk will accept us if we adopt their values. He declared those statements full of the contents found in a cesspool. On a roll, he related: blacks are more in tune with the ideals of America they are. Further, this --- --- --- --- country was built on our backs. We have fought and died for the love of America, have bought into its Western-style democracy and Christianity, so much so we have adopted their pagan religious rite of symbolic cannibalism— eating flesh and drinking blood; even their atypical sexual practice of dining at the "Y" and sitting on the low stool.

For a split second, there was a weird silence in the shop. Suddenly as if on cue, the shop roared with laughter. Cleansed but somber he asserted, since time immemorial, we have refused to realize that the brotherhood of the chosen men and the American Dream was never meant for us.

Another participant wondered and asked how whites who are a minority in world population gained control, forced their will, lifestyle, and grant themselves divine status, universal entitlements, carte-blanche to fulfill their self-proclaimed manifest destiny, of the non-white world. Another participant quipped, simple; and elaborated. If you control the media, writers, researchers, historians, delete whatever you consider against your best interest, adding only what is necessary to enhance, verify and justify your scheme, what would you expect? The pen is mightier than the sword. To illustrate, along with the sacking of Iraq, original books were burned, new ones written to support the ideas and values of the invaders. Further, if you tell a lie long enough, often enough, the lie becomes an accepted truth. The weapons of mass destruction are a classic example of a horrendous lie. You think about the "how," all shrouded in the divine inequality, individualism, divide and conquer syndrome supported by anti-egalitarian doctrines.

Every person present at the shop that Saturday seemed fired up and eager to vent. One person was fuming; seemingly frenzied by the behaviors and practices he called "the cult of the Human Dog." Before he began his tirade, he wanted everyone present to know it was nothing personal; his aim was not to create ill-will. He just wanted to draw attention to the vile and vulgar practices of the cult. He wanted to know what it was trying to accomplish. It is obviously not committed to developing wholesome principles to address the many ills in the black community. It is not a protest group. Then what does it hope to accomplish—just another unwitting barrier to black unification. Its goal is control the mindset and behaviors of many blacks only to support and justify licentiousness, lecherousness, irresponsibility and unaccountability. Members embellish sexual prowess and female degradation. They proudly greet each other with an assortment of specialized names—hound dog, soup dog, doggie-do, little or big bow-wows, to mention a few.

He now managed a wily smile when he stated the human dog has little in common with Spike, the cartoon dog in the Tom and Jerry cartoons—Spike teaches, protects and loves his offspring. More especially, cult members' behavior becomes models for many young and impressionable children. Continuing of equal importance is the fact cult members stymie responsible, accountable moral obligations of responsible men.

Somewhat reticent but equally animated, he focused on the cult's females. He noticed they openly greet each other with the "B" word.. In fact, they are highly offended when anyone other than their members greets them with that provocative "B." In that case, he opted to call them "Loosies." Loosies behaviors parallel their dog counterparts. Their roll is vital to the cult's survival by having children out of wedlock, abject parenting, poor socialization skills and animal behaviors. Unfortunately, the cult and similar bonds and other frictions keep the structure of the black family in a constant state of flux.

There is an old saying when everyone is participating excitedly and undaunted in one's venting, it must be a full moon. In the excitement, a young man, impeccably dressed, Brooks Brothers clad, giving a yippy appearance, unnoticed, quietly entered the shop, sat and passively waited for the next available barber. [Later it was found he was employed by a prestigious brokerage firm.] Apparently, the fall-out from the exciting venting propelled him to join the venting. He stated he was new to the neighborhood; his uncle had recommended this particular shop. Continuing, now he understood why. Besides getting an excellent haircut, stimulating conversations, here was an ideal place to unwind. The young man was deeply agitated by what he called "the time mystique." [The regulars were flabbergasted not by his pet peeve but his manners; they were so accustomed to seeing young men wearing their trousers at half-mast and expressing themselves in Ebonics.] Elaborating, he wanted to know what divine power had passed on and willed or claimed assigned cardinal virtues and omnipotence to time. Without the slightest doubt, time is an invaluable asset to mankind—languages, chronological measures, historical epochs, eras, as well as rhythms and cadence. His issue was not with time as a standard only when it is used as a cure-all for the social evils in our society.

Our clairvoyant leaders on both sides of the "color curtain" have declared since we are a multi-racial society it takes time to extinguish racial problems and social injustices. As a result, time is a perfect subterfuge for their inept apathy, indifference, inertia and delphic behaviors. Moreover, he feels that recognizing the motive and intent of our leaders' actions or inactions are crucial to understanding the American way. White leaders are handicapped by their indebtedness to the Bitch Goddess of Success; fear of her wrath cannot afford to get morally involved. Their indelible counterparts are caught in a similar bind. They are hogtied by their ingratiation of the whole middle class, fealty to integration, see no need to seek elsewhere for redress. Time, like integration and civil rights, without moral backup is ludicrous, degrading, mendacious—the zenith of deceit.

Sensing the need to bring everyone down from the emotionally charged atmosphere, an astute venter decided to present a lighter side by expressing similar ideas and thoughts through humor:

Joke #1

Dr. A. Winfred Smith, a renowned black nuclear physicist, was on his way to Massachusetts Institute of Technology for a conference. Dr. Smith had a fear of flying so he opted to take a train. Arriving at the station ahead of time, tired of reading, he was hard pressed to find ways to pass the time. To start, he decided to weigh himself. He dropped a coin in the slot and waited for the printout. After reading the printout, he was dumbfounded. It read, "You are a nigger nuclear physicist on your way to MIT for a conference and your weight is 184 pounds. [Beneath his conscious level, Dr. Smith saw himself as a shining example of the American Dream—his accomplishments.] Rationalizing, it was an obvious flaw in the programming; the scale's mechanism was not properly aligned. To test his belief, he decided to try another scale; got similar printouts; the third, the same. Somewhat agitated and bewildered, he went upstairs to try another scale at a different level. He dropped the coin in the slot and waited for the printout. It read, "You are still a nigger, nuclear physicist, you are still on your way to MIT for a conference, you still weigh 184 pounds, and you damn stupid nigger PhD, you just missed your train."

Joke #2

Two black men were in the park and ran out of ice. So they went to the ice house. There were two ice houses in the same block—one black-owned, the other white. The buyer bought the ice from the white owned ice house. On the way back to the park his buddy asked, "Say, man, why didn't you buy the ice from the black man?" The buyer took a long stare at his friend and retorted, "The white man's ice is colder."

Joke #3

During recess, two sixth graders were assembling their model airplanes, experimenting and solving problems associated with flying—ground speed, air speed and wind speed. One student played the role of an air traffic controller, the other a pilot. The controller reported "You have a tailwind of 27 mph. You want to make a ground speed of 185 mph. At what air speed should you fly? Together, using the equation a + w = g, were working to solve the problem. Before they were finished the bell rang—recess over. One student in disgust retorted, "Let's put up our materials and go to that math class and count those beans!"

Joke #4

Two elderly black men were sitting at their usual spot—the porch of the general merchandise store playing checkers. A student was coming home from school; it was his spring break. On the way home, he had to pass the store. One of the players saw him coming, asked "Wasn't that the boy the community had pooled the money to send him up north to school?" His partner bobbed his head, "Yep." To make sure, as the lad approached the store, he asked, "Ain't you the boy the community potted up money to sent you to school?" The student replied, "Yes." His partner "out-of-the-blue" asked him to speak them some learning. Caught off guard, the student said the first thing that came to mind," (πr^2) [pie, r, square] and went on his way. The checker players thought for a second or two, finally one said to the other, "We wasted our money on that boy, everybody knows pie are round and corn bread are square."

Now that calm has been restored, the next participant voiced his choice. He wanted to share with us his encounter with a fascinating, brilliant Brazilian from Behia. He described him as a combination of soothsayer, imam, sage, herbal doctor; the kind of person the West has stereotyped as a witch doctor. They exchanged pleasantries. He was excited; meeting an American and he was equally enthused meeting him. He found the Brazilian's wit matched his humor. He was not overtly concerned with racism per se, rather with seemingly difficulties people of color have adjusting to Western proclaimed democratic practices, more especially black Americans. They do not have a realistic concept of self and how they are suppose to fit such societies.

He was disturbed, bewildered, and animated when he talked about the role of citizens in a democracy—black and white. For example, he stated they lack the understanding, commitment, responsibility, and the true goals of a democracy, and seemingly unaware they are charged with seeing that the goals are met. They do not hold their leaders accountable and responsible for their deeds or misdeeds. Now, completely relaxed and comfortable, their ineptness even allows their leaders to think for them. On a roll, their laizzey-faire attitudes permeate every fabric of social behavior in English-speaking societies. They even allow their children to just grow. They have no sound guidance, no defined approved "rites of passage," family or community sanctions. They lack humane social graces, respect for themselves, elders or women, no limits, all shrouded in a kind of inane adolescent mystique. I nodded in agreement; however, saying to myself, blacks in the U. S. do not have cultural means or ways to remediate such practices.

After a few Brazilian libations, with what I interpreted as an inspired chuckle, he sang "drinking rum and coco-cola, going everywhere in the world, working for and protecting the Yankee dollar." Now his broad grin quickly gave way to a robust laugh. He said, "You know, Amigo, blacks living in such countries remind me of those 'Ladies of the night' who work in a brothel, the harder they work the more they get taken advantage of." On that note, the sagacious leader and I gave our respective "until we meet again." He stated he was determined to visit the land of enchantment—U. S. and myself back to fascinating and charming Brazil.

Sunday, we returned to the place where it all got started—our favorite unwinding spot. Many patrons showed up to continue their venting, eager to vent. One brother's pet peeve was that enigmatic phrase "Let the Buyer Beware." He described that folkway as a "con" of the highest order-a nice/nasty supreme, sneaking in a hint of sarcasm, he was sure the Bitch Goddess of Success danced a jig. Continuing, that con opened a can of swindlers, charlatans, unaccountable corporations, robber barns and a host of unsavory human parasites— including lay, cleric and many unprincipled omnipotent, clairvoyant researchers. Their sole objective, he maintained, is to hoodwink the gullible public, fill their coffers and insure their La Dolce Vita. Using unscrupulous business practices, taking advantage of lax "watch dog" agencies, a trusting public, legal loopholes and special privileges, they are able to fleece people and remain afloat. Ethnics never enter into their schemata. For example, Enron's unscrupulous behaviors and the savings and loan debauchery have taken millions from a hapless uninformed people depriving them of their pensions, "nest-eggs," jobs and insurances, without compensation, to mention a few.

Huge agricultural combines use genetic engineering to increase the yield of farm products, fatten livestock, fish, poultry, our food supply and to increase profits. Such technology has become our way of life. However, generic engineering has raised some serious social issues. An important one is food safety. We have observed thousands of people becoming ill, even dying from contaminated foodstuff, not primarily from restaurants using unsanitary practices. Tons of vegetables, meats, poultry, can goods and medicines are recalled on a regular basis. In addition, children have become emotionally scarred. They have become adults physically and remain children mentally without a clue as to how to deal with their programmed growth.

Drug companies have joined that august scientific conclave. They boast of incredible claims—feed more people, eliminate harmful pesticides, healthier foods, and advances in medicine to arrest or cure all manners of ailments and other lofty claims. What about the side-effects?

Another serious issue is the area of control. CDC, USBA and other control agencies are years behind the new technologies. They do have the funds or manpower to get the job done. Further, our elected officials are too inflexible to deal effectively with the problems. In addition, they are stymied by legal loop-holes and corporate pressures.

At some point, the whole concept of "Let the buyer beware" borders lunacy. How is it possible for people who struggle with reading a newspaper, taught from infancy not to think for themselves, understand corporate, legal and scientific jargon. The poor and the elderly are betrayed by the same institutions they have revered for generations. The problem, more importantly, how can the public in general protect itself from the ravages of the people in the know?

The next venter, a super-senior had the honor. He chose so many memories—his view of Black history. He began by stating Black history should be a daily routine in addition to a monthly ritual. It is a way of life far more than reciting poetry, singing and dancing, slogans, marching, eulogizing past comrades and lauding individual accomplishments. Its all-encompassing, learning from the past, trying to understand the values of forefathers, profiting from their mistakes, and aligning ourselves with those values. Further, to learn as much as we can about ourselves and community, helping everyone who needs help whether they ask for it or not, guarantee that help is there 24/7, and do not make the community suffer because we are too proud to ask for help.

In a somewhat nostalgic trance, he wondered how was it that we became doctors, lawyers, teachers, and other professions when there were no integrated schools, and how the cognitive delayed and special education labeled children survived. Snapping out of it, he directed us to follow him down memory lane, a time before an era he described as the neo-Dark Ages, a time before integration became our security blanket. Super flies dressed in Jesse James frocks, high-heeled male sneakers, "sporting" Jeri-curls became our heroes. A time before gangster leans and eulogizing Freddys became a folkway. A time before "cloud-nine" became our earthly Nirvana, "Who Let the Dogs Out" became a number one hit and gangster raps destroy. "If I Had a Hammer"; before the "Getting Over on the Man" mystique became our philosophy and having children out of wedlock became a virtue. A time before "uncles" became amoral, Mms. Jonses abandoned their marital and civic responsibilities; canine manner negated common courtesies. A period before we patterned our dress code, manners and social graces after jail inmates. A period before industry and honesty were considered vulgar.

Continuing, he wanted us to pay close attention to the "when"—the Black community in The Day. First of all, we seldom locked our doors; there was no need, brother's keeper was a reality. Fear of hobnobbing was non-existent, professional, non-professional and clergy lived in the same neighborhoods. Frankly, we had little or no options. We had few places to go. We lived in the true black-belt. The flip side of that scenario, we had each other. Nothing was perfect, mind you, under the circumstances our community was safe and workable; the differences were specific, formal accountabilities and responsibilities. We acted instead of reacting to impending problems. Beat policemen and other professionals knew the neighborhood, and had a pulse on the community; of equal importance, we were all on the same page. We didn't concern ourselves with the "wannabees." Fathers were in charge of their households. They set the moral standards for child rearing, not the impersonal state-mandated directed hot-line. The "don't put your hand on my child" malarkey was unheard of.

Every adult was a parent with guidance responsibilities regardless of surnames. Every parent was an adult. As a matter of fact, youngsters who had to be reprimanded for inappropriate behavior told their parents were caught in a double-bind. Sanctions were also applied by their respective parents. Families ate together, not in shifts, and had home-prepared meals. Moreover, any adult or child who happened to be visiting at mealtime ate with the family. Fathers worked. Mothers took care of the home. Grandparents were not primary parenting agents; they were overseers and child spoilers. More especially, there was only one hat per household or family unit.

What happened to change that mindset? Well, volumes have been written in an attempt to answer that question.. Nevertheless, from my lay perspective: when mothers become fathers, fathers become mothers, and extinct, children become parents and premature adults, black became beautiful without a portfolio. Further, faulty insights, unwitting reward systems, displaced values, status seeking, inertia, apathy, and indifference swarmed the black community like locusts leaving in their wake a virtual "no man's land" and the family in disarray. As an afterthought, I would be remiss if I didn't mention that jobs were plentiful and there was dignity and pride in an honest day's work. I realize one cannot recapture the past; however, one can certainly learn from it. In the meantime, thanks for the memories.

Back to the barbershop. The shop as usual was bubbling with eager participants wanting to be heard. One brother chose the "getting over the man" mystique" as his pet peeve. From his experience, he believed the statement should be reversed—the man is getting over on us. For example, we pay $150 to $200 or more for gym shoes, $300 and more for started jackets and other professional sports look-alike clothes. Our unwitting buying practices, superficial statuses, and fragile self-concepts force us to spend our limited funds on dictated styles and fashions. Therefore, we buy to satisfy our wants and beg for our needs, never realizing that the beggar is at the mercy of the giver. We are still flailing, wailing, weeping, and drowning in our tears of despair and dependency. We own no means of production; we have no economic, political or cultural base.

With a seemingly exaggerated puzzled look, he wondered how we came up with the "getting over on the man" folly. Was it adopted to avenge Freddy or just a feeble excuse not to do legitimate work and develop good work habits? For sure, we are getting over on each other. Moreover, the man has a protective shield we cannot penetrate. As a result, we have developed and used "cons" of every description, devised vile, vicious traps to snare each other. We have reversed the Robin Hood legend. We rob, cheat and kill each other and romance the man's behaviors. Whatever the motive, one thing for sure, that mindset has been an imposed debilitating curse.

At the shop, another patron sat patiently, yet anxiously waiting for people to arrive. At length, he began his spill, stating our leaders have been trapped and strangled by their own misgivings, delusions and myths. Their main focus should be on finding solutions to our many problems rather than blaming the leaderless masses solely for destruction in the black community—moral and emotional.

Another practice that has given him the flux is how leaders have not taken the best ideas of the past and present intellectual giants, collectively devised a plan and framework for developing a national black cultural family comparable to other sub-cultural groups. To him it is a vulgar practice to blame others for your own ineptness. As long as we allow others to tell us who we are, see ourselves through their perception, we will be forever riveted to hope; eternally divided with shattered self-concepts and self-hatred. In his opinion, only blacks can save blacks. We must collectively develop our own cultural institutions—institutions that will have the responsibility for pinpointing, developing moral and spiritual values, positive self-images, wholesome self-concepts, setting standards of moral conduct, enforceable sanctions, and to build in the community a variety of humanizing experiences. Then, and only then, will we see little black boys and girls, adults—male and female—holding hands chanting, "We have overcome."

A patron getting his hair cut, listening intuitively bounced from the chair in a robust voice and manner, stated he had a pet peeve. Eager to vent, he asked the younger venters to bear with him as he took us back to the civil rights legislation of the 50's and 60's, such a visit would shed some light on our present problems. He warned us never to ignore or dismiss history or historical perspectives. America made token efforts to address civil rights issues only to quiet domestic and supposed international pressures. As a result, those laws were not real changes only reflections of that mindset. He admonished us to be extra careful about putting all of our trust and faith in laws; they have a quaint way of reinforcing the same practices we are trying to extinguish. Moreover, it would be foolish to say there were no social and economic gains as a result of civil rights legislations. Indeed, "middle class" blacks made some significant strides in those areas. However, many of those gains were nullified by anti-civil rights legislation. More especially, the ignored masses got what they always get, used, abused, and blamed. Where do they go for redress; "cloud=nine" hope forever to travel the Yellow Brick Road; meandering and isolated?

We are now beginning to hear from a few "certificated Americans." One of the new-comers stated he has come to realize what we have the least of will help us make the most of—unity. My pet peeve, he stated, was actually a kind of confession—a re-birth in moral commitment. He admitted being engulfed by rugged individuals and strangled by designed euphonious promises. Continuing, it is very easy to get caught up in that elitist camouflage. At every level, we seem to lack the ability to distinguish between what should be, and that which is actually practiced. We continue to boast, flaunt and revere the American way as if it were a symbol of true democratic principles. He asked how is it possible to have a real democratic society when some people are more equal than others. Special privileges and inequalities are staunch enemies of a true democracy. In theory, America is beautiful; however, the American way is ugly, getting uglier, fast becoming most ugly at home and abroad. Yet, America is home. Here we exist, survive, but not live.

His main concern was how to live in a land of disparities; a challenge for all of us. Although he had no definitive answers, he was more than willing to share his thoughts, convictions and experiences. We can deal with the challenge, dismiss it, self-destruct, and tuck our tails, hide and/or run. "I ran." As he continued, I shuddered as he aired his remorse. He realized the very reasons he fled to suburbia had caught up with him. For his unwitting sojourn, he lamented, "You can run but you can't hide."

It is relatively easy to be hoodwinked, bamboozled and mesmerized by America's promises. Our learned predecessors spent centuries trying to get America to mend its nice/nasties by moral persuasion, to no avail. They finally realized the futility of trying to morally influence a people who have a flagrant disregard for the precepts of The Sermon on the Mount. Moreover, they dismissed moral strategies and declared we must seek other avenues for redress. Before they departed, they saw the "light." Now we are the torch-bearers. By following the light—the new path—we can retire hope, bypass dead=ends, and circumvent the Yellow Brick Road.

He felt that before embarking on our new journey it is imperative to eliminate blaming, self-righteousness, apathy, and indifference, and concentrate collectively on the best itinerary, ideas and plans. It would be difficult to travel without a thorough understanding of the American way—such awareness will allow us to recognize and deal effectively with shrewd political strategies and stratagems.

Next, we need to prioritize our problems. Start with the community, critically examine and eliminate continuous amoral practices—practices we have unwittingly skirted, shunned, overlooked and accepted as a way of life. For example, using our off-springs as trophies, wrecking their lives to enhance pathetic male bragging rights, and seeing all women as prostitutes and men as pimps.

The next was labeled "the heredity cult of soliciting, conning, loitering, preying, panhandling and boostering." To illustrate: 24/7 a countless number of men, women and children swarm the parking lots, "L" stations and currency exchanges, intimidating, conning and badgering shoppers in search of hand-outs, prey and suitable spots to sell their ill-gotten wares. For years, we have been guilty of patronizing and perpetuating t hose practices by buying their ill-gotten wares, keeping them afloat and intact. Evidently, our zest for saving money has replaced moral conduct. Moreover, if we don't start dealing, at every level, with ourselves openly and honestly we are going to remain at a moral impasse.

Now, with a slight pause, in a seemingly reflective mode, acknowledged the fact that a few of us were allowed in the kitchen and got a minute slice of the American pie. However, the majority of us cannot get past the kitchen police. It really doesn't matter how much of the pie we acquire, we will never get a tinge of whiteness nor its concessions. In other words, we black/white Americans with our portfolios. The moral of that metaphor "Get your own." He glanced around the shop, "I now yield the floor to my friend, Albert." Albert was caught off guard, but still managed a pleasant smile.

Al began by stating his spill would be brief. He was smarting over the fact, at every level, we as a people are still using random copying solely as a means for solving our problems. To him, copying was neither moral nor amoral. His primary focus was on the intent of the copier. Moreover, since time immemorial, eclecticism has been the mainstay of civilizations. Nevertheless, he was convinced when copying is used as a cop-out, a subterfuge to disguise slovenliness, ineptness, lack of initiative and self-worth, inaccountability and irresponsibility are debilitating obstacle to real progress. What is more, a copier lacks the moxie to separate good from bad, real from unreal, and is tactless. To support his claim, he shared with us a pitiful example: Years ago, when he was in school, a fellow student sat next to him at a final exam and was copying from his paper. The student was so intense in his copying he inadvertently copied his name—turned in his test booklet. The ensuing embarrassment did not faze the copier in the least. He was content with using his brain. We find ourselves in an analogous situation. We are still content with allowing others to do our thinking, planning and deciding what is best for us. Are we so destitute of "thinkers" we must look outside ourselves to find a neo-Moses to steer us through the Promised Land? Copying is definitely not a coping skill.

The next venter, with a smile of approval, heard about our ghetto-networking, came to check it out. Apparently, the format was to his liking. He felt comfortable enough to participate. His pet peeve was the unbridled power of money. He was convinced money in our society is far more than a medium of exchange. He felt in tackling the money problem without a doubt was stepping or trespassing on sacred, hallowed, forbidden grounds; claimed squatter's rights and proceeded. Moreover, the reverence for money rises sublimely over the tenets of moral conduct. Therefore, we kill, rob, cheat, deceive, extort, hock our souls, betray families, friends, and neighbors and become dream majors for that exalted devotion without any sleepless nights. To support his supposition he consulted C. Wright Mills. Mills stated:

> For of all possible values of human society, one and only
> one is truly sovereign, truly universal, truly sound, truly
> and completely acceptable goal of men in America. That
> goal is money and let there be no sour grapes at it from
> the losers.[85]

That mindset, he stated, was a clear manifestation of our devotion and commitment to money.

We have and continue to delude ourselves in believing money will be our rites of passage to moral acceptance. We barely have enough money to last from payday to payday. To think we will have enough money for our redemption was light years away from reality. He acknowledged the fact that a pitiful few of us reach the rich plateau, even then, they can do nothing more than adhere to the basic concept of middle class assumptions—the accumulation of material things. Let's face it, we are at the bottom rung of the economic ladder. According to Mills in *Power Elite*:

> On the bottom level of the money system one never
> has enough money which is the key link in the hand-
> to-mouth way of existence. One is, in a sense, below
> the money system—never having enough money to
> be firmly a part of it. On the middle levels, the money
> system often seems an endless tread mill; never gets

---

85   Mills, *Power Elite*, op. cit., p. 164.

enough; $8,000 this year seems to place one in no better straits than $6,000 the last . . . . . For the very poor, the ends of necessary never meet.[86]

As such, we have to search elsewhere for redress. Continuing, he was aware that culturally speaking we are black/white Americans. We have no choice. Therefore, we accept and cherish the system. To think otherwise is self-defeating, tantamount to heresy, sacrilegious, un-American and disloyal. He was, not in the least, concerned with changing the system, rather our mindset. In closing, he advised us not to self-destruct. There was/is a non-threatening way out. Two things it seemed to him will be the key to survival. One, to critically examine and evaluate our blessedness claim. Blessedness without moral responsibility was the height of Pharisaism. Two, collectively concentrate on helping each other to be the best he or she can be. Only then we'll have a rich experience.

Moving right along, everyone was antsy and in a festive mood. This will be our last gathering until after the holidays. Afterward we are going to our favorite unwinding spot for a few libations and jovial jibing and joshing; the owner was preparing the snacks. Although the scene was anxiety riddled, no one lost sight of the fact respect and consideration for others are the essence of common courtesies. So the new venter was welcomed with open arms. Being perceptive, he sensed the mood, vowed to make his compliant, short, light and direct. He was annoyed and agitated at our continuing wacky, funky, willy-nilly, vile and vulgar behaviors he described as being characteristic of the American self. Momentarily, he seemed preoccupied with how to present his issues without being trite, absurd, irrational or just plain foolish. So he came up with a novel approach. Everyone was to imagine seeing our social practices and behaviors in our society through the eyes of a non-American. (That he surmised would free us from guilt, and freeze our biases.) Ready! He called in a loud voice. We would see the following:

1. People running around like Keystone cops trying to get rich to be somebody.

2. People on both sides of the "color curtain" still trying to negate nature's work. To illustrate: Blacks with natural colored complexion, curly hair, spending bundles on bleaching and straightening compounds trying to look as white as they can. Whites with natural straight hair,

---

pale complexion, lying in and following the sun, spending fortunes on lotions and curing doodads, trying to get as black as they can.

3. Pro-lifers randomly killing obstetricians to save lives.
4. Leaders initiating, condoning the destruction of the life-styles of non-Westerners to make them free.
5. Blacks claiming blessedness and afraid of each other—children included.
6. Women dressed only to cover the minimum to be legal, walking with Little Sally Walker's movements, jogging at dawn or dusk, reporting they got attacked.
7. Invading "freedom soldiers" taking on the behavior of frenzied sharks at the smell of blood, killing civilians as well as "enemy" soldiers.
8. Our Western-style love and marriage is a many-splendored thing until we say "I do." After reality sets in it's now a terrible thing, producing arguments galore. The gist of basic conflicts, she shouts, "All you want is what's under my dress." He retorts, "So! You ain't got nothing under your hat."

He suggested we return to our eyes, the listing would be endless. Moreover, he recognized we all are smitten by the oracles of Apollo at Dephia and the wannabeeism of the Lady without means in Victor Hugo's "The Necklace." Now, sensing the festive mood was waning, simply stated "Let's go."

The Marketplaces – An Overview

There were several features that made our stylized marketplaces so precious: (1) ideas, thoughts, opinions expressed, for the most part, come form individual insights and experiences, not primarily from books or authenticated authorities; (2) our demeanor was shrouded in the brotherhood of man concept. As a result, there were no inferior or superior statuses, only persons with different accountabilities and responsibilities; (3) nothing was allowed to befuddle, muddle or sabotage our vision. Everyone was about talking, sharing, respecting each other's ideas, thoughts and opinions. Venting to us was an excellent cleansing and unifying practice.

In general, in my muckraking posture, I found a countless number of people on both sides of the "track," sincere, honest, longing to be heard, air their pet peeve, recognized and appreciated. On the downside, I encountered many apathetic, discourteous, arrogant, defiant, indifferent, self-centered persons who were welded to ostrich-like behavior and/or "The Three Monkeys" syndrome. Such practices were so pervasive they could be labeled folkways. That mindset, not primarily racism, creates formidable barriers to harmonious dialogue, empathy and unity for "have-not" Americans. Nevertheless, listening to, sharing comments, thoughts, ideas, frustrations and open-mindedness of our "untouchable" was an exhilarating, invigorating, informative experience, an experience that will be forever imprinted in my memory. Undaunted, I pledge to continue and expand the marketplaces.

Chapter XIV

CONCLUSION

"HAVE-NOT" AMERICANS across the board stay so high on supposed democratic ideals that they are prevented from acting responsibly to make those ideals a reality. That state, along with their individual stylized concepts of rights, have clouded their vision and perpetuated a false sense of their role in a true democratic society. As a result, accountability and responsibility, the mainstay of a democracy, have been flagrantly disregarded. Without those pillars, they are at the mercy of the governing class or elites. They seemingly have unconditionally and graciously accepted ;their assigned statuses as pawns and prey. Indelible Americans, in addition to being trapped in that net of compliance have been stranded upstream in that proverbial polluted creek without a paddle, always waiting for the life guards of the American way to rescue and set them free—wailing, praising and depending on the "way from whom their contrived blessings flow.

Money addition not adherence to true Christian and/or democratic principles is the essence of the American way. Greed, inhumanness, individualism, planned obsolescence, mass production, middle class assumptions, war, poverty, and racism are necessary for its survival. The schools as other institutions are charged with protecting, preserving, interpreting, imparting and imprinting the system, regardless of its shortcomings. Therefore, we delude ourselves in believing that Americans will develop the right moral and mental attitudes toward lesser-Americans and social justice.

Teachers have been and continue to be, hogtied, strangled and pressured to honor their mission. Such a commitment oftentimes paralyzes creative and humanistic teaching. Moreover, it pressures them to, in many instances, compromise their moral construct, and short-change themselves and children. Regardless, many find ways to circumvent those pressures and do a terrific job. As a retired teacher, I was privileged to have worked with teachers who were creative, talented, competent, motivated, inspirational and principled. At this juncture, I would like very much to share with you a letter written by one of those teaching giants and music virtuosos at Kenwood Academy to the "Five-Plus-Five" retiring teachers, Ms. Lena McLin. Over the years, I have not been in contact with that Grand Lady and do not have her permission to publish the contents of her letter. However, I am positive she would have given the ok. In my mind, the letter is a classic. Moreover, not to share it, keep it for my eyes only, would be a misdeed beyond selfishness, so here it is! (on page 80)

It would be ludicrous to think, suggest, assume, or hint that racism does not impact the lives of Americans. How much of an impact would be pure speculation on my part? However, it is my contention that racism by design has been allowed the luxury, in and of itself, to dominate and dictate our thought patterns and behaviors. As such, it has created an all-encompassing subterfuge, perpetuated a unique "I can't do it, because of" syndrome; a gigantic security blanket for everyone's aberrant, irrational, base behaviors, and camouflaged real problems.

In my opinion, there are too many factors that have a greater influence on society than racism per se. For example, the ability to think for oneself, make wise choices, responsibility and accountability are crucial to problem-solving and the governmental process. Without that understanding, we are prone to repeat the same mistakes over and over. Further, reacting instead of acting to problems has reached the panic stage.

5/6/94

Dear Fellow Teachers:
You have been:

Loyal
Diligent
Compassionate
Courageous
Dynamic
Daring
Wise
Joyful
Confident
Hopeful

in spite of the untrue picture painted over and over again about teachers.

Your personal dedication to Knowledge and to your Students has shaped many lifes.
Your Teaching will always be reflected in those to whom you un Covered and reveal Knowledge.
In the words of an old Christmas hymn, thank you, we love and appreciate you, So:
"Oh Come, Let us Adore you!"
4.25

For you have Charted
the path for many who
Can Now Overcome.
God Ever Bless You.
Your fellow Teacher,
Lena McLui

Some typical examples; of that claim are Katrina, in-school tragedies, unsafe bridges, railways, and workplaces to mention a few. Can those happenings be the fault of or attributed to racism? If not, who or what is responsible.

Flipping the TV channels one evening I found an advertisement that added relevance to my accusation—two inspectors making a routine check of a huge hydro-electric dam discovered a crack in a wall. They scribbled something on the report pad, patched the small crack with chewing gum, finished the report and departed. Similar practices and behaviors are witnessed throughout our society; the patching approach to solving problems. Dr. Paul L. Wachel in his book *Race in the Mind of America* emphasizes the fact:

> Our problems are too severe and our challenges too great
> to afford us the luxury of trying to attack them without
> full awareness of what they are and where they came
> from. Unless blacks can find a way to face the pain of
> seeing fully what has been done to them, and whites can
> face the guilt most of us would prefer to rationalize or
> deny we are in for many more years of great danger.[87]

Black leaders seemingly have been too unyielding, too opinionate to cope with the problems in the black community. Men of the cloth have been too busy building heavenly mansions. The black masses have been too gullible, the white community too pre-occupied with the demands of the Bitch Goddess of Success and certificated or legitimate blacks have been exhausted chasing their white counterparts. Evidently, Americans are suffering from a rare visual defect, no one is as perceptive as a Capp's comic character, Pogo. "We have seen the enemy and the enemy is us."

We know there are a countless number of students who enter the public school who are talented, creative, intelligent, responsive and aware of the social injustices in our society. In spite of that fact, no one seems to acknowledge or realize the school has done little to develop and exploit those abilities. Instead, it has consistently blamed the students for its blunders. The school is still unyielding, tenaciously adhering to its policy of using traditional teaching methods and dated curriculums. Small wonder the "usual" has and continues to create serious problems for the school system. We know not all black families are dysfunctional. Far too many are and have created serious problems in the community. Moreover, we know we still have many seemingly small problems unabated have blossomed into "biggies." Misconceptions and confusions of manhood and womanhood have contributed to the

87   Wachtel, op. cit., p. 164.

stockpile of debilitating barriers to wholesome moral development. They are not given or ceded. They are earned titles veiled in responsibility, accountability and moral behavior.

My thoughts, ideas and opinions have been greatly influenced by my encounters with mounds of nice/nasties. That experience did not become a crutch, rather awareness and the joy of learning from those encounters. More especially, they led me to try extremely hard to show "invisible Americans" the lay of the land without overloading them with historical facts, scientific jargon, statistical data, analyses and the usual. Further, I have tried hard with my presentation not to give the impression that I am talking down to the reader. I am sure some will think my thoughts, ideas and opinions are good, to some good not good enough for society as a whole; to others, they are not real, unprofessional and bar-roomish. Still others I hope will begin to recognize how we use deceit to attain advantages, heighten our differences, ignore the magnitude, the pervasiveness of our problems, and realize our problems cannot be resolved by pretending they do not exist and at the same time revering the usual.

My mission was to explore and expose some of our nice/nasty behaviors, get people connected by sharing ideas, thoughts, opinions, and raise questions without blaming, ridicule, fear, anger or envy. Moreover, each story, joke, venting echoed that mission. All dealt with the what is, not what the is should be. In general, the writer's perception of the "should be" is based on a vision taken from the book *The American Way*, the author's view:

> A country in which the citizens cooperate with their common concerns, respecting one another's differences of opinion and beliefs, respecting one an other's differences of cultural aspirations, letting the musicians have their way and the artists theirs, and the artisans theirs, without blame attaching to anyone. When people in other countries would look to America as a place where reason and harmony prevail, welding us together into the most powerful people in the world—not powerful by the sword, but spiritually powerful by our having attained knowledge, sympathy and tolerance for the people who live on the same street with us, and for our fellow citizens in this continental country.[88]

William (Bill) Goins

---

88   Booker, Hayes, Straus, <u>op. cit.</u>, p. 10.

Epilogue

THE APOCALYPSE NOW

THE CURRENT crisis situation in the black community did not happen overnight. For years no serious attention has been paid to our seemly progressive chronic problems, nor has there been any realistic plans for their solution. They have developed from our misdirection, our applauding, congratulating, extolling and admiring deviate behaviors. Moreover, our contrived blessedness, blinded individualism, apathy, scape-goating, and the polarization between the "certificated" and "non-certificated" blacks have made generous contributions to our stock-pile of agonies. We appear to have lost track of who we are, where we have been and where we might be going. The intensity of those behaviors have and continue to keep the community irresolute, fickle laden, morally barren, hampered, hapless, harried, handicapped ;and embarrassed. This internal incoherence is still hovering over the black community. Perhaps it is time to stop debating "which way to go" and ask which way will create the least friction and bring positive changes.

Observation has shown the futility of racial integration as the sole means for solving black Americans' problems. Forced integration has not, will not, and cannot work. The aim of the integration movement has been worthy, but lacks collective commitment to make it a reality. The goal is well-meaning, but design naive. More especially, the movement was, from its inception, doomed to failure because America was not ready to grant blacks moral status equal to mainstream Americans. More importantly, the pillar of society-religion – the keepers and purveyors of moral behavior, refused to collectively support the movement. One must recognize that:

> The structure of American society can easily defeat, check, negate, balance out and control integration on any level. It can at the same time permit whatever amount of token integration is necessary either to let off steam as it were, or to satisfy the gradualist, negro or white that progress is indeed being made.[89]

Many of our learned intellectuals, many years ago, recognized the duplicity, the moral contradiction and recanted their integration posture in favor of a national black cultural group.

I found from my marketplace travels to suggest, hint or mention national black cultural group conjures up a feeling of impending doom. Contrary to mounds of research, personal observations showing that integration cannot be a cure-all for our problems, many people still cling tenaciously to the movement. They were extremely uncomfortable with the idea of abandoning integration as our only way for redress and the fear of traveling in uncharted waters. From my perspective we would not abandon integration, just put the movement on hold for a "spell." Integration is the end we seek and strive for; however, presently it is not the wherewithal for attaining that goal.

Nevertheless, the fear of the group ideas was/is seemingly embedded in our psyche. Granted the unknown has an uncanny way of evoking anxiety, myths, superstitions and a medley of irrational fears. Regardless, those strong emotional reactions cannot and must not be used as a cause for our inhumane relationships. For example, the bitterness with which we see and deal with each other on a daily basis demonstrate our contempt, maliciousness, mendaciousness, apathy, crab-like behaviors, envy, murder, assorted disaffections and inhumane practices. Evidently, we view each other as a tainted people. How, then, can we rid ourselves of those seemingly chronic infectious practices and chart a realistic course toward our ultimate goal? Perhaps finding answers to the following questions may help us to shed our inhumanity, non-cooperation, isolation, establish moral identification, and become riveted to the concept of brotherly love.

(9.)   When are we going to have the courage to acknowledge that we make/made a tragic mistake by abandoning each other and

---

89   Cruse, op. cit., p. 203.

blaming our children for their actions and reactions to the moral desert we had a hand in creating?

(10.) Do we have to be experts to have an opinion on how things should run?

(11.) Are we obligated to follow and defend leaders who make us victims for their irrational thinking and unwitting behaviors?

(12.) What should be the schools' approach to social inequality?

(13.) How can we mend the break between "have and have-not" blacks?

(14.) How can we get people to face their problems and recognize their underlying causes?

(15.) How can we "break-off" our romance with deviate and wanton behaviors?

(16.) Do we continue to wail, mourn, pray, "hide our hands," bask in contrived blessedness, piety; patiently, but battered, wait for a new redeemer?

(17.) When will our intellectuals, in addition to doing research, writing articles and books for themselves, step down a notch and help lay folk get organized and rally around genuine community issues?

(18.) Are we going to continue giving carte blanche to any spokespersons who are forceful, colorful orators, who make huge sweeping promises they cannot keep and disregard their past performances and misdeeds?

(19.) When are we going to realize we don't have a boatload of options in dealing with our problems?

(20.) Will we ever recognize the fact in America control of the community has always rested with groups not with the federal government?

(21.) When are we going to stop seeing and using biological differences as a symbol of superiority and inferiority?

I do not believe our problems are irremediable and our directions irreversible, nor do I think we are so destitute of talent to find solutions to our own problems. We simply lack the structure, directions to synthesize our organizations, coordinate our programs and activities. More especially, we do not have a design to harness our energies to stimulate, incite people to "junk" their "can't do" mindset, join forces and become an integral part of the united mending process.

To illustrate, we have a countless number of splinter "savior" organizations and programs; each establishing its own agenda without thought or cooperation with each other; each competing, vying for control and monies form federal, state and local governments. We know from past experiences we cannot find solutions to our problems form laws and in-house jockeying by our leaders. There can be no real progress or programs, "doing our own thing" until our individual interests can be subordinate to the welfare of all.

Despite changes in vocabulary, we are still in the same old "stew." Still running around like keystone cops going in all directions, looking in all the wrong places, searching for quick fixes and bandage approaches to problem solving. It is time for us to put quick fixes, patching, random searches on the back-burner, concentrate collectively on developing plans, methods, for solving our problems and community. Moreover, we have been so preoccupied with holding America accountable for her misdeeds, we have conveniently barreled over our own insatiable bad behaviors. Simply put, it is a nice/nasty to hold America accountable, responsible for her errant ways when we cannot and do not have the means to address and extinguish our own misconduct. It is time to stop trying to conceal reality; stop crusading and take a "long" hard look at ourselves.

We are seen collectively. Instead of developing and using that given grouping for our purposes, we opted to use individual progress as a substitute for collective cooperation. As a result we are a pseudo-group without portfolio and no group savvy. To quote "The Great White Chief," who in that instance did not speak with "forked tongue": "A house divided against itself cannot stand." The same truism applies to a community. In unity there is strength.

Therefore, if we are to have a viable community, a means for influencing policy-makers, keeping our leaders accountable and responsible to remediate our problems, establish a power base, participate in any meaningful dialogue and coalition with other American groups, we need a national black cultural group. There would be no reason or need to fear anomaly or anonymity. People would not have to give up their religion, social group, and political beliefs to be a part of the group. The goal of the group would be not to turn people away, rather to develop a coherent policy of unification without loss of diversity and individuality. Such a group would bring all of our institutions under one umbrella, guaranteeing a unity of purpose. Further, it would open new avenues for change, new possibilities for openness and reasonable plans for reconciling our differences. It would motivate, maintain high moral standards and emphasize human values. Everyone in the community would be able to participate in all of the programs and activities. In education, the school and community would be one and the same. The community would be actively involved in solving its own problems and in improving the quality of life for everyone.

Without a doubt, our problems are too severe and pervasive for our continuous pussy-footing. Why not research our limited options, mistakes and mis-directions and collectively find a means for extinguishing our energized despair and re-claim our community. To me, a national black cultural group seems the logical start. We have nothing else which to build the future except by correcting the mistakes of the past.

My main purpose is to incite, encourage and emphasize the need to pursue and find the best plan or plans for correcting our imbalances and unifying the community. Once we have been collectively committed to such a plan, it is imperative that we all be on the same page physically, morally, socially, politically and jointly duty-bound to support and guarantee compliances. Then, and only then, will the bell toll all over the black community at our re-claimed moral construct, brotherhood and community. Now we would, in a meaningful way, be able to join our counterparts' groups, work together to re-claim the democratic, moral principles and practices America so proudly and boldly boasts. That mission accomplished, the peal now, will be heard throughout the realm.

References

Chapter I

Baker, Hayes, Straus. *The American Way*. Chicago: Willett, Clark & Co., 1936.

Crow, Lester D., Crow, Alice. *Child Development and Adjustment*. New York: The McMillan Co., 1962.

Fisher, Louis. *Gandhi*. New York: Mentor Books, 1954.

Frazier, E. Franklin. *Black Bourgeoisie*. New York: Simon & Shuster, 1963..

Harris, Thomas A. *I'm Ok You're Ok*. New York: Avon Books, 1967.

Johnson, James Wheldon. *The Book of Negro Spirituals*. New York: Viking Press, 1925.

Leckie, Robert. *The Wars of America*, Vol. II. New York: Harper and Row, 1957.

Schimke, David, "Heaven Can't Wait." *UTNE* (March-April) 2005.

Tannenbaum, Frank. *Slave & Citizen*. New York: Random House, 1946.

Chapter II

Curse, Harold. *The Crisis of the Negro Intellectual*. New York: The New York Review of Books, 1967.

Dudziak, Mary L. *Cold War Civil Rights*. New Jersey: Princeton University Press, 2001.. Leckie, op. cit., p. 43.

Chapter III

Federal Register, Vol. 70, No. 33 (February 18, 2005).

Fitzgerald, <u>op. cit.</u> pp. 75-77.

Gans, Herbert J. *The Uses of Poverty, the Poor Pays Social Policy*. New York: Random House, 1974.

Gottschalk, Louis; Lack, Donald. *Transformation of Modern Europe*. Chicago: Scott, Foresman & Co. 1954.

http://enwikipedia.org/wiki/poverty_line.

http://www.angelfire.com/ca3/jphuck_216_html

Mintz, Morton; Cohen, Jerry S. *Power Inc.* New York: Viking Press, 1956.

Roper, Richard, *A Persistent Poverty, Dream Turned Nightmare*. New York: Pheen Press, 1991

Tawney, R. H. *Religion and the Rise of Capitalism*. New York: Harcourt, Brace & Co., 1926.

Chapter IV

Baker, Newton D.; Hayes, Carlton, J. H.; Straus, Roger Williams. *The American Way*. Chicago: Willett, Clark & Co., 1936.

Brody, Don. *The Iron Triangle*. New Jersey: John Wiley & Son, Inc., 2003.

Elyon, Gilboa, "The Panama Invasion Revisited—Lessons for the Use of Force in the Post-War Era." *Political Science Quarterly*, Vol. 10.

Fakiolas, Efslothios T. "Kennan's Long Telegram and NSC-68. A Comparative Analysis." *East European Quarterly*, Vol. 31, No. 8 (January 1948).

Fitzgerald, Michael. "The Permanent War—Militarism and the American Way of Life," *UTNE*. (March-April), 2005.

Gottschalk, Louis; Lack, Donald. *Transformation of Modern Europe*. Chicago: Scott, Foresman & Co. 1954.

Mills, Wright C. *The Power Elite*. New York: Oxford University Press, 1956.

Mintz, Morton, Cohen, Jerry. *Power Inc.* New York: Viking Press, 1956.

Shulman, Ken. "The Soul of Resistance: Civil War Parallels in U.S. and

Iraq." *Christian Science Monitor* (Commentary- Opinions), August 28, 2005.

Chapter V

Abraham, Mitrie, Rabbany. *Wise Men From the East and West.* New York: ;Houghton Mifflin Co., 1922.

Carey, James W., Quirk, John J. "The Electronic Revolution." *The American Scholar,* Vol. 39, (Summer 1970).

Kirk, John. *Defeat of Presidential Powers and National Character.* New York: Simon and Shuster, 1975.

Mills, John Stuart. *Dissertation, Discussions, Political, Philosophical and Historical I.* New York: Haskill House, 1925.

Mills, Wright C. *The Power Elite.* New York: Oxford University Press, 1956.

Sullivan, Leonard, Jr., (U.S. Assistant Secretary of Defense (1974-76). *Time* (Letters), July 12, 2004.

Steiner, Claude. *Scripts People Live.* New York: Grove Press, 1974.

Wurmer, Leon. "Drug Abuse: Nemesis of Psychiatry." *The American Scholar,* Vol. 41, No. 3 (Summer 1970).

Chapter VI

Bell, Derrick. *Silent Covenant.* New York: Oxford University Press, 2004.

Frazier, op. cit., pp. 135-8.

Chapter VII

Cruse, op. cit.

Frazier, op. cit., p. 135.

Ibid., p. 26.

Ibid., p. 108

Henry, Rick. "Stop Lying to Ourselves," *Afro-American Chronicle* (Commentary) March 4, 1996.

Schlesinger, Arthur; Boorstin, Daniel. "The United States of America—In

These Times." www.inthesetimes.com/article/3094.

Tannenbaum, op. cit.

Chapter VIII

Baker, Hayes, Straus, op. cit. pp. 77-8.

Bell, op. cit., pp. 97-107.

Crow & Crow, op. cit.

Frazier, op. cit., pp. 81-3.

Cruse, op. cit.

Frazier, op. cit., p. 135.

Ibid., p. 26.

Ibid., p. 108.

Gold, Stephen, F. "School-Community Relations in Urban Ghettos." *Teacher College Record*, LXIX (November 1967),

Guilford, S. P. *The Nature of Intelligence.* New York: McGraw-Hill, 1967.

Hofstader, Richard. *Anti-Intellectualism in American Life.* New York: Vintage Books, 1963.

Learner, Janet W., *Children with Learning Disabilities.* Boston: Houghton Mifflin Co., 1971.

Mills, C. Wright. *Power Elite.* New York: Oxford University Press, 1956, pp. 303-324.

Mills, C. Wright. *White Collar: The American Middle Class.* New York: Oxford University Press, 1957.

"Problems with Drop-outs." *North/West/South Gazette, Inc.*, Vol. 21, No. 12.

Ross, James I. *A Ghetto Principal Speaks Out.* Detroit: Wayne University Press, 1974.

Wachtel, Paul L. *Race in the Mind of America.* New York: Routledge Press, 1996.

Chapter IX

Lerner, op. cit., p. 73.

Sa Via, John; Ysseldyke, James E. *Assessment.* Boston: Houghton Mifflin Co., 1998.

Ibid., pp. 5-10.

Lerner, op. cit., p. 72.

Chapter X

Bell, op. cit., pp. 97-107.

Baker, Hayes, Straus, op. cit., pp. 77-9.

Chapter XI

Hofstader, op. cit., pp. 309-12.

Mills, C. Wright, op. cit., p. 329.

Crow and Crow, op. cit., pp. 423-29.

Ibid. pp., 482-5.

Decker, Randall E. *Pattern of Exposition* (Editor's excerpt); "The Ghetto Cop," from Dick Gregory's book *The Shadow that Scares Me.* New York: Little, Brown and Co., 1966, pp. 26-35.

Steiner, op. cit., pp. 156-7.

Chapter XII

Chapter XIII

Mills, *Power Elite*, op. cit., p. 167

Ibid., p. 162.

Chapter XIV

Baker, Hayes, Straus, op. cit., p. 10.

Wachtel, op. cit., p. 164.

Printed in the United States
by Baker & Taylor Publisher Services